MW00365478

DAKOTA BURN

D.V. BERKOM

For Sandy —
Thanks for coming out!
Enjoy —
DVB

DAKOTA BURN
A Leine Basso Thriller
Copyright © 2019 by D.V. Berkom
All rights reserved.

ISBN: **978-0-9979708-9-0**

This book is a work of fiction and any resemblance to any person, living or
dead, any place, event or occurrence, is purely coincidental. The characters and
story lines are created from the author's imagination and are used fictitiously.
No part of this book may be reproduced, or stored in a retrieval system, or
transmitted in any form or by any means, electronic, mechanical,
photocopying, recording, or otherwise, without express permission of the
publisher.

Published by

First print edition September 2019
Cover by Deranged Doctor Designs

Author Website: dvberkom.com

Derek van der Haar eyed his empty beer and wondered how he managed to wind up in a seedy strip club in Nowhere, USA. A shitty CD player pumped out an old rap song as a dark-haired stripper with a back tat of a butterfly defied gravity on the chrome pole in the middle of the tiny stage. The stench of spilled beer, mixed with the dozen unwashed, overexcited white boys grabbing their crotches and wolf whistling had come close to pushing him out the door into the frigid North Dakota night.

But first he needed to find Bart.

He waved his glass at a passing waitress. She smiled and headed toward him. The Madonna-worthy breast implants strained her low-cut T-shirt with each perky step. Her nametag read Corrine.

"Another beer?"

"Yeh." He set the glass on her tray.

"Alaskan Amber?"

"Spot on, Corrine."

The waitress cocked her head as she replaced the damp cocktail napkin with a dry one. "Where're you from, darlin'?"

"A little continent called Africa."

"Really? What are you doing in this godforsaken place?" she said, looking like she meant every word.

"Hunting."

A piercing whistle broke through the already raucous crowd, coming from a beefy guy in the group of drunk bros near the stage.

"Need some drinks over here," the guy yelled.

Corrine sighed.

"Be right back with your amber." She disappeared into the crowd.

Derek settled in to watch the show. The purple and pink lights aimed at the stage didn't do the dancer any favors. The "well" between her and the drunk bros appeared to be narrowing, as they jostled each other closer to the action. The bouncer, a massive guy named Bruce with tatted arms the size of oil rig pistons, started toward the group. A tight black T-shirt with a green shamrock and the words "Lucky's Bar" printed on the front stretched across his torso, giving him the gravitas of a wrecking ball.

The bros backed off.

Didn't have a death wish, apparently.

A tiny back room of the club—more like a closet, really—served as the lap dance emporium. The night before, Derek had stumbled into the room by accident. One bleary-eyed customer continually handed his "private" stripper twenties whenever she stopped moving. She'd slide her dress back on and repeat the same routine of slithering her hips and shoulders like a drowsy Marilyn Monroe. The dance lasted all of two minutes. Then the next twenty would disappear and she'd start over. Like a mechanical doll, Derek thought.

Pretty good wages. Shit working environment.

But Derek didn't come for the strippers. Sexual fantasy wasn't the only thing a guy could find at Lucky's Bar. When he told Corrine he was hunting, he'd meant it in a broader sense. While most who braved January in the northland came looking for work or for the ice fishing, he sought an altogether different prey.

One more drink. If he hasn't shown by then, I'm gone.

Good to her word, Corrine returned with another beer. He paid in cash, included a generous tip, and she scooted off to take care of the rest of the crowd. Derek sipped his drink and scanned the room, searching for the man he'd met the night before. He studied the business card in his hand.

Bart Grantham Enterprises

Products you can trust! *Procurement of the following items:*

Beaver

Mink

Fox

Bear Gall Bladders

Mountain Lion

Bobcat

Quick turnaround. Call for quote.

The fourth item on the list had caught Derek's eye, prompting his return to Lucky's. Wild black bear gall bladders were hugely popular in Asia as a component of traditional medicine, but possession could get you jail time in North Dakota. He marveled that the man had the balls to include them on his business card. Poachers in Tanzania and Kenya weren't quite as stupid as good ol' Bart. Derek figured Fish and Wildlife would be interested in his whereabouts.

He'd make sure Bart's card displayed properly on the body.

Derek drained his second beer, threw some cash on the table, and rose to leave. Before he had one arm inside his coat, a man appeared at his elbow. Dwarfed by Derek's six-foot frame and muscular physique, the rail-thin interloper had the distinctive facial scarring and rotted teeth of a chronic methamphetamine user. Derek took a step back to get upwind and shrugged his coat on the rest of the way.

The other man cut his eyes side to side and motioned for Derek to lean in closer. Wary, Derek turned his head so he could hear him.

"You looking for pussy?"

Derek resisted the impulse to walk away and cocked his head.

"That depends. What's on offer?"

The man raised his chin and replied, "A sweet young thing I *know* you gonna like."

"Where?"

Meth Guy nodded toward the door. "Out back. Ain't part of Lucky's stable."

"Lucky know about that?"

Lucky, a bottle blonde in her mid-sixties with a voice like a chainsaw, owned the place and acted as talent manager—at least, that was what one said in polite company.

Meth Guy's gaze flickered around the bar, as though Lucky herself might materialize right then and there. "Yeah, you know, maybe I'll just move along here—"

Derek put his hand up. "Hang on a minute, brah. I didn't mean anything. Just curious. She runs a tight ship."

Meth Guy bobbed his head. "Don't I know it." His shoulders inched down. "You interested?"

"I might be. Can I get a preview?"

The other man nodded, then started for the entrance, looking back twice to make sure Derek followed. Derek readjusted the forty-five concealed in his waistband and followed him out the door.

He sure as hell didn't intend to get rolled.

The icy air hit his lungs like death itself. Didn't matter how long he stayed, he could not get used to what he dubbed the "North Dakota Freeze." He missed the hot savannah of Africa, missed the hazy mirages that morphed into a pride of lions resting in the shade of a tree, or a giraffe nibbling on the tender leaves of an acacia.

But his calling had brought him to North Dakota oil country, and he had a job to do. He actually hoped Meth Guy would try to rob him. He'd been on good behavior for over a week and could use the adrenaline kick.

He followed the other man around to the back of the bar and across the dirt parking lot. Apparently, there'd been a sale on T-111 siding and gray-blue exterior paint, and everyone decided to stock up. He'd seen the same exact color on a shit-ton of other buildings in town.

No surprise there. North Dakotans were nothing if not frugal.

Meth Guy stopped at the side door of an older model cargo van idling in the lot. The lone security light missed the dented white vehicle by a good six feet, and there were several dark places an accomplice could hide. Derek scanned the area but didn't detect any threats.

"Inside." Meth Guy stood next to the idling van, his hand on the door. "Forty dollars and she'll suck your dick clean off. You want something else, you gotta pay."

"I wanna see the goods first, yeh?"

Meth Guy slid the door open. He flicked on his phone light, illuminating the interior.

A metal screen separated the cargo area from the front seats. Huddled against the back wall of the van on a bare mattress sat a girl that couldn't have been more than fourteen years old. Dressed in a skimpy baby doll outfit, her dark hair hung limply around her face. Multicolored bruises peppered her arms and legs, and dark bags accentuated her fearful eyes. Bile rose in Derek's throat, but he tamped down the anger.

For now.

"Well?" Meth Guy shoved the door closed.

"She's not what I'm used to."

"You want younger? I got you covered, bro. Just say the word."

"She looks like a junkie."

Meth Guy shook his head emphatically. "She ain't no junkie. And her slot's pristine, I guarantee it. Check her out if you want. That squaw's clean as a whistle."

"Just like you, right? You runnin' her?"

Wary, Meth Guy took a step backward. "Yeah, I'm runnin' her. What's the problem?"

"Think about cuttin' a guy in, maybe?"

"I don't need no partner, if that's what you're gettin' at."

Derek pulled out the forty-five and aimed it at the other man. The whites of Meth Guy's eyes gleamed as he raised his hands in the air.

"Afraid that isn't what I'm getting at. I just needed to know if you had someone else hanging around, waitin' to take my money."

Meth Guy shook his head so fast Derek thought it might spin off his neck. "No, sir. I'm a sole proprietor. We can hammer out a deal, if that's what you're lookin' for."

Derek pulled out a pair of Flex-cuffs and secured the other man's hands behind his back.

"The fuck you doin'?"

"Call it a public service, asshole." Derek opened the side door of the van and shoved him inside. The young girl winced as the pimp landed on his face. She glanced at Derek and then back at the floor of the van. In that one short moment, confusion and fear and an unfathomable bleakness met his gaze. An anvil landed in his gut.

So damned young.

Meth Guy struggled to his knees and threw himself head first toward the open door. Derek caught him by the shoulders and heaved him back into the van. He stuffed the forty-five back in his waistband, then cold-cocked him. The skinny man's jaw made a cracking sound and he slumped to the mattress.

Derek took off his coat and held it out to the girl. After a moment's hesitation, she accepted and put it on.

"You want to ride up front?" he asked.

She nodded. Derek stepped aside as she gingerly made her way out of van and into the passenger seat. He slid the door closed and climbed in the driver's side. He gave her what he hoped would be interpreted as a kind smile. She stared at the floorboards, not meeting his eyes.

"What's your name?" he asked, his tone gentle. She reminded him of a baby dik-dik he'd found in the bush the year before, after its mother had been killed by a pride of lions. He'd bottle fed the thing like it was his own kid and had been rewarded with a strong young antelope that took joyfully to the wild. He'd been sad to see it go, but happy to give it back to the wilderness.

"Mimi."

He barely heard her tiny voice, but it was enough.

"You got family, Mimi? Someone I can call?"

Her eyes brimmed with tears as she shook her head. "No." She cut a look at Meth Guy and shivered before turning back to stare out the windshield.

"Don't worry about him. He won't hurt you again."

Derek shoved the van in gear and drove out of Lucky's parking lot. *Just great, Derek. Now what?*

Locating Ol' Bart the Gall Bladder Trafficker had just taken a backseat to bottle feeding another dik-dik.

2

L eine Basso stepped off the plane in Williston, North Dakota, looking for a bar.

She needed antifreeze. She got vending machines. When she asked one of the employees where she could get a drink, the woman shook her head.

"Closest place is town. Too bad you didn't wait to come when the new airport's up and running. I hear there's gonna be a restaurant with a bar."

"Thanks." Leine walked to the entrance and pulled out her phone. A text from Derek told her he'd be there soon, that he'd been held up in traffic. Traffic? In a town with a population of thirty thousand? She dropped her bag on the floor and stared through the window at the drifting snow. A brilliant blue sky capped the frosty white landscape, stark in its simplicity.

Deer traffic, maybe.

She'd met Derek in the hold of a cargo ship destined for Tanzania. He'd been a poacher back then, trafficking ivory and rhino horn. During the course of their brief partnership, he'd had a "come-to-Jesus" moment and decided to turn his life around by tracking other poachers.

By the looks of the macabre necklace he'd sent her, he didn't just track them.

Landing in Williston had been a first. She'd never had a reason to travel to North Dakota—land of endless prairie, bitter cold, and, she'd heard, bison. Oil rigs dotted the landscape like alien birds digging for food. If not for Derek's phone call she'd be back in LA, putting the final touches on the first graduating class of the SHEN Academy. She smiled at the thought of Jinn proudly holding up the certificate of excellence she earned during her training. She'd certainly come a long way from her days as a poor street kid in Tripoli.

And it appeared that her daughter, April, had finally found her niche. The twenty-five-year-old had gone from a traveling vagabond to an aspiring novelist studying at NYU to one of the best mentors at the academy. A fierce pride filled Leine whenever she thought about "her girls."

But Derek had found Leine's weak spot and talked her into making the trip.

The Bakken formation, known simply as "The Bakken," was a geological anomaly which caused the current oil rush plaguing Williston. The good citizens of Williston were now characterizing their home as a hotbed of the seven deadly sins. The area had been a magnet for roughnecks and unsavory types since the first oil boom in 1951, and again with the latest, which started in the early 2000s. The influx of money and men with nothing to do but work, drink, fuck, and fight had brought a Wild West lawlessness to the small towns ringing the Bakken with an emphasis on greed, lust, pride, and envy. Prostitution soon blossomed, followed close behind by sex trafficking.

Leine understood Derek's reticence to hand over Mimi. Traumatized by what she'd been through, she had understandably clammed up, refusing to answer his questions. He didn't feel comfortable delivering her to the lone anti-trafficking agency located in Williston, and insisted Leine fly in to question both the girl and the man who'd been acting as her pimp.

At least Derek hadn't killed him. Yet. Although he had made some comment about not being a fan of catch and release.

Ten minutes later, she and Derek were on a two-lane highway in his white Ford Super Duty pickup, headed for the town of Hansen, population 1,500. The endless traffic gave her the first taste of the boom—Leine lost count of the number of oil trucks on the road.

"Thanks for coming," Derek said. "Not exactly Africa, right?" He gave her the once-over and added, "You haven't changed."

"You have." The skin around his eyes had started to sag, and he wore jaded like an old coat. The cocky, ex-poacher ladies' man she knew in Tanzania had left the building. "How are Alma and Hattie?" Alma and Hattie ran Rafiki, a wildlife rescue camp in Tanzania.

"They were good the last time I saw them. I haven't been back in a few months."

"And Zara?"

Derek stared straight ahead. A muscle twitched in his cheek. "According to Hattie, she's doing all right."

"You don't stay in touch?" Derek and Zara had been an item at one point. Leine wondered what had happened.

"She doesn't approve of my lifestyle."

More likely, Zara didn't approve of Derek's deadly vocation of eliminating poachers. Leine could relate. Santiago Jensen, the love of her life, was a homicide detective for the Los Angeles Police Department. Needless to say, he didn't agree with her particular brand of justice.

Understandable, but not something she was willing to change.

"Tell me about Mimi," Leine said, changing the subject.

"Says she was born on a reservation in Montana, but got taken away from her biological parents."

"Did she say why?"

Derek shook his head. "She landed in a foster home, but that didn't work out, so she ran away and hitched a ride to the Bakken to get a job. She'd heard restaurant owners looked the other way when it came to underage hires."

"And she found out otherwise."

Derek nodded. "Pretty fast, too. Some woman offered her a place to stay, but it came with strings attached." He shook his head. "The girl clammed up after a few questions. Maybe you'll have better luck."

"What about her handler?"

He scowled. "A waste of space. All I could get out of him is that he talked Mimi into working for him. Outright lied to her. Said he'd get her a legit job, that the money would be insane. And it was, for him. I'll wager most of his ill-gotten gains went up the proverbial crack pipe."

"An addict? You haven't given him access to any drugs, have you?"

"Wouldn't think of it. He can rot in hell, far as I'm concerned."

"So he's in withdrawal?" she asked.

Derek nodded.

"Getting him to talk shouldn't be too difficult as long as psychosis isn't an issue. How long do you think he's been using?"

"Fuck, I don't know. Forever? He looks pretty rough, yeh? You can find out yourself."

They drove through town, which boasted three bars, a strip club, the Wagon Wheel Café, and a tiny grocery, and continued into farm country for a few miles. He took a right off the highway and followed a gravel road for a quarter mile before turning down a dirt driveway. They pulled into the expansive front yard of a modest white farmhouse with a screened-in porch. A towering silver and red silo with an attached barn loomed in the backyard.

Leine glanced at Derek. "You live here by yourself?"

Derek nodded.

"I thought housing was tough to find in these parts."

He shrugged. "Right place, right time, I guess. Used to be a dairy farm. Some oil company swooped in and offered the owners fuck-you money for their mineral rights." He gestured at a series of distant pump jacks in the field behind the house, lazily pumping away. "The family left for the tropics. No one's seen them since."

"That happen a lot?"

Derek shook his head. "Most folks lease their land. It can be great money, but not earth-shattering. You do see a lot of new pickups, though. It's mainly the oil companies that make the big bucks now."

"How much oil is produced here?"

"I've heard different numbers. Depending on the source, somewhere around one-and-a-quarter million barrels a day down the pipeline. Reserves are guesstimated to be over a hundred billion barrels, plus a massive amount of natural gas."

Leine whistled. "That's a lot of cabbage." She grabbed her bag and followed Derek to the enclosed back porch and into the house.

The Formica countertops and white metal cupboards gave the kitchen a 1950s vibe, as did the diner-style metal table and chairs. Ruffled curtains with little bees and flowers hand-stitched on them graced the window over the deep ceramic sink, reminding her of a photograph in a country home magazine.

"Nice curtains. Make them yourself?"

He shrugged. "I got bored."

"Seriously?"

"Fuck no. What do you think?"

Leine smiled. "Just checking."

Derek rolled his eyes. "Your room's upstairs."

He led her up the steep, carpeted stairs to the second floor and pointed to one of three small bedrooms.

"That one's yours. I'd avoid the one next to the stairs."

"Yours?"

"Let's just say it contains a welcome gift for unwanted guests."

"Got it."

A full-sized bed with a handmade quilt, a six-drawer dresser, and a nightstand made for a cozy if crowded room. A shallow closet took up one wall. Wood paneling from the seventies covered the rest, with an occasional framed print to break up the space. A small bathroom could be seen down the hall.

Leine dropped her bag on the bed. "Where's Mimi?"

"Probably out for a walk."

"And the pimp?"

"In the barn."

"Show me."

"First, I have a surprise for you in the nightstand."

Leine went over to the bed and pulled out the drawer. Inside she found a six-inch tactical knife, a waistband holster, and a new-looking Glock 19 with a suppressor and three extra magazines.

"Aw. You remembered. How sweet." She donned the holster and slid the Glock inside. The knife and extra magazines went into a side pocket.

Derek gave her another grin and nodded at the stairs. "Let's go get some intel."

3

They walked out to the white clapboard barn and entered through a side door. The smell of old hay, dust, and dried cow shit hit Leine hard, and she stifled a sneeze. Derek led her through a room that had once been used as storage for milking equipment, but which now sported an old holding tank and a forest of spider webs. A field mouse scurried past, its tiny squeak magnified in the empty space. Derek startled when he saw it and shuddered.

Leine laughed. "Big Game Hunter weirded out by a tiny rodent? That's rich."

"Little bastards are death traps. Do you know what kind of fucking diseases they carry?"

"Not as many as your mouth." Leine shook her head and followed him through to the back of the barn.

Weak daylight shone through a dirty, broken window, partially illuminating the gloomy interior. An emaciated man with scars on his face sat on a hay bale, handcuffed to a metal cow stall. His ancient green army coat sagged over a pair of dirty jeans. Worn cowboy boots completed the ensemble. A gray wool blanket lay on the floor beside him. The black collar he wore around his neck looked strangely out of place in a barn in the middle of the heartland. Then again, a man cuffed to a cow stall wasn't exactly normal.

Derek kicked at the bale, rousing the man. "Hey, asshole. Someone here to see you."

Sweat slicked the man's gaunt cheeks. He shivered and glanced nervously at Derek, then Leine.

"Didja bring the Sara Lee?"

Derek leaned against a nearby stall and crossed his arms. "Remember what I told you? You give me something I can use, you get the Sara Lee."

"Ah, man. I'm jonesin' for coffee cake. Bring me some. I promise I'll tell you whatever you want to know."

"Not a chance."

"Shit, dude. It's only a few dollars. What's your problem?"

Derek moved toward him, his body tense. "You."

"Down, boy," Leine said. Derek relaxed and took a step back.

The addict turned to look at her. "You his boss?" He cackled and glanced at Derek. "Got your women fightin' your battles for you, pussy?"

"I wouldn't piss him off if I were you," Leine warned. "I'm here to make sure you actually survive. If it were up to him you'd be dead already."

The man narrowed his eyes. "Who the fuck are you?"

"That isn't important."

She walked over to Derek and asked in a low voice, "What's with the collar?"

Derek grinned. "Electric shocks. In case he gets out of hand." He reached in his pocket and brought out a small remote. "Wanna see it in action?"

"I take it the cuffs aren't enough."

Derek shrugged. "You can never be too careful."

A shudder coursed through the prisoner, and he doubled

over with a wheeze. She glanced sharply at Derek, but he shook his head. He hadn't activated the collar.

"You're looking kind of rough," Leine said, moving closer to the prisoner. "Answer some questions and we'll alleviate your pain."

"How about gettin' me some of that painkiller right now?" He nodded at Derek. "I'd be able to think straighter."

"What's your name?"

He averted his eyes.

She squatted next to him. "We need to call you something."

"Scarf," he mumbled.

"Scarf? What kind of name is that?" Derek asked.

"It's a nickname, okay?"

"And it means—?" Leine asked.

Scarf hesitated before answering. In a low voice, he replied, "When I eat, I scarf my food."

Derek snorted.

"Okay, Scarf," Leine said. "Where are you from?"

"Texarkana."

"What brought you here?"

"What do you think? Money." Scarf shrugged. "Drugs."

"Who did you work for before you went out on your own?"

Scarf continued to stare at the floor. He shuddered again, the involuntary movement wracking his emaciated body. She looked at Derek again. He showed her his empty hands and shook his head.

Once the shuddering passed, Scarf said, "Weren't nobody else. The bitch is lying."

Derek moved in and seized him by his jacket collar, lifting him off the bale. "By bitch, you mean that little fourteen-year-old girl who trusted you?" Scarf's eyes bulged as he struggled to suck in air.

"Derek." Leine warned.

He gave a disgusted snort and dropped the junkie back onto the hay bale. Scarf leaned forward, hacking and gulping air.

Leine studied him for a moment. "If you want to live, you're going to have to tell us who you work for. I can't promise Derek will stop next time."

"You think I care?" He shivered. "I don't score pretty soon, might as well be dead."

Derek pulled out a small plastic baggie containing a white substance and showed it to him. "You want some of this?"

Gaze riveted to the packet, Scarf visibly swallowed as he tracked its movement. "Give it to me."

Derek shook his head. "Not until you give us something, brah."

Scarf closed his eyes. "I can't."

"Yes, you can," Derek countered.

"No. I. Can't." He practically spit out the words.

"Why?" Leine asked. "It's not like you have much of a choice."

"Because I'll be dead." His voice reverberated through the empty space.

Leine and Derek exchanged glances.

"I thought you didn't care," Leine said.

"I don't care about the dead part. It's the how that I'm afraid of."

"What if we promise to protect you?"

Scarf's laugh landed hollow in the dank barn. "That's a good one. Protect me. Yeah." He lifted his chin. "How you gonna protect me when they're everywhere? Shit, they probably already know I'm here."

"Who are they?" Leine asked. "Tell us and we'll have a better chance to keep you safe."

"If they're everywhere, how did you manage to go off on your own?" Derek asked. "And steal their property?"

Scarf dropped his chin to his chest. "I ain't on my own. I made that shit up to keep Mimi in line."

"How big of an organization are we talking about?" Leine asked.

He shook his head. "How would I know? I'm just a peon. They don't tell me shit."

"Then give us whatever you know. If you cooperate, Derek will hand over that baggie."

Scarf's gaze skated to Derek's. "Yeah?"

Derek nodded.

Minutes ticked by. Leine could tell by the look in Scarf's eyes that he was struggling mightily with the decision to rat out his employer for the packet of drugs.

Finally, he made a decision.

"What the fuck. I'm dead anyway." The junkie hacked up what sounded like a hairball and spit on the floor. "I deal with a dude named Sean."

"How often?" Leine asked.

"I meet him once or twice a week outside of town at the old grain elevator."

"What happens then?"

"I hand over ninety percent of the cash from the girl, he hands me enough crystal to get me through."

"Except enough doesn't last anymore, does it?"

His silence gave her the answer.

The door to the milk room opened and a young girl walked in. She wore an oversized down coat, rubber boots, and a knit cap. She gasped when she saw the three of them in the dusky light.

"Sorry. I didn't know anyone was in here." She turned to leave.

"Mimi, wait." Derek gestured at Leine. "There's someone I'd like you to meet."

Leine moved so the girl could see her. "I'm Leine. A friend of Derek's."

Hands shoved inside her jacket, Mimi studied the former assassin. Her gaze flickered to Scarf, then back to Leine. "You're here to help me."

"Yes."

She nodded at the prisoner. "What about him?"

"We're questioning him," Leine replied.

"Find out anything?" she asked.

"Not much."

"He's afraid."

"Of what?"

"Of Sean and his guys."

"Should he be?"

Mimi shrugged. "I'm not. I'd kill them all if I could."

Leine had heard talk like that from other trafficked victims. She didn't doubt the girl meant every word.

"What can you tell me about Sean?" Leine continued. "Does he live in town?"

Another shrug. "He's around. You could ask the girls at Lucky's. A couple of them freelance for him."

"How many people are there? Is he the only boss?" Derek asked.

"Stop talking, Mimi." Scarf gave her a warning glance. She ignored him.

"A bunch. One time I saw him with, like, nine other guys."

"Did any of them stand out? Act like a boss?" Leine asked.

"Sean was the only one. The other guys would act all like, cool around him, laugh at his jokes, that kind of thing."

"Do you know where any of them stay?"

She nodded. "They used to take me there. It's just outside of town—"

"Shut up, bitch," Scarf growled. Mimi turned on him.

"And what? Do what you tell me? Yeah, *that* worked out, didn't it, Scarf?" She glared at him, her breath coming fast.

"You ungrateful piece of—" Scarf strained against the handcuffs, trying to get at Mimi. The kid took a step backward, clearly afraid. A split-second later, he let out a strangled cry and sank back onto the bale, cuffed hands clawing at the collar. He closed his eyes and groaned. His hands dropped to his lap as his ragged breathing slowly returned to normal.

Derek walked over, grabbed him by the hair, and yanked his head up so he could look him in the face.

Scarf's eyes opened to slits.

"Put another finger on her or any other girl and I'll cut your hands off."

Scarf coughed. "Fuck your collar. I'm not a dog."

Body rigid with anger, Derek let go of his hair and walked away.

"I trusted you." Mimi's small voice echoed through the room. Tears glistened in her eyes. "I thought we were friends."

Scarf glowered at the floor. "Ain't no kinda friends in this fucking place." Silence underlined his statement.

"Look," Leine said. "I get that you're afraid of repercussions—"

Scarf shot her a look. "I told you, I'll be dead. But Mimi's got a chance, small as it is." He nodded at the girl. "Get her out of here. Take her someplace safe. They won't stop. She's their property."

"Then tell us more," Leine insisted. "Who are 'they'? How big of an organization do they work for? Is it local? National? International?"

Something shifted in his eyes.

"International?" she prodded.

Scarf shook his head. "I'm not sayin' nothin'. Not until I get me some of that pain reliever your flunky's got in his pocket."

Leine gestured for Derek to join her. "It's cold," she said in a low voice. "I'll take Mimi inside the house to warm up. Why don't you finish questioning Scarf, see what you can get out of him?"

"What do you want me to do with him?"

Leine glanced at their prisoner. "I think he'll give us more, but we have to earn his trust. Make him think we're on his side. Let him have some of the meth. We can come back in a little while. And no more shocks."

Derek rolled his eyes. "Fine."

Leine walked over to Mimi and smiled. "Let's go inside and have some hot chocolate."

4

L eine and Mimi walked outside into the frigid air. Leine squinted against the brilliant blue sky, letting her eyes adjust from the darkness of the barn. Mimi crossed her arms against the cutting wind rattling the dried corn stalks in the field.

They were several feet from the back porch when a car door slammed shut in the front yard. Leine gestured for Mimi to freeze as she withdrew her gun and moved where she could see the driveway.

Four men in tactical vests had just exited a shiny black four-door pickup. The man in the lead had a semiautomatic pistol with a suppressor. The other three were armed with AR-15s. They headed for the door.

The lead gunman made it to the front porch first and signaled the second man, who hung back and waited for the other two to make their move. The first gunman eased his way up the concrete steps, gaze riveted on the door. He paused for a moment, then slowly turned the handle. Cracking the door open, he hesitated, then slipped inside. The second man followed while the third took a position on the steps, face out, scanning for threats. The fourth headed around the side of the house.

Leine sprinted back to Mimi.

"Come with me."

Mimi's face drained of color. "Who is it?"

Leine propelled her toward the barn. "Not sure, but they aren't friendly." Her terse comment left the young girl silent.

They raced across the yard and around the side of the barn. Leine stopped outside the broken window.

"Derek," Leine called, her voice low and urgent.

Derek appeared out of the gloom. "What's wrong?"

"Four gunmen. I'll hide Mimi, then you and I need to set up."

He glanced at Mimi. "You okay in the dark?"

"I guess," she said, the wariness returning. "Why?"

He turned to Leine. "Storm cellar—north side of the barn. She'll be safe there."

Scarf craned his neck, trying to see behind him.

"The fuck's going on?" he said.

"We've got company."

He stilled. "It's them." The fear in his voice serrated the air. "They fuckin' found me."

"Make sure he can't warn them," Leine said. Derek nodded and disappeared.

With a quick look behind her, Leine slipped around the back of the barn with Mimi in tow. An overgrown bush concealed two weathered doors set in concrete in the ground. A padlock to the cellar door lay open on the hasp. Leine slid the lock free and heaved on one of the doors to reveal crumbling concrete stairs leading into a dark cellar.

Mimi balked at the yawning black expanse.

"I'm not going in there," she said.

"You won't be here long. I promise. But you need to stay out of the line of fire."

"Line of fire?"

Leine prodded her down the steps into the cool, dry room. The space had a dirt floor and chiseled rock walls. She directed her phone light toward the back, illuminating a twin mattress with an old hurricane lamp next to it on the floor. Remnants of dead spiders and canned goods peeked from the crevices.

"Sit tight. Shouldn't be too long," Leine assured her. "Don't come out unless Derek or I tell you to."

"Can you leave the light?"

"Of course." Leine handed her the phone. "If you hear anyone outside, be sure to turn it off, all right?"

Mimi nodded.

"I'll knock twice, then twice again so you know it's me."

Leine quietly lowered the door and scattered loose hay and broken branches over the outside of the cellar. Then she checked the path leading to the doors. The frozen ground didn't allow for clear footprints.

Satisfied she'd removed obvious signs of activity, she rounded the corner of the barn. Derek had taken a position near the house, using a bushy evergreen for cover. Leine joined him.

"What are we looking at?" he asked.

"From what I could see, three AR-15s, one suppressed pistol. Two entered the house, the third one's on point at the entrance. The fourth headed for the back of the house."

"He's inside." Derek gestured at the back door. "Vests?"

"Yes."

He removed a hand grenade from his side pocket and gave it to her.

"How should we play this?" she asked. They hadn't had a chance to discuss the kind of security he'd already set up.

Derek tipped his chin toward the second floor. "One or two

of them should be meeting the welcoming committee. I'd like to set up an *arrivederci* committee for the others." He nodded at the grenade in her hand. "I'll take care of the front door, if you'll do the honors here at the back." He pointed to a set of nails sticking out on either side of the back door, near the bottom. A roll of what appeared to be fine gauge wire hung from one of the nails, with an empty can attached to the wall nearby.

"Will do."

Derek made his way to the side of the house and disappeared. Leine moved to the back step. Alert for movement inside the kitchen, she pulled the grenade from her pocket and removed the safety pin, then inserted the grenade into the empty can. It was a perfect fit, and kept the spoon depressed, which kept the grenade from exploding. She unwound a piece of wire the width of the door plus a bit extra, strung it across the expanse, wrapped it around the nail on the other side, and secured it to the neck of the grenade. She tested the tensile strength and, satisfied, moved to a position with a clear view of the back door.

The blast from upstairs shook the house to its foundation. Breaking glass and shouting erupted from the second floor. A man's voice screamed, "Trap!" Footsteps thundered down the steep stairs.

"Get the fuck out!" another man shouted.

A second blast from the front of the house was louder than the first, cutting the screams short.

Silence.

Assuming Derek took care of the gunman guarding the entrance, there could be one or two more, unless either explosion did double duty.

Leine waited a moment, but no one came through the rear. She moved to the back door and paused to listen. Not detecting anyone in the kitchen, Leine detached the wire connected to the nails and eased the screen door open. She froze and listened. Nothing. She reconnected the end of the filament wire to an anchor point inside the house and continued into the kitchen, 9mm leading the way.

Once there, she stopped again and listened. The ceiling creaked above her.

He's upstairs.

She continued into the house, stopping at intervals to listen. When she reached the front room, Derek materialized from her left. The grenade had blown a chunk of the front porch out, leaving shards of glass and wood splinters scattered across the front yard. A bloody gunman lay facedown on the snow-covered yard. The man who'd been covering the front lay face up a few yards from the first. A bullet hole marred his forehead. There wasn't a third body visible.

She acknowledged Derek and lifted her chin at the ceiling. Derek nodded, and held up one finger, confirming there was one gunman left. He cut a glance toward the kitchen. She signaled to let him know she'd armed the door.

The ceiling creaked again.

They exchanged glances. Derek indicated via hand signals that he would take the stairs and that she should cover the second-floor windows from outside in case the gunman tried to escape.

Derek eased up the stairs as Leine slipped out the now-obliterated front porch. Picking her way through the rubble, she moved to one of the gunmen lying on the ground and checked his pockets. She found the key fob for the pickup, a cell phone, and a sidearm. He'd obviously been caught by the grenade in Derek's *arrivederci* plan—glass shards, pieces of concrete, and splinters were embedded in his skin.

She checked the other corpse, the man who'd taken the outside position, and retrieved his weapons and cell phone.

She worked her way around to a vantage point that gave her a good view of the farmhouse, including the back. The side she didn't cover had a gaping hole from the first explosion and didn't offer any way to climb down. Two of the back windows on the second floor opened onto the porch roof, while the ones on the other side required a steep jump.

It didn't take long before a second-floor window slid open and a man climbed onto the porch roof. Leine moved closer to keep him in view, waiting until both of his hands were occupied. He slung his AR-15 over his back and lay flat on his belly, then dangled his legs off the edge.

"Drop the gun." Leine's voice cracked through the air.

The man froze.

"Now."

Derek poked his head out the second-floor window and grinned. "Looks like we've got ourselves a squirter, yeh?"

"Looks like it." Leine aimed at the man's legs. "Throw your weapon to the ground and then lower yourself from the roof. Now."

The man hesitated until it apparently dawned on him that he wouldn't be able to shoot his way free. He shrugged off his AR-15 and let it fall.

"Now lower yourself to the ground, nice and easy." Leine picked up the AR and slung it over her shoulder.

Derek climbed out the window and crossed the roof, covering him with his gun as he did. "You heard the lady. Move."

The man shimmied off the roof. With both hands on the gutter, he lowered himself until he dangled, then dropped the last few feet. Derek followed.

"Take off your vest."

The man complied with her request and dropped his tactical vest on the ground, leaving himself in a long-sleeved T-shirt, cargo pants, and hiking boots. He stood maybe five feet seven, all lean angles with a buzz cut and blue eyes. A sharp wind from the north careened through the yard and he shivered.

"Who sent you?" Leine asked.

Derek aimed his forty-five at his head. "The lady asked you a question, mate."

The man glared at him.

"Looks like our squirter has quite an attitude, yeh?"

"He's not going to tell us much." Leine nodded at his ankles. "Secure the prisoner. Check for a backup weapon."

Derek seized the man's wrists, zip-tied them behind his back, and patted him down. He confiscated a knife from his waistband, a cell phone, and a small pistol tucked in an ankle holster.

"Who do you work for?" Leine asked.

The man remained mute. His stance and expression reminded her of military.

Derek tapped the guy's phone screen. He gave Leine a sharp glance and turned the device toward her. "He called for backup."

The screen showed several texts, the last of which read, "Send BU."

"Let's get him inside."

Derek grabbed the gunman and dragged him into the barn. Leine followed and helped secure the prisoner to a cow stall a few down from Scarf. The look that crossed between the two could have frozen the tundra.

"You two know each other?" Leine asked.

Scarf nodded. "Yeah, man. He's one of the enforcers. Was it just him? Or did they send more than one?"

"Why do you ask?"

"They usually run in packs."

"We took care of it. But more are on the way."

Scarf's eyes bulged. "Why the hell did you bring him out here? Shit. They find me an' him together, they'll kill me for sure."

Derek shrugged. "I guess you should have thought about that, yeh?"

"Got any more grenades?" Leine asked. "And wire?"

"Yes, ma'am." Derek jogged to a work bench and opened a drawer from which he produced two more hand grenades and a roll of thin wire. He came back and handed them to her.

"Drag that hay bale over next to him." Derek did as she instructed. Leine hollowed out a depression in the bale and nestled one of the grenades inside. She then attached the thin wire to the pin and unspooled several feet.

Derek grinned. "That's quite an enema."

Leine glanced at the gunman. "Hope you've been working your glutes."

The look of alarm on his face told her he understood what she had planned.

"Sit him down."

Derek shoved the gunman onto the bale and the grenade. Although the barn couldn't have been more than forty degrees, rivulets of sweat streaked the man's face.

Scarf eyed his compatriot. "That thing goes off, it'll take me with it, too. Thought you wanted information?"

"Again, should've thought of that before," Derek said as he threaded the wire through two eye bolts near the floor that were attached to a stanchion. "See how that works?"

"I'm not a dumbass. It's a trip wire." Scarf glared at Derek. "At least give me the baggie."

Derek continued his work, not bothering to reply.

"You're going to deny a dying man his last wish?"

Again, Derek ignored him.

"That should do it," Leine said, satisfied with the trip wire. "Tape their mouths shut. I'll get Mimi. You get the truck."

"My pleasure." Derek returned with a roll of duct tape and proceeded to rip off a piece for each prisoner.

Leine walked outside and around the corner to the cellar. She swept away the branches and hay, knocked twice, then twice again, and opened the door. Mimi blinked from the sudden onslaught of sunlight and gave Leine a hopeful look.

"Can I come out now?"

"Yes. More company's coming, but if we're lucky we'll have enough time to get you away from here."

"Where am I going to go?"

"Haven't thought that far ahead yet." At the look of panic on the young girl's face, Leine added, "We'll figure something out. Don't worry."

5

L eine glanced out the back window of Derek's pickup at the receding farmhouse. The rubble pile that had once been a front porch along with the gaping hole on the second floor reminded her of a war zone.

But we're in North Dakota, not Libya.

Mimi sat in the back, staring glumly out a side window. She looked delicate, exhausted.

Derek turned onto the highway and headed for town. Three identical pickups—all new, all carrying at least three men—screamed past, kicking up dirt as they careened around the corner onto the driveway and barreled toward the farmstead.

Won't be long now, Leine thought.

Derek pulled to the side of the road and waited. A short time later, a faint *boom* clapped toward them like thunder. Thick black smoke curled into the sky and obscured the silo. Derek and Leine exchanged a look.

"How many ya think that one got?" he asked.

Leine glanced behind them. "Two for sure, maybe more. Whatever happened, they'll be looking for you."

Derek nodded. "Yeh. We have to get Mimi out of town first. Then I'll come back and do some digging."

"I don't think that's a good idea, Derek."

The indignation on his face almost made her laugh.

"Why not? It's not like these animals know my face."

"What name did you use to rent the farmhouse?"

"A pseudonym. Derek Van der Haar's still in play."

"Cash?"

Derek nodded.

"Okay. Say no one knows your real name. This is small town country. There is no anonymity. The Afrikaner accent is enough of an anomaly. The cops'll be all over you once they get wind of the massacre at the farmhouse."

"What's your point?"

"My point is I'm relatively unknown, except for the woman I spoke to at the airport. I'll find out what we need to know. You make sure Mimi's got a safe place to lay low. You should do the same. At least for a while."

"I have a friend at Lucky's who might be a good source. A dancer."

"What's her name?"

"I think it's best if I did the talking with this one. She and I have an...understanding."

"How do you know she'll be honest with you?"

Derek gave Leine a look. "I know, okay? I don't want to brag, but she's into me."

Leine stifled a smile. "Well, then, you should definitely talk to her."

"I know some of the girls." Mimi slid forward in her seat. "Can I help?"

"Absolutely," Leine said. "One of the best ways is to give us whatever you can remember about Sean's organization: names, dates, schedules, who's who, that type of thing."

"Sure. I can do that. But where are we going now?"

"I have a contact in Williston who helps people like you find a place to stay. Her name is Brenda. She knows what you've been through. She's been through it, too."

Mimi leaned back in her seat. "Okay, I guess."

"You talked about a place Sean would bring you outside of town, where part of the organization met. Can you show us where that is?"

"Take the next right and follow the road past the old grain silo. I'll show you where to turn."

Derek did as she instructed and turned onto an older county road, its surface pitted from overloaded machinery using a throughway never intended to support such heavy loads. They passed miles of barbed wire fencing, telephone poles, and dozens of pump jacks, lazily pumping away, punctuated by holding tanks squatting on the flat, treeless prairie. Every few miles, one of the rigs would flare, burning off natural gas. Even with the windows rolled up, the smell of crude permeated the air.

"Does that ever go away?" Leine asked.

Derek shrugged. "You get used to it."

There was a kind of stark beauty to the landscape, Leine decided. No fancy landscaping or expansive mansions to mar the view: just fields filled with stubble from crops long since harvested, oil rigs, and the occasional farmstead with a huge barn and soaring metal silo proclaiming civilization. She wondered for a moment what people in these parts did for fun —the landscape and community were so different from her upbringing in Southern California. Fishing, she supposed, and hunting, horseback riding. She'd caught glimpses of a couple of small rodeo arenas.

Many of the families in the area were farmers and cattle ranchers, which implied hard work for much of the year. People found things to do, to be part of, coming together as humans have done for thousands of years.

Besides, most everyone was online. The internet had become the great equalizer.

They passed a large number of trailers set up in a grid pattern across the flat landscape. A chain link fence surrounded the perimeter.

"Why do I think that's not your normal mobile home park?" Leine said.

"Man camp." Derek nodded toward a larger mobile set up near the entrance. "The foreman lives in the larger structure, while the smaller ones bunk oil rig workers. This particular company's privately run. The mobile office is located in the foreman's place, so he shares with administrative staff during the day. Has the run of the place at night, though."

"No luxury there."

Derek snorted. "You'd be right about that. Once all the existing rentals were taken, it was a race to set up as many camps as possible. When word of good paying jobs spread, housing the huge influx of workers became a headache for the locals. Most of the families who were here before the boom aren't real happy about the rise in crime and overcrowding that came with all this prosperity. Kind of a love-hate relationship."

"I'll bet."

Mimi pointed to a dirt road in the distance. "Take the next left after the mile marker. The road will lead you to the place I told you about."

They drove past and Leine made a mental note of the location. The road itself disappeared around a low-lying hill.

"Not much cover," she mused. Derek nodded.

"Looks like a night job," he muttered.

"Can you describe the place? How many buildings? How many people were there? Is there security?"

"It's kind of like the camp we just passed, but smaller."

"Is there a fence?" Leine asked.

Mimi nodded. "Yeah. A tall one, but you can see through it. It's locked all the time, though."

"Is it a chain link fence? Like the kind around the last camp we passed?"

"Taller."

"Got it. How many houses are there?"

"A bunch."

"Like five? Ten?"

"Ten, maybe? I don't know if someone lives in all of them, though. I was only there at night, usually, so I couldn't see much."

"Are there cameras?"

"I'm not sure. Maybe."

"Thanks, Mimi," Leine said. "That's very helpful."

"There were a lot of guys." Her voice trailed off.

Leine turned in her seat to look at Mimi. "Was it just you, or were there other girls?"

She stared out the window. "It wasn't just me," she said, her voice barely above a whisper.

"I'm sorry that happened to you, Mimi." Leine's heart went out to the girl. "No one should have to experience what you did, ever."

Tears sprang to Mimi's eyes and her face reddened. She didn't say anything—just stared out the window at the passing landscape.

"It's going to be all right, Mimi."

Mimi wiped the tears off her cheeks, but didn't answer.

Leine watched her for a moment, then turned around to give her space.

Derek tapped the console to get Leine's attention. "Does this place we're bringing her to have some kind of mental health program?"

"They have protocols in place, although the organization survives on private donations and volunteers, so it's pretty basic. At least it's something. According to Brenda, the state of North Dakota doesn't consider her enterprise important enough to allocate public funds. She claims it's because the governor refuses to acknowledge human trafficking exists at a level that requires action."

"There's a task force mentioned on the state's website."

Leine shrugged. "Brenda says it looks good online, but in practice there's not much being done. I checked and none of the websites have been kept up to date. I think 2016 is the last year that had any kind of actual statistical reporting."

"Yeh, you know the people I've come in contact with in the area seem like good folks. I wonder if they know what's happening in their backyards?"

"Likely not. I've spoken with people all over the country who are shocked when I tell them human trafficking occurs in their area. Most believe it's something that happens in Thailand, or Saudi Arabia, or some other faraway place. Not the United States."

"Sounds like somebody needs to do some educating."

"That takes time. And money."

"You'd be surprised what goes on around here for money," Mimi said, breaking into the conversation. "There's a lot of cash getting thrown around. But none of us girls ever get to keep any of it."

"Which is one of the ways traffickers keep you on a short leash so they can exploit you."

"What am I going to do when we get to this place you're talking about?" she asked, her expression bleak. "I don't have money or any place to go."

"What about your parents? We could bring you back home."

"My parents are dead."

Leine fell silent. "I'm sorry."

Mimi wiped the tears from her cheeks and shrugged.

"What about relatives?" Derek asked. "Aunts? Uncles?"

Mimi shook her head. "There's no one."

Leine held out her hand. After a moment's hesitation, Mimi's fingers curled around Leine's.

"I will make sure you have a safe place to land," Leine said. "I work with an organization in California that matches kids and families. If there isn't a local family available, we'll look until we find a good fit for you. Either way, you'll be safe."

"You promise?" A glimmer of hope dawned in the young girl's eyes.

"I promise," Leine said.

6

J ustice "The Body" Norquist set his beer down on the table and let out a loud belch. The massive belt buckle he wore proclaiming his one successful bronc ride eight years ago peeked out from underneath his ample belly.

Although the temperature would be considered frigid by anyone's standards, Justice insisted on eschewing outerwear and instead wore his favorite worn cargo shorts and a black MMA T-shirt with the sleeves cut off, revealing beefy, undefined biceps. He hadn't been working out much lately—his employers kept him too busy busting heads.

And there'd been a lot of heads to bust lately. Guys with nothing to do but work could sure get into a lot of trouble.

Go figure.

He wished he would have been tapped to ride along to the farmhouse with the enforcers—a team of trained dudes brought in when shit got real—but Sean had told him he needed Justice to hold down the fort while the A-Team did their thing.

Shit, man. He wanted so badly to be on the A-Team, he could taste it. He was ready. He'd been practicing, especially with his AR-15 and the Glock. But he'd also been learning moves. Not the stuff they taught down at that namby-pamby dojo in Williston. That shit got old real fast. He didn't want to learn the basics first. He wanted to vault over that beginner shit and learn the good stuff.

YouTube was his friend.

Besides, whenever he talked about what he may or may not have done to some idiot at the man camp, Gloria'd get all hot and nasty for him, and that was worth more than money, far as he was concerned.

He shifted in his seat, trying to make the boys comfortable. Damned if he didn't get a hard-on every time he thought about Gloria. Justice had enjoyed his share of girls, but Gloria was something else. One of the regular strippers at Lucky's, she knew moves he hadn't ever seen on the porno sites he frequented. And he frequented a lot. His cheeks grew warm at the thought of the last time they were together. She'd pulled something on him he would have sworn he'd never, ever do, but damned if that butt plug didn't work as advertised.

The door to the trailer banged open, shaking Justice out of his reverie. In walked Cooper, one of the enforcers that went to the farmhouse in the second wave.

"How'd it go?" Justice asked. The scowl on the other man's face told him not well.

Cooper opened the fridge and grabbed himself a beer, popped the top, and chugged it down. He crushed the can and tossed it into the garbage near the sink before he sat heavily in the chair across from Justice.

"Not good, buddy. Not good at all."

This was new for Justice. Normally, the enforcers wouldn't give him the time of day. Now one just revealed they'd fucked up. The perfect A-Team wasn't so perfect after all.

"What happened? Was that pussy-Aussie there?"

Cooper frowned. "Dude's from Africa, not Australia." He

shook his head when Justice gave him a blank look. "Never mind. No, he wasn't there. But A-Rod and Scarf were."

Justice sat up in his chair. "What was that piece of shit doing there?" Scarf had been a running joke to everyone except Scarf. When Sean told the waste of space to run the little res slut to see where things went, everyone made bets he'd be on the unemployment line before the end of the week. He'd surprised them all.

"The guy took Scarf when he grabbed Mimi. Tried to get intel out of him is my guess." Cooper dug out a cigarette and lit up. "Turns out the dude's some kind of ex-military or something. The house and barn were booby-trapped."

"Like how?" Justice leaned forward, elbows on his knees.

"Fucking grenades, man. We lost A-Rod, Jam, Grunt, and Watts. Billy's got pieces of grenade lodged in his leg."

"Shit! Four enforcers down? Aw, man, we gotta find this fucker." Justice rose from his chair and started to pace.

"Calm the fuck down, will you? We're workin' on it. Ain't no way this motherfucker's going to skate after that."

"What happened to the girl?"

Cooper shrugged. "Don't know. She disappeared with the guy."

"Then we gotta find both of them." Justice turned his chair around and sat astride, leaning against the back. "Let me ask around. I bet I can find out where they went."

Cooper took another drag of his cigarette and appraised him coolly. "We'll see, man."

"C'mon. I know I can find out shit."

"You gonna ask Gloria?"

"How do you know about that?"

"Shit, man. Everybody knows about you and Gloria." Cooper leered at him. "She as good as they say, Mr. America?"

Part of Justice wanted to talk trash about his girlfriend—

could he even call her his girlfriend? He wasn't sure. But part of him wanted to keep the details private. Make it their own little thing. The latter won out.

Justice gave him what he hoped was a mysterious smile. "I'll never tell."

Cooper guffawed, but then sobered. "Yeah, we gotta drill that motherfucker. Find out where he's got Mimi." He stubbed out his cigarette and stood. "I'll talk to Sean, see if there's something you can do."

"Cool. Thanks." Justice tried to look calm, but his heart pounded with excitement. He was getting tapped to help the enforcers!

"Go ahead and see what Gloria knows about this guy. Maybe she can ask around, see if he let anything slip during his time in town."

Justice nodded. "Will do."

Cooper grabbed another beer from the fridge and left. Chin resting on the back of the chair, Justice twirled in place, his mind working feverishly. He wouldn't only ask Gloria to check out where the African dude went. He'd conduct his own little investigation, find him, and get Mimi back.

And then he'd fuck the guy up.

"THAT'S THE ONE," LEINE SAID, INDICATING A SMALL, SIXTIES-ERA ranch home on the outskirts of Williston. A burgundy colored, older-model Kia Sorrento was parked in the driveway. Plastic flowers decorated a planter under the picture window at the front. The deep-green siding with white trim had seen better days, and the front porch still had its original boot scraper embedded in the concrete. Patches of dirt peeked through the scarce snow covering the yard.

Derek, Leine, and Mimi exited the truck and walked to the front door. An unobtrusive sign in rainbow colors in the corner of the window proclaimed the house to be a safe zone. Leine rang the doorbell and waited. Moments later, a woman wearing an oversized sweatshirt and leggings opened the door and peered out.

"Brenda?" Leine asked. Lou had mentioned Brenda was in her late twenties, but the stooped shoulders and deep lines around her eyes made her look closer to forty.

The woman nodded. "You must be Leine." She turned to Mimi and smiled. "And you must be Mimi."

Mimi nodded and moved closer to Leine.

Brenda sized Derek up and asked, "And you are?"

Derek grinned his most disarming grin. "You can call me Derek."

"He's the one who called me," Leine assured her. "He's good people."

Brenda gave him an apologetic smile. "Can't be too careful. Come on inside." She opened the door and stepped aside to allow them in.

Two dark blue velour recliners and a flower print sofa clustered around a wood and glass coffee table. An upright piano with a mismatched bench stood against one wall. An early seventies-era dining table with chairs for six filled the far end. Colorful banners with Native American symbolism decorated the walls, along with a massive dream catcher in the front window. The residue of fried eggs and bacon scented the air, making Leine's stomach rumble.

"Please, have a seat." Brenda indicated the recliners and couch. "Can I get you something to drink?"

"Can I have some water?" Mimi asked.

"Of course." Brenda looked at Leine and Derek. "Anyone else?"

"I'm good," Leine answered. Derek shook his head.

"Be right back." She disappeared through a doorway into the kitchen, leaving them alone.

Derek grabbed one of the recliners and Mimi took the other. Leine sat on the sofa.

"Am I staying here?" Mimi asked.

"I'm not sure about the setup yet," Leine said. Often, victims were housed away from the main intake office so that traffickers and ex-boyfriends wouldn't be able to find them, when and if the organization's location was discovered.

"Doesn't sound like anyone else is here." Mimi moved to the piano bench and plunked a couple of keys.

Brenda returned with a glass of water for Mimi and sat on the couch. "Mimi, would you mind joining us?"

Mimi drifted over to the recliner and sat down.

"Mimi was just asking if she'd be staying here or somewhere else," Leine said.

Brenda cleared her throat. "About that. I'm sorry, but I'm closing up shop."

"You're what?" Derek shot her a glance.

"I had a visit late last night. Three men with guns told me to stop what I was doing or they'd burn the place down." Tears welled in her eyes. "At first I was angry, but then I got scared. These men weren't joking, and they had assault rifles. This place has become a target. I can't risk using the house anymore. I'm putting it up for sale and hoping for the best."

"What will you do?" Leine asked.

Brenda shrugged. "If I get a decent price, then I can take the money and set up somewhere else. Somewhere they won't find me. I'll figure something out."

"Won't that make it difficult for victims to find you?" Derek asked.

"I have some contacts in town. I distribute flyers with my

contact information at the strip clubs and bars, although traffickers basically live at those places, so I'm not sure how effective that is. Face-to-face works the best."

"How do you think these men found your house?" Leine asked.

"I'm not sure, although someone could have followed me. It's a small community. A few people know what I do." Brenda sighed. The lines around her eyes deepened. "I have to go out and connect with people, or the girls will never find me."

"You're brave to stay and help, after what happened to you."

Brenda's eyes flashed. "I'm not about to let them win. They shouldn't be able to exploit girls for their own purposes. There has to be a way to stop them. Stop *it*."

Mimi moved to the couch and sat beside her. "I'm glad you're here." She turned to look at both Leine and Derek. "Isn't there some way to help?"

"I'll give Lou a call," Leine said, "see if there are some resources he can spare."

"I'd appreciate that." Brenda smiled at Mimi and covered her hand with hers. She turned to Leine and Derek. "The problem isn't just trafficking. It's in the way people treat the land. All these big corporations care about are profits. They disregard the sacred. Anyone who doesn't care about Mother Earth doesn't care about people—women, especially. Rampant greed undermines our culture, our heritage." She studied Mimi. "Who are your people?"

"Northern Cheyenne."

Brenda nodded, smiled. "Lakota."

Mimi's shoulders relaxed as she returned the smile.

Derek stood and walked to the window. "You know, we could install a little surprise in case they come back..."

Leine shook her head. "Yeah, probably not a great idea.

We've already done enough in this county. If they haven't already, they'll be calling in SWAT or the FBI next."

Brenda looked a question at Leine.

"Things got a little out of hand where Derek and Mimi were staying. Suffice it to say we won't be going back."

"Ah. Okay."

Leine checked her watch. "It's getting late. We should get to a motel and figure out our next move."

"There are a bunch of places to choose from. I'd go with either the Ramada Inn or Hawthorn Suites," Brenda offered. "They're a couple of the bigger places. You probably won't attract attention at either one."

"Thanks." Leine rose to leave. Derek and Mimi did the same.

"I'm sorry I couldn't help you, Mimi," Brenda said as she walked them to the door. "It's been hard. Especially when no one wants to believe this is happening in their own backyard."

"You're not staying here, right?" Derek asked.

Brenda shook her head. "I'm going to a friend's. Those guys scared the hell out of me, and believe me, I'm not easily scared."

"Probably a wise choice."

The three said their goodbyes, and walked to the pickup. Leine opened the door and paused.

"What?" Derek asked.

"I assume those men were related to the thugs who came to the farmhouse."

"Wouldn't be surprised. How many traffickers can there be in one place?"

"If they're anything like the scumbags I've dealt with in the past, they're territorial in the extreme. They don't let anyone else muscle their way in, preferring to squash the competition. The money's too good."

"You need to talk to Chloe. She's super nice," Mimi said as

she climbed inside the pickup. "She tried to help me before... before Scarf pretended to be my friend."

"Who's Chloe?" Leine got into the rig and closed the door.

Derek answered for her. "One of the dancers at Lucky's."

Leine shot him a look. "You know her?"

"She's the one I told you about."

"You need to be careful contacting her. I'm pretty sure whoever sent the thugs to the farmhouse is a little pissed off right now. You're *persona non grata* at this point."

"I've got her mobile number."

"Does she have any ties to Sean? Would he monitor her communications?"

Mimi scooted forward in her seat. "I don't think she likes him. Most of the girls don't."

"She never said anything to me about him," Derek said.

"How much influence does he have over Lucky's dancers?"

"Lucky isn't a pushover," Derek said. "Sean tried to force her out of the strip club, but so far the old gal hasn't buckled."

"Lucky must have good security."

"From what I hear she's connected to somebody big back east."

Leine nodded. "Well, then. I know who I need to talk to next."

7

L ucky zipped the bank bag closed and handed it to her bouncer, Bruce.

"Make sure you deposit it before the bank closes."

Bruce gave her a nod. "No problem, Lucky. You need me before my shift?"

Lucky shook her head. "Not tonight, hon." She opened the cash register and handed him a fifty. "Go have a nice dinner with your girlfriend, what's her name."

Bruce accepted the cash and grinned. "You sure you don't want to be my date?"

"Go on, get outta here." Smiling, she waved him away, sending him out the door. He sure as hell knew how to make a gal blush. If she was thirty years younger she'd definitely give him something to think about. With a sigh, Lucky turned back to her laptop. Analyzing revenue trends wasn't sexy, but it was the next best thing.

Lucky shook a cigarette out of the pack next to her laptop and lit up. Ever since the engineers figured out a cheaper way to get oil out of the Bakken, business was up two thousand percent. That's the way things went in a boomtown. One year you're eating shit off of politicians' shoes, the next you're flying high and no one can stop you.

She wouldn't have it any other way.

Lucky and her stable of ladies had filled a vacuum—the other strip club operating in town went tits up, literally, after the last boom bottomed out, and couldn't fund a reopening. Enter Lucky and her East Coast connections—a group of old-school mobsters that set her up in the former club, promising to help her expand as soon as she showed a profit.

That was two years ago, and she'd made a hefty profit both years. It was hard not to, what with the overabundance of single, bored, horny men, pretty strippers, hookers, and booze. Hell, the food she served—if you could call it that—was an afterthought. All cheap, pre-frozen appetizers that only needed a microwave or a toaster oven. No one cared. Early on, one of the waitresses had come to her with the idea of expanding the menu, but Lucky stopped her cold. The overhead stank, and spoilage would have been too much of a concern.

Besides, Lucky knew she wasn't anything other than a madam who ran a covert stable of prostitutes out of a titty bar in Small Town, North Dakota. Wasn't much sense in Lucky's trying to be an upscale supper club. She didn't want to hire more waitresses, for one thing. Most of the dancers worked two-week contracts except for a couple of regulars. No full-timers, no insurance or set wages, no paid time off. Kept things fresh for the customers.

And cheap for her.

"Hey, Lucky." Chloe waved as she walked in the door. A dry cleaner bag with her costume for the evening was draped over her arm. "You hear about that big explosion outside of town?"

"I sure did. That's the most excitement we've had around here in months."

"Any news on where or what caused it?"

Lucky shook her head. "Should be hearing something soon, though. News carries fast in this town."

"Sure does." Smiling, Chloe shook her head and continued to the changing room. Lucky watched the Nordic blonde disappear down the darkened hallway, and then returned to her numbers.

That girl was a find. Not only a pro dancer who didn't do drugs and showed up when she was supposed to, Chloe was also working toward becoming a paramedic. Lucky just wished she could talk her into turning a few tricks. The boys from the Bakken liked big, strong blondes with back and shoulder tats— there wasn't a night that went by someone didn't offer big bucks to take her home. They'd both be rich.

Who was she kidding? The boys from the Bakken liked women, full stop. And Lucky was already rich.

Not that her financial health was general knowledge.

Lucky liked to keep an air of mystery around her. Nobody except the IRS knew her full name—and that was how she liked it. Everyone just called her Lucky. If an inquiring mind dug a little deeper, they'd find that Lucky, aka Louise Morgen, aka Lulu Morgenstern, came from a long line of certified public accountants who worked for certain connected individuals on the East Coast. When it came to where the bodies were buried, Lucky could recite from memory every single bank account number she'd ever accessed.

Turned out, an eidetic memory did a fine job of keeping her alive when circumstances may have predicted otherwise.

Which was why she didn't push for expansion. Monty, her backer in the east, was not happy with the way Sean conducted business and stood ready to send in some muscle when the trafficker set up his "man camp." Lucky had talked Monty out of it, citing her ability to shut the usurper down using her contacts at the police and sheriff departments.

Damned if Sean didn't get to them first. Apparently, underage girls were a thing for a couple of the top brass. Lucky could only shake her head in disbelief. Didn't they know Sean recorded every one of them? Talk about leverage. These days, schtupping a stripper was everyday stuff, but, thankfully, doing a kid still carried shame in the public eye.

Lucky didn't have that kind of leverage.

She'd been close to calling in the cavalry, but held off. Rumor had it Sean was either connected to somebody powerful out of Manhattan, or some *loco* south of the border. She hoped the rumors were just that—rumors. She couldn't imagine some billionaire from the City would be interested in doing business in Hansen, North Dakota. And any time the cartels came into town shit went downhill fast.

The Wild West had nothing on those assholes.

Masters of operating underground, like worms, whenever the cartels came to town their credo of lawlessness and brutality became the norm, pushing the remaining citizens out of their homes and communities. Profitable businesses that wanted to stick around ended up paying outrageous vig just to keep their doors open. Damned if she'd allow some drug cartel hood to shake her down. That's when she'd call in the East Coast boys.

She really hoped it wouldn't come to that. Hansen would never survive the fallout.

Lucky glanced at the time on her laptop and lit another cigarette. Smoking wasn't allowed in public places in the great state of North Dakota, but as long as she didn't allow customers to smoke during the hours of operation, no one gave her any trouble.

The door opened and a wall of frigid air swirled in. Lucky squinted at the visitor and frowned. The woman wasn't anyone she'd seen in town before.

Lucky appraised her visitor. Her reddish brown hair and

piercing green eyes coupled with the tall, athletic body screamed earning potential. Lucky could see putting her on stage, or better yet, turning her out. The Bakken boys would lick their way over glass shards for a ticket to ride that. The way she carried herself reminded Lucky of one of Monty's bodyguards, without the bullshit macho attitude.

Now that Lucky thought about it, she could set her up as a dominatrix with a full set of leathers and a bullwhip—branch out into the whole BDSM thing. She'd heard tell it was quite the money maker. A few of the regulars might go for that. She'd have to bring it up in conversation, depending on why the woman was there.

The woman threaded her way through the tables and chairs waiting to be set up for the evening. Lucky closed her laptop and leaned back.

Then again, maybe not. The closer the other woman got, the more the dollar signs in Lucky's mind turned to lead. The look in her eyes told Lucky she'd seen—and done—some things, things that altered a person's core.

This woman was no hooker. Or dancer. Lucky would bet her life on that.

Maybe Monty had decided to send out some muscle to give her a hand.

"Can I help you?" she asked, crossing her arms.

"Maybe." The woman stopped a foot away and surveyed the bar, her expression neutral.

She exuded an underlying current Lucky couldn't quite place—something that made her antennae twitch. This definitely wasn't someone to fuck with. She'd have to watch herself.

The woman returned her attention to Lucky and said, "You've got a problem. I want to help."

Lucky waved at the bar. "You talking about this place? If so, there's no problem." Maybe sending Bruce away hadn't been such a good idea.

"We have a certain enemy in common."

Lucky narrowed her eyes. "Did Monty send you?"

The woman ignored the question. "I hear an asshole named Sean's been trying to take over and run his little enterprise out of here."

Still suspicious, Lucky answered, "I'm listening."

"I'll make you a deal: you get me information about his organization—where he operates, who and where his muscle is, who's backing him—and I'll take care of the rest."

Lucky shook another cigarette out of the pack and lit it off the old one. "What's this going to cost me?"

"Nothing, other than time." The woman produced a business card with only a phone number and handed it to her. "My cell. Text or call when you have something."

"What if I don't trust my girls? Be pretty hard to get the information without tipping off our mutual enemy." *What if I don't trust you?*

The woman shrugged. "Then we can't help each other." She turned to leave.

"Hold on, hold on. I didn't say that was the case, did I?" Lucky's gut told her this woman would get things done—that she could work her, giving Lucky the advantage over Sean.

The woman turned back, waiting.

"Look, Sean's been a pain in my ass for months now. He's always trying to poach my customers and my girls. Hell, he even had one of his guys working the parking lot this past week." She shook her head. "If you can help me get rid of his ass and all it'll cost me is time, you got yourself a deal." Lucky held out her hand.

The other woman shook it and nodded at the card still in Lucky's other hand. "Any of your dancers have something specific they want to tell me in confidence, have her call or text. I'll set up a face-to-face."

Lucky took a drag off her cigarette and blew smoke toward the ceiling. "Will do."

The woman turned to leave.

"You got a name?"

"Leine." The woman opened the door and walked out, leaving a whirl of gritty, freezing North Dakota air in her wake.

ater that evening
L   Derek stood next to his rig in Lucky's parking lot,
waiting for Chloe. The remaining vehicles belonged to
the bouncer, Chloe, and the bartender. An SUV idled near the
front door. He stamped his feet, trying to feel his toes again. In
all his thirty-eight years, he'd never experienced temperatures
this low. The sub-zero air literally took his breath away. But he'd
been sitting too long and was determined to outlast the Dakota
Freeze. Hell if he'd let Mother Nature win.

The other dancer on shift that night came out of the bar and
climbed into the waiting SUV, her laughter cut short by the door
slamming closed behind her.

Unable to bear the cold any longer, Derek opened his door
and was about to climb inside when Chloe appeared at the
entrance.

"G'night, Bruce," she called as she walked toward the
parking lot. He'd parked next to her Toyota Corolla, making sure
she knew he was there. She looked up and their eyes met. She
smiled. A warmth spread through him, the frigid night
forgotten.

He smiled back, waiting for her to reach him.

"I didn't think you'd be by tonight," she said, stopping a few inches away. White puffs of warm breath punctuated her words.

"I like to keep you guessing."

She chuckled. "My place?"

"Gonna have to be. Mine's not in very good shape at the moment."

She gave him a questioning look and cocked her head. Then the confusion cleared and her eyes widened. "The explosion? That was your place?"

Derek looked at the brilliant stars dotting the sky and nodded. "Yeh, you know, I probably won't decorate with hand grenades next time." He shrugged. "Lesson learned."

Chloe shook her head in disbelief. "Holy shit, Derek. Four of Sean's guys are dead." She scanned the parking lot. "Rumor has it he's looking for the guy who did it. All his thugs are. You've got to leave. Tonight."

"Not gonna happen."

She searched his eyes. "You're not afraid, are you?"

"Nope. Sean's a thug. I've dealt with worse."

"Where are you staying?"

"Got a room at the Ramada. It's not fancy, but it works."

"I can't be seen going into a hotel with you. You know how people talk."

"Then I guess we'd better go to your place."

He followed her to a little ranch-style house on a quiet residential street and parked in the detached garage. She ran her car in next to his and closed the door. He met her in the kitchen, a cheerful little space painted bright yellow with sky-blue curtains at the windows. Cherry cupboards. Stainless appliances. Dark granite counters. A wooden table with four chairs waited expectantly in the breakfast nook.

"You hungry?" she asked.

Derek grabbed her by the waist and pulled her to him. "Only for you."

She smiled and put her arms around his neck. Their lips met, and for a moment Derek lost track of where he was.

He broke away first.

"What's wrong?" she asked, concerned.

"Nothing." He was going to have to ask her sooner or later, but he didn't want to spoil the moment.

"Well, then, I think you should follow me." She removed his coat and hers and hung them both on a hook by the door. He followed her through the house to her bedroom, intending to broach the subject with every step, but his body had other ideas.

DEREK TRACED THE OUTLINES OF CHLOE'S BODY WITH HIS GAZE. The white moonlight shining through the window caressed her hips and spilled down the lines of her long, lean thighs, dropping into dark shadow at the base of her knees. She sighed softly in her sleep and shifted under the blankets, as though aware of his scrutiny. His body stirred again, and he turned onto his back to look at the ceiling.

He didn't want to involve her in the things he and Leine were doing—didn't want to put her in danger. Except that was exactly what he'd done just by being here, by meeting her outside of the club.

How could he make sure she was safe? She liked her job, raked in the tips, allowing her to continue studying. Derek didn't want to put a wrench in her plans.

And yet.

Would it be so bad if she quit dancing? I could take care of her until she got her license and found a job.

He closed his eyes and muttered a curse. Who the hell did he think he was? Some Great White Hunter come up from Africa to save a pretty woman from a life of questionable circumstances? He rolled his eyes at what Leine would have thought. That kind of Neanderthal reaction didn't do anyone any good.

Chloe sighed again and rolled over, her hand falling lightly on his chest. Every part of him wanted to kiss every part of her, wake her up, and do everything all over again.

Let the woman sleep, Derek.

He eased her hand from his chest and slipped out of bed, too restless to sleep. How should he raise the subject? Just tell her he rescued the kid and now he wanted to destroy Sean and his despicable organization?

Yeh, probably not. Too harsh. Chloe didn't strike him as the vengeful type. She had guts, though, he'd give her that. He'd seen her fight off customers when they got too grabby, and she handled the drunks pretty well. It wasn't like Bruce the Bouncer could always be there for her. Sometimes the guy had to deal with disturbances in another part of the club, small though it was.

No, he'd have to come at it a different way. Softer, less angry. Even though Derek seethed inside. How anyone could use children for sex was beyond him. The world could be a dangerous and nasty place—he'd been around and seen quite a lot of the dark side. But using children like that made the bile rise in his throat.

And made him wish for easy access to an assault rifle.

"Penny for your thoughts." Chloe grinned at the well-worn saying, her skin gleaming in the moonlight.

Derek moved back to the bed and slid under the covers, relishing the warmth of her naked body.

"I'm afraid a penny won't get you much," he answered, the tips of his fingers trailing down her torso. He touched her in a sensitive spot and she gasped. He smiled to himself. She was definitely ready again. He gently pushed her onto her back, planting kisses along her stomach and inner thighs.

Afterward, they lay with their legs entwined. Her head rested on his shoulder.

"What happened at the farmhouse?" she asked, her finger tracing a circle around his right nipple.

Derek sighed. "Remember when I told you I've dealt with dangerous people?"

She nodded.

"Well, let's just say I learnt some valuable lessons about being prepared."

Chloe smiled. "Like a Boy Scout, you mean?"

When he gave her a puzzled look she burst out laughing. "Always be prepared? No? Sorry. It's an American thing." She snuggled deeper into his embrace. "So this preparedness involved explosives?"

"You could say that. It's more about the element of surprise. In case someone comes after me or someone I love."

"I heard you're helping one of Sean's girls."

"Her name's Mimi. She's barely a teenager."

She sat up and grabbed a glass of water from the night stand. "He's known for running younger girls. But I didn't know they were *that* young." She offered him a sip, but he shook his head. She drank deeply, replaced the glass, and sank back into his arms.

"From what we've gathered," he continued, "most are under fifteen."

She looked at the ceiling. "Who's we?"

Derek waved her question away. "Someone who deals with these kinds of things. Our priorities aligned, so we're working together."

"What kinds of things?"

"Sex trafficking."

Chloe sat up and pulled the sheet around her. "You're sure that's what's happening?"

Derek threw a couple of pillows behind his head and lay back against them. "I don't know what else you'd call it. Sean's holding underage girls against their will and making them have sex with whoever pays him. I'd say that's the very definition of sex trafficking."

Chloe pulled her knees up and wrapped her arms around them. "I knew he sometimes skirted the law using sixteen- and seventeen-year-olds, but he claims they came to him looking for work." She shook her head. "It's not up to me to be the morality police. If they wanted to turn tricks to make money, who was I to say anything? I knew where they were coming from."

"What do you mean? Underage is underage."

She picked at a fingernail, avoiding his eyes. "When I was a teenager my home life wasn't good and I had to leave. I was sixteen and on the street. I met a lot of people who had to do extreme shit to survive." She looked at Derek. "But if what you say about Sean is true, he needs to be stopped."

"You want to help?"

She studied him for a long moment. Derek didn't say anything, letting her think it through.

Then she nodded. "As long as you promise to lay low."

"You're not the only one to suggest that."

"What do you need me to do?"

"Get me whatever information you can on his operations. When, who, what, how, where. Where he does business. How does he deliver the girls? Where does he get the girls? Who does he work for or is he the big kahuna? What's his schedule? Anything will help."

"I can do that."

"Be careful. If Sean finds out, you'll have a target on your back."

She sighed and stared at the ceiling. "I know. I want to do this. I can't stand the idea of him using girls against their will." Her voice vibrated with anger. "Anything I can do, I will. I'll talk to Lucky. I know he's been trying to intimidate her into letting him run girls out of the club."

"We've already got that handled. My partner talked to her earlier this evening. She's on board."

"So, do I get to meet this mysterious partner?"

Derek smiled. "Yeh. I think you'll like her."

9

L eine checked the time on her phone. Derek and his girlfriend were due at the Soaring L Truck Stop but hadn't shown yet. She sighed and glanced out the large picture window at the restaurant's parking lot. She'd already memorized the makes, models, and license plates of each car, SUV, and pickup parked next to the diner. So far, the lunch crowd consisted of Leine, two truckers, three families, and an elderly couple.

Derek's Super Duty pickup wheeled in next to the front door of the diner and parked. A few minutes later, Derek led Chloe past the front register to the back of the restaurant where Leine waited in a booth. They took off their coats and sat down across from her. Chloe was the first to speak.

"Hey," she said, extending her hand. "You must be Leine. I'm Chloe."

Leine shook her hand and glanced at Derek. "Could you have chosen a more out of the way spot?"

Derek grinned. "You did tell me to be careful."

"Careful, not insane." The drive to the lone truck stop had

taken Leine over an hour and a half. "Let's hope the food's good."

"Where's Mimi?" he asked.

"Lou called with a contact in Minot. Brenda offered to drive her there."

Derek inclined his head. "One less worry, yeh?"

The waitress stopped at their table and handed them menus and waters. "Coffee?" They all said yes. She poured three cups and then headed back to the kitchen. "Just give me a holler when you're ready," she called over her shoulder.

Chloe studied the menu. "How did you two meet?"

"Derek?" Leine said, letting him take the lead.

"On a ship from Bangkok to Tanzania. You might say our interests aligned so we ended up working together."

"Derek helped me find a backpacker who'd been trafficked," Leine added. "He almost lost his life a few times."

Derek waved her comment away. "It wasn't a big deal. Leine's a big reason I switched my focus from hunting big game to something far more satisfactory."

"A mutual admiration society." Chloe smiled. "That's a good basis for a working relationship."

Leine studied Chloe. She didn't notice any nervous tics or movements, and she looked Leine directly in the eyes. Leine's first impression told her she could be trusted and that she would be a solid entrée into the world of Lucky's exotic dancers.

But she'd been wrong before. *Trust, but verify.*

"How do you feel about what Derek's asked you to do? You're aware this kind of fact-finding is dangerous, especially with a man like Sean?"

Chloe nodded. "I've been in this business a long time. I've dealt with a lot of different people. Some good, some not. Sean is definitely the latter. Most of the dancers stay away from him and his guys. Who wants that kind of trouble?"

"Does he show up often?"

She shrugged. "He comes sniffing around every once in a while, especially when Lucky gets in new talent. The younger, the better. Although, I had no idea how young."

"That's why Chloe's on board," Derek interjected.

"No one should exploit young girls," Chloe said. The steel in her voice revealed a molten anger under the surface. "I'm no innocent, believe me. I've done my fair share of questionable shit. But holding girls against their will is one step too far."

Leine sipped her coffee. "I appreciate your conviction, but this job hinges on you remaining neutral around Sean and whoever else you come into contact with. If he's anything like the traffickers I've dealt with, he gets one whiff that you're fishing, he'll either disappear or try to disappear you. Can you handle that?"

"I can. I will."

The waitress stopped at the table and Chloe fell silent.

"Make up your minds yet?" she asked.

"Three specials?" Leine said, looking at the others.

Derek and Chloe nodded. "Works for me," Chloe said.

The waitress smiled and headed back to the kitchen. "Three specials it is."

Leine leaned forward. "Do you have a gun?" she asked Chloe.

"I do, but I haven't practiced in a while."

"What kind?"

"Glock 26. It's small, but it's all I've ever needed."

"How often do you carry?"

Chloe shrugged. "When I first got it, I carried it all the time. Now, not that often."

"You might want to go to the gun range and get some practice in. Keep it with you."

Chloe looked at Derek, then at Leine. "I'm going to need more protection, then."

"We don't know at this point. But both Derek and I would feel better if you had some way to defend yourself if the need arises."

"I'm a black belt in karate, if that helps."

Derek glanced at her in surprise. "You never told me that."

Chloe shrugged again. "I don't talk about it much."

"That's good," Leine said. "How often do you train?"

"I work out at the dojo in Williston twice a week."

"Keep up your normal routine," Leine said. "If you go to the dojo on Tuesdays, go to the dojo on Tuesdays."

"I can do that."

"Good. Now tell me how Lucky's works. Most of the dancers are on contract, right?"

Chloe nodded. "Two weeks, usually."

"Derek tells me you're more or less permanent. How did that happen?"

"I worked a couple of contracts, made sure I didn't cause any trouble. I showed up on time, didn't do drugs, changed my routine so the customers wouldn't get bored. A few months back, she hired me on as a regular. I have my shifts and fill in when someone doesn't show or needs time off."

"Money's obviously good."

"I don't do it for my health."

"I imagine the customers aren't the easiest bunch to deal with."

Chloe rolled her eyes. "Adding alcohol doesn't help things. Most of them just need to let off steam, usually. Sometimes things get out of hand, though. Good training for being a paramedic, I guess."

"Are you from around here?" Leine asked.

"A little town in Montana you've never heard of."

"Try me."

Chloe studied her. "Havre."

"Been there."

"Seriously?"

"Highway 2. As I recall, the population hadn't hit ten thousand."

"Just passing through, right?"

Leine nodded.

"That's pretty much what it's known for. My turn." Chloe took a sip of her coffee. "Derek told me a little about what you do, but he was pretty cagey on the details. What's your story?"

"Not much of one, I'm afraid." Leine sipped her coffee. "I worked as a security consultant for several years. A client asked me to find a kid who'd been abducted. The head of the anti-trafficking organization I'm with now is an old friend and I reached out to him for help. He did. We found her. He asked me to join him. I did."

"Security consultant, huh?" Chloe smiled. "I've heard that one before. But it's usually from some dude with a bunch of tats and an attitude."

"Not this time."

Their waitress appeared with three plates balanced on her arm, each with a club sandwich and french fries, a pickle spear and a lettuce leaf. She carried a coffee pot in her other hand. She set them down without incident and refilled their coffee, then pulled a bottle of ketchup from her apron pocket and set it in the middle of the table.

"Anything else?"

"No, thanks," Leine said.

"Take your time, guys." She flipped their tab facedown next to Leine and moved on to another table.

Leine took a bite of her pickle. "How do you want to do this? I'd prefer not to wire you. It wouldn't work too well at the club for obvious reasons. We could set up a dead drop, or give you a burner phone to use. Or both."

"Sounds very spy-like." Chloe picked at a piece of bacon from her sandwich. "A dead drop is a secret place where I can leave a note, right?"

"Right," Leine said.

"Why can't I just pass it along to Derek? We see each other a couple of times a week."

"We're assuming Sean's looking for Derek," Leine replied. "You two should probably keep your meetings to a minimum, and definitely out of town. The dead drop is a safety feature, in case you get into trouble."

"We can set up a signal that one of us will check daily," Derek added. "Twice a day, if we need to. That way if Sean or one of his thugs gets suspicious, you can let us know."

Leine pulled a cell phone from her pocket and slid it across the table. "Use this in case you need immediate help. It's been programmed with the number to my mobile, which I have with me at all times. Don't let it out of your sight. Call, let it ring once, hang up, and call again."

Chloe slipped the phone into her pocket. "Tell me a scenario where I'd need the dead drop. Seems like the phone is enough."

"In case you lose the phone, or Sean confiscates it. Or if you think you're being monitored."

"Monitored?"

"Listening devices, video surveillance, that kind of thing."

Chloe shook her head. "Why would I have to worry about something like that?"

Leine cut a glance at Derek before answering. "Because at this point we don't know who we're dealing with. Could be

Sean's just your run-of-the-mill trafficker. Could be he works for someone else. Someone bigger, more connected. Until we know, we need to be careful."

Chloe arched her brows and looked at Derek. "Is there something you're not telling me?"

Derek shifted in his seat. "Nothing for certain, so don't worry. Yet. Like Leine said, we're just being careful."

"There's still time to change your mind."

Chloe held Leine's gaze. "I told you I'm in."

"All right." Leine picked up half of her club sandwich. "Let's establish a signal and a code word, in case things get dicey."

"Got it covered," Derek said. "Chloe can place her Christmas cactus in the living room window. It faces the street, so we'll be able to see it."

"And if I can't get home but it's important?"

"Call or text me," Leine answered.

"Okay. What if I get into trouble and need you yesterday?"

"That's when you text me your code word," Leine said.

"Which is..."

"Let's make it simple. How about Dakota?"

"Dakota. Got it."

They finished their sandwiches and grabbed their coats. Leine paid for lunch before she followed them outside to the parking lot. She stopped next to Derek's pickup.

"Derek will show you the dead drop on the way home." She nodded at the white pickup. "You should probably trade in your truck. Assume Sean and his men know what you drive. I passed a dealership on my way here."

Derek nodded at his rig. "Do you know how many white pickup trucks there are in this area alone?"

"I imagine quite a few. But I'll guarantee Sean's got his goons watching every white Super Duty pickup they can find. Make it difficult for them to find you."

"Yeh, you're probably right." Derek sighed, looked at Chloe. "You got time to stop?"

Chloe tucked an errant strand of hair behind his ear. "I always have time for you."

10

Brenda set the cruise control on her Kia Sorrento and settled back. The drive to Minot would take around two and a half hours. She glanced at Mimi and smiled. The girl looked relaxed for the first time since they'd met.

"Thought we'd have a late lunch when we got there. What do you think?"

"Okay."

"Any preference?"

"Do they have a Dairy Queen?"

Brenda grinned. "You bet they do. What's your favorite dessert? Mine's the Peanut Buster Parfait."

Mimi thought about it for a second. "I want a Butterfinger Blizzard."

"Ooh, yeah. That's a good one, for sure." Brenda put on her blinker and passed a black four-door pickup, settling into the lane in front of it before she reset the cruise control a few miles over the speed limit.

"How did you get into...what you do now?" Mimi asked.

"I trusted the wrong guy." Brenda shrugged. "I believed him

when he said he loved me. Turns out, he just loved the money I could make him."

Mimi watched the snow-covered scenery skate by, lost in thought. A moment later, she turned to Brenda and said in a soft voice, "Why did they do this to us?"

"I don't know, honey," Brenda said, searching for the right words. "Some people are just bad. They don't have any respect for women or girls, or for the law, or the land. Guys like that think we're only good for one thing and figure it's their right to use us that way."

"Like a piece of furniture."

Brenda nodded. "Like a piece of furniture. I know for a fact the guy who tricked me never loved anything. Took me a long time to figure that out, though."

"So you ran away?"

"I did. It got so bad I couldn't look myself in the mirror anymore. I felt myself sinking lower and lower. I tried using, but it only dulled the pain for a little while. Once I came down I was usually worse off than before I got high. I was circling the drain." She stared out the windshield. "Who knows what would have happened if I hadn't left?"

"There were other girls like me, but it still felt like I was the only one who had to do the bad things." Mimi clasped and unclasped her hands.

"I felt the same way. I was locked up in a hotel room outside of town," Brenda said. "A couple of other girls were there, too. I could hear them through the wall. I don't know what happened to them. We had our own rooms, although that sounds a lot better than it was."

"They never let me stay in one place," Mimi said. "Sometimes they'd drive me around in a van with a mattress." She blinked back tears. "I felt so—dirty. A lot of the men hurt me." She stared at her hands as tears spilled onto her cheeks.

Brenda reached for her hand and held it while she cried. She didn't say anything, afraid of interrupting the moment. After a few minutes, Mimi's sobs slowed. Brenda squeezed her hand.

"You're safe now, Mimi. We're going to find you a good place to—"

The back window exploded as something slammed into them from behind. The Sorrento surged forward. Mimi screamed. Brenda gripped the wheel, struggling to stay on the road. She floored the accelerator and shot ahead just as the vehicle behind them tried to smash into them again. Brenda braved a quick glance in the rearview. The black four-door pickup she'd passed a short time before loomed in the mirror.

"What the hell?" Were they pissed off at her for passing them? Really?

She glanced at the speedometer. The needle hit 80, 90, then 100 miles an hour. Cold sweat pooled under her arms and slicked her palms. "Hang on."

Her face pale, Mimi squeezed her eyes shut and gripped the armrest.

The black pickup kept pace easily. Arms rigid, Brenda pushed the Kia faster and faster, hoping, praying she could outrun whoever was trying to run them off the road.

Up ahead, a motor home lumbered along the highway. Brenda leaned on the horn and swerved into the fast lane, blowing by them at 110, hoping the driver would have the sense to call the highway patrol. The black pickup followed at a distance, accelerating once it passed the RV.

"I need you to do something for me, Mimi, okay?"

Eyes still squeezed shut, the girl nodded.

"I need you to reach in my purse there on the floor and pull out my phone. Then I need you to call nine-one-one. Can you do that?"

Mimi opened her eyes. She leaned over, pulled the purse onto her lap, and started digging through the compartments.

"It should be in the front pocket."

Mimi unzipped the pocket. The pickup slammed into them again. Mimi screamed and the purse launched onto the floor, scattering the contents. Brenda floored the accelerator, pushing the Kia past its limits.

"That's okay, honey." Brenda's voice shook. "Try again, okay?"

Tears streaming down her cheeks, Mimi nodded. She leaned over, groping through the purse's contents.

Should have had the Bluetooth fixed. Too late now. Brenda shifted her gaze from the rearview to Mimi's progress finding the phone. The pickup stayed a few feet off her bumper, never losing ground, easily keeping up. Her stomach sank at the loud whine coming from the Kia's engine. *How long can I keep going before something breaks?*

Brenda plowed on, gaze riveted to the road ahead as the flat, icy landscape screamed past. How much further to Minot? She hadn't been paying attention. If she could get someplace where there were people, she might be able to make it to the police or fire station. Where was the station in Minot?

Finally, Mimi sat up in her seat, brandishing Brenda's cell phone.

"I found it!"

"Dial nine-one-one. Hurry."

Mimi nodded. She swiped the screen, found the phone icon, and pressed it before punching in the emergency number.

The black pickup accelerated and slammed into the Kia's rear quarter panel, sending the SUV careening across the highway.

Mimi screamed again. Brenda gritted her teeth and tried to steer out of the spin, but the Sorrento hit an icy patch and spun out of control. A second later, the tires hit dry asphalt and the SUV somersaulted into the air. The purse and its contents rocketed off the floor.

The Kia slammed down on two tires and rolled across the highway, landing roof down in a shallow ditch.

11

C hloe finished her routine to thunderous applause and slipped off the stage. *Full house tonight,* she thought, gathering her tips. She made her way down the hall to the tiny dressing room Lucky had set up for them.

Two brightly colored posters greeted her when she opened the door. The one on the left, Chloe's favorite, showed a deserted, white sand beach in the Caribbean with clear, turquoise water, a calm blue sky, and deep green palm trees. The one on the right had two Vegas showgirls in full costume standing next to a black limousine in front of Caesar's Casino. Pink ostrich feathers and sparkling headdresses sprouted from each of the dancers. The words, "Viva Las Vegas!" ran diagonally across the poster in hot pink.

Gloria, the next dancer on the roster that evening, sat at the makeshift dressing table putting on her makeup. Her dark hair, creamy skin, and raunchy routine had won her a coveted space on Lucky's permanent list. Chloe liked her well enough, but steered clear whenever Gloria tried to get her to go out with some friend she'd just met. Chloe suspected she wanted to lure her into tricking by introducing her to the life gradually, but Chloe wasn't buying.

All evidence to the contrary, Chloe had a soft, romantic heart. The idea of having sex for money didn't appeal to her at all—something so intimate being used as commerce struck her as much too cynical in a world filled with cynics. She wanted someone to woo her—send her flowers, take her out to dinner, treat her nice. Derek had come the closest so far. When they first met he'd been the perfect gentleman. So much so that one night after dinner and drinks at the Wagon Wheel, Chloe took the bull by the horns and brought him back to her place.

The seduction had gone well, and they'd been seeing each other since. She wasn't exactly clear on what he did for a living when he wasn't going after sex traffickers, although hunting seemed to play a big part. Truth be told she didn't really care, as long as he was employed and happy.

She'd had enough with unemployed and unhappy.

"How'd you do?" Gloria pursed her brightly colored lips in the mirror and turned her head side to side, checking herself out.

"Good crowd," Chloe replied. She never let on what she made. Revealing her tips tended to bring out the beast in a lot of the dancers, and she didn't have time to fuck with perceived inequity or victimization. The ones who turned tricks on the side rarely let on what they made. By the looks of their clothes and cars, it was a lucrative gig. Gloria definitely fell into that category. Despite the unforgiving and frigid North Dakota landscape, she drove a brand-new, blood red Mazda Miata convertible.

At least it had heated seats.

Gloria rose from the folding chair and adjusted her costume. Tonight she looked like a sexy Annie Oakley—a cowboy hat, vest, and a pair of leather chaps sat atop pasties and a sparkly Gstring. She'd added a holster, two plastic revolvers, and a hobby horse on a broomstick as props. The shiny snakeskin boots were a nice touch.

"You'll kill it tonight. Lots of wannabe cowboys out there."

Gloria grinned and drew the two revolvers. "Li'l Annie Wood-maker at your service, ma'am." She pulled the trigger on one of the guns and a white substance shot out the end. Chloe squealed and jumped back.

"What *is* that?"

Gloria wiped the gun with her finger and licked it off. "Vanilla yogurt. Yum."

Chloe rolled her eyes and laughed as she moved to the dressing table. "You're one in a million, Gloria."

"Aren't I though?" She watched as Chloe opened a jar of cold cream and applied it to her cheeks and forehead. "You know, there are a lot of nice young gentlemen who would pay a shit-ton for an hour with you."

"I told you before." Chloe pulled tissues from a box on the table and proceeded to wipe off her makeup. "I'm not interested. I make enough dancing."

"You always say that. Wouldn't you like to pay off your student loans quicker? You'd be debt-free by fall. I guarantee it."

Chloe tossed the tissues in the garbage and glanced at Gloria in the mirror. "What makes you think I'm not already there?"

"Because," Gloria answered, "if that were true, you'd be long gone."

"Look." Chloe turned in her chair to face the other woman. "I don't want to work for some asshole who takes a bunch of my earnings just to keep me safe from other assholes. That doesn't make any sense. Why would I give my hard-earned cash to anyone else when it's me doing the work?"

Gloria leaned against the door and crossed her arms. "It's the same as tipping the bouncer. Or the bartender."

Chloe shook her head. "No, it's not. I tip Bruce because I want to, not because I have to. Besides, he's a good guy."

"So's the guy I work with."

"Who is it?"

"If I tell you, you have to keep it to yourself, all right?"

"You know me. I don't talk."

Gloria nodded. "I'm working for Sean."

Chloe widened her eyes and her heart rate ratcheted up a notch. *This might be something Leine and Derek could use.* "Really? I thought—doesn't he run younger girls? Like really young?"

Gloria shrugged. "I don't know about that. I do know it's really good money. Apparently, there's going to be an opportunity for travel, too. He's got a boatload of muscle, so there's no chance of a bad trick. They're well trained."

"What kind of money?"

"Depends on what the client wants. You'd be upper tier, so it'd be damn good."

"Like drop your jaw good?"

Gloria laughed. "That all depends on what would make your jaw drop, honey."

A sharp knock rattled the door. "Gloria, you're on," Bruce called.

"Thanks, darlin'." Gloria checked herself once more in the mirror and put her hand on the door. "Think about it, would you? I can set up a meeting with Sean anytime. Just let me know."

"I'll think about it." Chloe smiled at Gloria's back as she left the cramped room.

There wasn't much to think about. She would definitely like to meet with Sean.

L eine looked up from the results of Chloe's background check on her laptop, her attention diverted by the local news station. The scene showed a burgundy colored SUV on its roof in a shallow ditch on Highway 2. She picked up the remote and turned on the sound.

A reporter with a microphone stood on the side of a highway in front of several patrol cars with their lights flashing.

"Earlier today, the Highway Patrol arrived on the scene of a horrific accident on Highway 2, just east of Williston. According to witnesses the driver of the SUV was being chased at speeds topping one hundred miles per hour by the driver of a black Dodge pickup. The driver of the SUV apparently hit a patch of ice and flipped the vehicle, landing in the ditch. There was one fatality. We're withholding the name of the victim pending notification of family. If anyone has information regarding this accident, please call the number appearing on your screen."

Brenda hasn't checked in yet. Leine grabbed her phone and tapped in her number. It went to voicemail. Frustrated, she hit speed dial and called Lou Stokes, the head of SHEN, the anti-trafficking organization she worked for.

"Lou, it's Leine. Have you heard whether Brenda and Mimi made it to Minot?"

"Come to think of it, I haven't."

"I asked Brenda to call and let me know as soon as they made it to the shelter."

"Let me call my contact there."

Leine waited while Lou called. A few minutes later he came back on the line.

"She never checked in. What's going on?"

"The local news station just reported a fatality on Highway 2 a few miles outside of Williston. They're not releasing the name of the deceased, but I've got a bad feeling."

"Ah, Christ. You think it might be them? What happened?"

Leine recounted the information from the local news. "Apparently they were being chased at high speeds by a black pickup."

"You think this Sean guy found out Brenda was taking Mimi to a shelter?"

"It's possible. I don't know how, but I'm going to find out." Leine closed her laptop and climbed off the bed. She retrieved her coat from the closet and put on her shoes. "They didn't mention another person—just the one fatality."

"Let me call NDHP, see if I can get something." If anyone could engage with the Highway Patrol, it was Lou.

"Thanks." Leine ended the call, then speed-dialed Derek.

"Have you heard anything from Brenda or Mimi?" she asked when he picked up.

"No, why?"

"Did you see the news about the accident on Highway 2?"

"Haven't been watching. You think it's them?" Alarm peppered his voice.

"I think so. We'll know more soon. Lou's checking into it."

MIMI KEPT HER HEAD DOWN TO AVOID INTERACTING WITH THE MAN in the driver's seat. The trauma of the accident still fresh, thoughts ricocheted around her head, leaving her with nothing but questions. Was Brenda dead? She never got the chance to find out.

She looked dead.

But what if she wasn't? What if she survived? Would she come for her? Tell Derek and Leine? How would they know where she was?

What was going to happen to her now? Would she have to go back to...that life?

Oh my God, oh my God, oh my God. She replayed the accident over and over in her mind, wishing for a different outcome than the one she found herself in now. The man hadn't said a word when he unbuckled her seatbelt and dragged her out through the window of Brenda's upside-down vehicle. He'd been rough, too. Her arm hurt where he grabbed her.

She braved a glance at the side of his face but didn't recognize him. *He must be one of them,* she thought. One of Sean's enforcers. She'd only seen one the night another girl got beat up by some man she'd been with. That same girl whispered to Mimi that the man dressed in black would teach the guy a lesson, let him know he couldn't hurt Sean's girls. Mimi had found some comfort in that. Later on, though, she found out Sean used his enforcers in other ways, too. Ways that none of the girls wanted.

Mimi squeezed her eyes shut, trying to keep from crying, but it was no use. The tears spilled down her face. She let out an involuntary sob and slapped her hand over her mouth. She would be punished for going with Derek, although she'd had no choice. How could she make Sean understand it wasn't her idea to be rescued? Maybe then he wouldn't be so hard on her.

She brushed aside thoughts of what lay ahead and clasped her hands in her lap. She stared straight ahead, determined to do as she was told, keep quiet, and maybe, just maybe she'd survive.

13

Leine paced the length of her hotel room, gripping her phone to her ear. Lou had just called back.

"Brenda's confirmed dead."

"What happened to Mimi?" Leine asked.

"Looks like they got her."

"Are we sure?" Leine stopped pacing and stared out the picture window at the snow-covered parking lot.

"Afraid so. An older couple in a Winnebago pulled over to see if they could help. Brenda was the only one in the car, and she was pronounced dead at the scene. Highway Patrol told me the couple said she'd blown past them while she leaned on the horn. A young girl was in the passenger seat. A black four-door pickup was riding her bumper. According to both of them, it looked like the pickup tried to force Brenda off the road."

"Did they get the license plate number?"

"The wife managed to get a partial. North Dakota plates. The HP's running them now, looking for a match with a black Dodge pickup." Lou sighed. "It has to be one of your guy's men. But how did they know?"

"Some scary guys with assault rifles paid Brenda a visit at the home where she did intake," Leine said. "She told us she was going to put it on the market and that she'd stay with a friend—she was too freaked out to stay at the house. They must have been watching her, knew her vehicle's make and model. They might have followed her and saw her pick up Mimi."

"Or, they didn't know. It could have been a fluke. Maybe the guy recognized the car and followed them."

"Maybe. Anything's possible. One thing we do know. Mimi survived the accident. Sean's goon wouldn't take time to get rid of a dead body. What did you tell HP?"

"After they verified that I was the director of SHEN, I explained that Brenda was transporting a victim of sex trafficking and I needed to confirm Brenda's identity and whether Mimi was in the car."

"So they know she's missing."

"They do. They assigned an officer to work the case. Any idea where they might've taken her?"

"She mentioned a place outside of town. I'll check it out tonight."

"Keep me posted. The officer's name is Sergeant Robinson. Feel free to contact him. I gave him your name."

"Great. Thanks."

"And Leine?"

"Yeah?"

"Don't take chances."

"Sure, Lou."

Leine ended the call and continued to pace. Derek had come to her room as soon as she called him. He sat in one of the two chairs by the window, a partially eaten Snickers bar in his hand.

"Want one?" he asked, producing another candy bar from his coat pocket.

"No thanks." She sat down in the other chair. "How do you feel about doing a little late-night recon?"

Derek raised an eyebrow. "You realize it's colder out there than the Arctic in the middle of a blizzard, right?"

"And that matters because...?"

"Never mind." Derek crumpled the empty candy wrapper and shoved it in his pocket. "It doesn't. The sooner we find her, the better."

DEREK CUT THE LIGHTS AS THE SUV COASTED TO A STOP. LEINE peered at the terrain through a pair of night vision goggles, picking out the gravel drive leading to Sean's man camp. High, thin clouds partially obscured the moon, giving their dark vehicle sparse cover in the wide expanse of prairie. The low, undulating hills Mimi had pointed out the day before lay between them and the camp.

"Let's go the rest of the way on foot," Leine said. "We can split up closer to the objective."

"Copy that." Derek parked his new rig, a forest green Suburban, and switched off the engine. He checked the overhead light to make sure it was turned off and then exited the vehicle. Leine did the same.

A field of stars littered the black sky. The crisp air hit her hard and she slid a dark knit cap from her pocket, pulling it on as she walked to the back of the SUV. A pair of tactical gloves went on next. Derek held the back door ajar. He handed her an AR-15 with a two-point sling, and three 30-round magazines, two of which she slid into the side pockets of her cargo pants. The other she snapped into the well of the assault rifle and pulled back the charging handle, chambering a round. She'd already holstered the loaded semiauto and had the hunting knife strapped to her calf.

"Here." Derek handed her a quick-release tactical vest,

which she put on under her down vest. A suppressor and extra magazines for the pistol went into the pockets.

He did the same with his, secured a bolt cutter to his belt, and attached a handful of zip ties to a snap link on the back of his vest.

"Let's hope we don't need any of this."

"Amen."

Derek eased the door closed, and the two of them set off over the frozen ground toward the camp.

A quarter mile from the rig they rounded the base of the rise and caught a glimpse of the camp. Leine and Derek each donned night vision goggles and scanned the area. A chain link fence surrounded the property, with a large gate near the front. Leine counted twelve separate structures. The largest one stood near the gate. No lights were on in the front trailer. Faint music and laughter could be heard somewhere on the other side of the compound.

"Good thing it's not as big as the oil company man camps," Derek said. "Those can house hundreds of workers. Way too many witnesses."

Each modular structure sported a set of stairs leading to a front door. Light peeked through a couple of the windows, illuminating cracks in the drawn blinds. Most of the trailers facing them were dark.

"Guard, two o'clock," Leine whispered. An armed gunman came into view patrolling the perimeter, a rifle slung over his shoulder.

A few minutes ticked by. Derek whispered, "Looks like it's just the one. The bigger question is, how many are inside and awake?"

"How many men generally live in one of those?"

"Depends on whether the rooms are singles, doubles, or quads."

"In other words, take a wild guess."

"Yeh. If this were a legit camp run by the oil companies, it'd be difficult to do recon without being seen. Oil workers don't have regular shifts. Some start at four in the morning, some work the graveyard shift, others work everything in between. A woman on the premises would be noticed."

"Sounds like a party on the other side of camp."

"Let's go."

Leine led the way past the front gate and around to the other side. As they drew closer, the music and laughter drowned out the sound of their footsteps.

They slowed as they reached the far side of the camp and went in low, stopping at the base of the fence. All the noise appeared to come from one particular trailer. Dark shadows crossed in front of the windows, backlit from the interior lights. The rest of the barracks were dark.

"I'll cover the party, get an idea what we're up against," Leine whispered. "Do recon and then meet me back here."

Derek nodded. He unfastened the bolt cutter and proceeded to cut through the chain link. When he'd cut a large enough slice, he pulled the fence apart so Leine could slip through, then squeezed in after her.

Leine sprinted across the compound and crouched below the window with the lights on, listening to the raucous laughter coming from inside the trailer. An old rock song from the seventies played in the background.

"So where's the entertainment?" The man's slurred words were met with laughter.

"Whatdya call this?" another man replied.

"I mean the *live* entertainment."

"Can't wait, huh?" said a third male voice.

Someone guffawed. "Shit, man, he's already got a chubby. What do you think?"

"Lemme text the guy. Shouldn't be long now."

Three people, minimum. Leine screwed the suppressor onto the barrel of her pistol and waited. A scuffling sound erupted near the entrance to the trailer. She moved to the front corner and peered around the edge.

A man lay sprawled on the ground in front of Derek. Less than a yard away two girls dressed in winter coats clung to each other as they stared wide-eyed at the body. Both wore snow boots. Leine put them at maybe eleven or twelve years old.

She slid the gun into her waistband and joined Derek and the girls at the base of the stairs.

"Dead?" she whispered.

Derek nodded. "Delivery guy."

"Don't be afraid," she said in a low voice to the two terrified girls. "We'll take care of you." Upon closer inspection, she realized they were closer to nine or ten. Leine tamped down the old, familiar anger and turned to Derek.

"They're waiting for them," she whispered.

"How many?" Derek muttered, his expression dark.

"I counted three voices. One guy slurred his speech. The rest sound wasted, too."

Derek clenched his jaw and took a deep breath. "Let's get the bastards." He moved toward the stairs.

Leine stepped in front of him, barring his advance. Her anger was white-hot, reaching its apex. She welcomed the laser-sharp clarity it brought. "First we move the gunman." She nodded toward the girls. "Then you're going to take them to the truck," she said in a low, clipped voice. "Wait for me there."

Derek opened his mouth to object but apparently thought better of the idea. Their eyes met and he nodded. They each took an arm and dragged the dead gunman to the side of the trailer, then returned to the front.

He squatted next to the girls, the smaller of whom had

begun to cry softly. "Don't cry, sweetheart. You and your friend here are going to be all right. Can you come with me? I'll make sure you're safe."

"What did you do to him?" the taller girl asked, nodding toward where they'd dragged the man.

"He went to sleep for a while. We should probably go before he wakes up, yeh?"

The girl nodded. "Okay." She slipped her hand in his and said to the younger girl, "It's okay. We can go with him."

"Will he take us home?" The little girl sniffed.

The tall girl glanced up at Derek, who nodded. She looked at the younger girl. "Yes, he will."

Derek shepherded the two girls away from the trailer. Leine waited until the three of them had gone through the hole in the fence and disappeared into the icy darkness before she ghosted up the steps. She paused at the door and tried the handle. It wasn't locked. Leine eased the door open and entered the trailer.

She stepped into a small, utilitarian kitchen with a sink, refrigerator, center island, and a stove. Digital zeroes blinked on a built-in microwave. The smell of freshly popped popcorn filled the small space.

Leine eased down the hallway past a utility room with a water heater and a stackable washer and dryer. Farther down the hall were three empty rooms with two bunks in each. The rooms all had a programmable lockbox on the doors.

Light glowed underneath the door of the room at the end of the hallway where the laughter and music could be heard. There was no lockbox. The metal tag on the wall read *Media Room*.

"When are the girls supposed to get here?" one of the voices complained. A different song thumped through bad speakers, drowning out another man's reply. Leine eased closer to the door.

"The guy ain't texted me back yet," a second voice said. "Soon, I expect. Ain't never been this late before."

"They're young, right? I don't want some old, sloppy pussy."

"That's a fact, brother. That's a fact."

"Damn well better be fresh for what we're payin'."

More laughter.

Leine kicked in the door.

Three men sitting next to each other in theater-style recliners looked up in surprise. Several beer cans and an empty bottle of cheap vodka stood on a low table in front of them. Popcorn littered the floor.

One of the men lay sprawled in his underwear, a bag of potato chips and a magazine on his lap. The cover showed a little girl wearing a pair of panties and too-large high heels. A movie played on the television on the opposite wall, in which a camera panned across the poorly lit scene of a young girl on a king-sized bed. The hairy back of an unidentified man filled half the screen.

Leine's rage spiked, screaming to be released.

She calmly aimed her semiauto at the three men. The odor of unwashed bodies and stale beer was overpowering.

The bleary expression of Underwear Guy changed to one of alarm as he recognized the threat and struggled to his feet. He raised his hands.

"Look, now, we don't want no trouble, right, boys?"

The other two nodded vigorously. One had the square-jawed, fresh face of a farm boy who was maybe in his twenties, and the other was a dark-haired, burly dude with an old-fashioned tattoo of a heart ripped in two on his biceps.

"Then you won't mind handing over your wallets and phones," she said, keeping her tone conversational. She grabbed the remote and turned off the movie.

Underwear Guy blew out a relieved breath. "She's just shakin' us down, boys. Give her your shit and we'll be all right."

"Seriously? Fuck, man. I just got paid," Burly Dude grumbled.

"Do it now," Leine commanded. "And give me your phones."

She kept the pistol trained on them as she picked up first one man's phone and wallet, and then the others. She placed them on the table next to each other and chose one of the phones.

"What's the password?" she asked, holding it up.

Underwear Guy blushed, and spelled out B-I-G-D-I-C-K. Keeping her gun aimed at them, Leine entered the password and accessed his saved pictures. She tapped open a file labeled *Entertainment* and paused. Bile rose in her throat. Hundreds of haunting images of young girls and boys in various sexual positions stared back at her. Her anger spiked again, but she took a deep breath and tamped it down.

Keep it together, Leine.

"What have we here?" She turned the phone toward Underwear Guy. "Your own private gallery?" After getting the other two to unlock their phones, she glanced through them. Each had similar images stored in their memories. She changed access on all three so they wouldn't require passcodes and slipped them into her pocket, then used her own phone to take pictures of their driver's licenses.

"What are you going to do with our cells?" Farm Boy asked.

"I'm going to deliver them to some people who will be very interested in your collections." Lou's contact in the FBI who headed the Violent Crimes Against Children investigative unit would be happy to bring charges against these lowlifes.

Underwear Guy blanched. "Is that why you took pictures of our licenses, too?" He glanced nervously at his compatriots.

"That's part of it. I also wanted to know exactly who you are and where you live."

Burly Dude stared at her in disbelief. "Why'dya want that shit? You coming to visit?"

"You better hope that I don't."

"Hey," said Farm Boy. "She hasn't taken any of the money."

"Shut the fuck up, Donnie," Underwear Guy hissed.

"You're right. I didn't. But I'll tell you what I am going to do. If I find out that any of you assholes ever abuse another child again, including your own, I will hunt you down—and I will kill you."

"Fuck you will." With a low growl, Burly Dude sprang out of his recliner and lunged for her.

He wasn't fast enough.

For Leine, the *thud* of the suppressed round entering his forehead wasn't nearly satisfying enough.

Both Underwear Guy and Farm Boy Donnie jumped to their feet and barreled toward her. Leine shot Farm Boy in the leg and used Underwear Guy's own momentum to throw him to the floor. The younger man screamed as his leg buckled. Underwear Guy sprawled face-down, arms and legs akimbo. He tried to rise, but she shoved him back down, wedged her boot on the back of his head, and ground his face into the carpet.

"Fucking A!" gasped Farm Boy as he stared at Burly Dude's dead body. "You can't—that's murder." He climbed up on his good knee, but froze when Leine leveled her semiauto at his head. His gaze shifted. Something flashed in his hand. He launched himself at her like he was diving into home plate. She fired. The round entered his eye socket and he dropped like a sack of rocks, shaking the trailer with his weight. A buck knife fell from his hand. She kicked it clear.

She would have preferred to make them all suffer by turning them over to the FBI, but the attacks sealed their fate. Leine didn't question her actions. She rarely did anymore. Their deaths didn't bother her in the least. These animals wouldn't learn, wouldn't understand their monstrous sins. She'd lost the small part of her that believed they could redeem themselves. She'd seen too many go back to business as usual.

As far as Leine was concerned, those who preyed on the innocent belonged in hell, if there was such a place. She was more than happy to help expedite the trip.

"Don't shoot. I—I've got money. Please—I'm too young to die..." Underwear Guy blubbered into the floor. The sharp tang of urine joined the other questionable odors in the room.

"Should've thought of that before, dickhead."

"We was just having ourselves a little fun," Underwear Guy said, his words spilling out in a rush. "Ain't no harm in that, is there?"

"If you don't know the correct answer to that, you belong in prison." She aimed the semiauto at his head. "Or dead."

He tried to squirm out from under her boot, but Leine bore down, applying more pressure until he stopped. She lifted her foot and kicked him in the ribs.

"Turn the fuck over, dirtbag."

With a soft whimper, the guy did as she commanded. "You won't get away with this." His voice came out somewhere between a whisper and a sob.

Leine squatted beside him. "Yes, I will. Though I do need something from you before I leave."

"W-what's that?" His voice held the faintest note of hope, as though he thought maybe if he helped her she'd let him go.

"First, I need to know how you find these girls. Is there a specific phone number?"

"The number's on the back of that free publication they got all over town," Underwear Guy continued, trying not to look at his dead friends. "You know the one, *The Last Page*?"

"Which number? There are quite a few to choose from."

"You gotta know who you're callin'. It's the one that says *Your Private Escort*."

"Okay. You call the number and then what?"

"Then you tell whoever answers the phone what you're looking for."

"What did you tell them tonight?"

"That me and my buddies was lookin' for a couple of girls to party. You just order what you want."

"I see. And did you order a certain age?"

"They know me pretty well. I've used them a bunch."

"Good to know. Second question. I'm looking for a girl by the name of Mimi. Thirteen, maybe fourteen years old, dark hair, medium height. A real sweet girl. Since you pedophiles tend to stick together, I figured you'd know all about who's available, am I right?"

Underwear Guy frowned. "I'm no prevert."

"You can't think the girls you were expecting tonight were over eighteen?"

He stuck out his lower lip. "That's illegal."

"Huh." Leine cocked her head. "So you're telling me what I saw here tonight—the movie, the magazine, the photos on your phones—is kinda like fake news?"

"Yeah. That's exactly right. You never saw no young girls." A gleam lit his eyes and he nodded vigorously.

Asshole. "You know who Mimi is?"

"Can't say as I do. But I can keep an eye out for her, if you want."

"She's a little old for you, though, am I right?"

Underwear Guy screwed his face into a frown. "That's not what I was sayin' exactly..."

Leine stood and leveled the gun at his head. "Too bad you couldn't help me find her. I might have let you live."

"Wait! Wait. Wait a minute here. You know, I might've...I might've seen her." He made a smacking sound as he licked his dry lips. "She disappeared for a while and came back, right? Long dark hair? Kinda skinny? One of the res girls?"

"That's the one."

"Yeah, yeah. Now I remember. Her picture was in the catalog online, but she ain't available right now. They's ramping up for the Super Bowl."

"Where's the party?"

"Heard tell he's going down to Phoenix."

"Good to know."

"You're gonna let me go, right?" Underwear Guy started to get up, but Leine pushed him back with her foot. The pent-up rage tugged at her, begging for release.

"Sorry. Not today, asshole."

"But you said—"

"I lied," Leine said, and pulled the trigger.

Twice.

14

C hloe checked herself in the mirror one last time. She wanted everything to go perfectly, which meant she needed to look good enough to get Sean interested in hiring her. Gloria had given her a couple of tips—he liked women who were confident, but not ballbusters. He also responded to flattery.

Pretty much like every guy.

"He'll love the tall Nordic look," Gloria had said, "but the tattoo could go either way."

Which was why Chloe chose a short, sapphire blue, form-fitting sweater dress, blood red fuck-me heels, and sheer thigh-highs. She hated wearing hose but figured it would give her legs protection from the bitter cold. The sweater dress did double duty—it was warm and covered the tat. She'd spiked her short hair with gel and kept the makeup to a minimum, assuming he'd appreciate the natural look. Besides, it took five years off her.

She'd texted Derek, letting him know she was going to a party at Sean's, but warned him not to show himself because his goons were looking for him. He texted back he'd be close by if she needed him. That worried her. She'd overheard one of Lucky's customers at the bar, a guy named Justice, asking if anyone had seen the Aussie who lived outside of town. Wrong nationality notwithstanding, no one had, of course. Derek kept a low profile since the explosion.

After one too many drinks, Justice had grown obnoxious and Bruce ejected him from the premises. He'd cussed a blue streak and swore he'd be back to teach them all a lesson. After that, Bruce had made it known he was packing.

Chloe sighed. Just another night at Lucky's.

Gloria pulled into the driveway in her Miata and honked. Chloe pulled on her long down coat and grabbed her purse. She glanced in the mirror one last time. *You're on.* She took a deep breath, exhaled, and walked out the door.

Cursing the stilettos, she gingerly maneuvered her way across the ice that had formed since morning. She made it safely to the car and climbed in without falling on her ass. A heavy beat thumped from the subwoofers in the trunk and she grimaced at the loud music. She had her fill at the club.

Gloria turned down the stereo and beamed at her. "Ready?"

Chloe nodded as she pulled at the hem of her dress. "As ready as I'll ever be."

Gloria backed out of the driveway and headed east. "You're gonna love his place. It's amazing."

"You didn't tell him I was totally committed yet, right?"

"I didn't tell him a thing. It's all up to you. If he likes you, you'll know." She grinned. "Either way, get ready to party. He knows how to throw a bash, believe me."

Good thing I coated my stomach, Chloe thought. She'd put some charcoal pills in her handbag, just in case the night got away from her. She didn't intend to overindulge, but she wasn't stupid. Shit happened.

Forty-five minutes later, Gloria turned into an asphalt

driveway and stopped at a gate flanked by two large brick columns and a guardhouse. She waved at the security guard, and the gate swung open.

As they wound their way up the drive, a large stucco house appeared on their left. There weren't any cars parked in front.

When Gloria didn't turn in, Chloe asked, "Who lives there?"

"The caretaker."

They crested a small rise and Gloria stopped so Chloe could take in the view. Below them stood the largest house Chloe had ever seen. Lights blazed from every window, lending a festive glow to the stone and wood framed mansion. Dozens of cars lined the driveway.

"See the lake?" Gloria asked, indicating a flat, frozen area arcing in a rough circle from the rear of the house.

"Which one is that?" Chloe didn't remember a body of water in this area. No other houses dotted the shoreline.

"It's man-made. Sean has it stocked with rainbow trout and Dolly Varden."

"Seriously? His own lake? Wow."

Gloria continued down the driveway, rolled up under the portico, and parked.

"Welcome to paradise, hon."

A man wearing a red jacket appeared at Chloe's window, and she jumped in surprise. Gloria guffawed.

"Babe. It's just the valet."

The man opened Chloe's door and offered his hand. She grabbed her purse and climbed out.

"Thanks." She took note of the security cameras trained on the front door and at various intervals along the width of the house.

He bowed and gestured to the entrance. "The party is through the double doors."

Impressed in spite of herself, Chloe made a face at Gloria,

who grinned back at her as they walked up the steps.

The doors opened onto a huge entrance hall, complete with marble floors, a massive crystal chandelier, and artwork that seemed familiar, but that Chloe didn't recognize. A jazz ensemble played unobtrusively at the far end, while waiters and waitresses wearing red, white, and black wove in and out of the crowd carrying trays of champagne.

Drinks in hand, several people milled through dozens of rooms, laughing, drinking, and chatting. Another man in a red jacket took both their coats and steered them toward an open door to their left.

"Help yourself to refreshments, ladies."

"Thanks," Gloria said.

Chloe followed Gloria into the packed room. Tall ceilings and a baby grand greeted their entrance. A gleaming wooden bar with a series of glass shelves stocked with top-shelf liquor ran along one wall. Two busy bartenders worked the three-deep crowd.

Gloria grabbed two glasses of champagne from a passing waiter and handed her one. She took a long drink and licked her lips.

"Yummy. If I'm not mistaken, Dom Perignon. One thing about Sean—he's top-shelf all the way." Gloria raised her glass for a toast. "To the beginning of a beautiful something."

"Skol." Chloe took a sip and rolled it around her tongue. "Pretty good," she added.

Gloria laughed. "Pretty good, she says. Sheesh. What, Dom ain't good enough?"

Chloe shook her head and giggled. "That's not what I meant." She scanned the room, instantly recognizing several regulars from the club. That could make things interesting. She usually didn't frequent venues where she might run into Lucky's clientele. She took another drink and mentally shrugged it off.

At least the younger customers weren't there. The older guys tended to be more inhibited.

Which was just fine with her.

"Come on. Let's sit." Gloria grabbed her hand and led her to a tall table with high stools that had just been vacated. The two women put their purses and drinks on the table and climbed onto the stools. Chloe tugged at the hem of her dress and made sure she kept her knees together. She didn't intend to give anyone a show tonight.

"What do you think?" Gloria leaned closer so she wouldn't have to yell.

"Impressive." Chloe took another sip of her champagne. "How many people live here?"

"Just Sean."

"Seriously? How many rooms are there, like twenty?"

Gloria shook her head. "I heard someone say there's over thirty. That's including six or seven baths."

"Who needs that many bathrooms?"

"Well, if you throw a big shindig like this one, the guests certainly do appreciate it."

Startled at the man's voice behind her, Chloe swiveled on her stool to see who'd spoken. Tall and muscular with a shaved head and dark brown eyes, their host stood just steps behind her. Sean had eschewed his typical khakis and golf shirt for a black Hugo Boss suit and dark blue tie.

Imposing and impressive, although not Chloe's type.

He held out his hand. "Sean Cumani. And you are?"

Chloe extended hers and said, "Chloe Olson."

Holding her gaze, Sean lifted her hand to his lips. "A pleasure, Chloe Olson." He kept her hand in his a moment too long before letting go.

The press of bodies in the room ratcheted up the temperature—or was it Sean's close proximity? She had to admit, he did exude confidence. She tried to unobtrusively wipe her palms on her dress—probably should have worn something lighter.

Chloe had only met him twice before, and not in any formal capacity. The first time, she'd walked in on an argument between him and Lucky at the club. She'd tried to back out of the room before they noticed her, but she was too late. They both stopped arguing immediately. Lucky clammed up when Chloe asked her later what had happened, telling her it was nothing.

It didn't feel like nothing.

The second time, he'd been at a party one of the oil execs hosted for the higher-ups in the city. Sean worked the crowd, talking with as many government officials as he could. During one of his rare down times, he'd offered to get her a drink. She declined, and left soon afterward. The mayor famously asked a reporter covering the event who the hell the young snake oil salesman was in the expensive suit. The reporter answered, "Someone very rich." At that time, no one knew the exact source of Sean's wealth.

Most still didn't.

"Welcome to my home." His gaze moved over her like a Zamboni on ice. A shiver laced up her spine.

"Quite the crib you've got here," she said, trying to cover her reaction. "It must have cost a fortune to build."

"Um, Chloe," Gloria said. "We don't usually talk about—"

"No, no, I don't mind," Sean said. "Yes, it did cost a fortune. But it was worth every penny."

"And it's just you?"

Gloria groaned.

Sean smiled. "Yes, it's just me."

"Must get lonely."

He ignored the comment and asked, "Would you like a tour?"

"You bet."

He offered his arm. Chloe threw back the rest of the champagne and set the glass on the table. She started toward the door but turned back. "Aren't you coming?" she asked Gloria.

Gloria shook her head. "I've already seen it. You go ahead. I'll be right here, people watching."

Chloe took Sean's proffered arm as they threaded their way through the crowd into the foyer. The two of them garnered a boatload of curious looks. The town gossips would have a heyday tomorrow, especially when they found out the blonde with Sean Cumani was a stripper at Lucky's.

"The marble is imported from Carrera, Italy," Sean said, pride obvious in his voice.

"The US doesn't have good marble?"

Sean chuckled. "That's a good question. I don't know, but I doubt it."

"Actually, did you know the Lincoln Memorial is made out of marble from Aspen, Colorado?"

"No, I didn't know that."

Chloe shrugged. "Lots of people don't."

"How did you learn that?"

"I'm a walking encyclopedia of useless information, I'm afraid. Comes with spending so much time studying."

"That's right. You're going to school to become a paramedic, right?"

She nodded. Interesting. Either he did his homework or Gloria clued him in. "I can tell you thirty ways to treat a wound, and throw in the best way to cook a lasagna."

"That must come in handy as a dancer."

Chloe gave him a sharp look. "Sarcasm about my chosen profession?"

"Never. I've seen you dance. You're good."

Even more interesting. He'd seen her dance. *That's not creepy, is it?* A tendril of doubt snaked up her spine. Was she getting in over her head? He obviously knew more about her than she did about him. And he'd watched her dance at least once.

They came to the bottom of a sweeping stairway and stopped.

"Shall we?"

The first hint of alarm swept through her. Chloe let go of his arm and walked past the stairs.

"I'd like to see the rest of the main floor, if you don't mind." Did he expect her to audition? Yeah, that wasn't gonna happen. But what if it tanked the deal? *Well, at least I know where he lives and I've seen part of his security detail. That should count for something.*

"Whatever the lady desires." Sean followed her past the stairway through an enormous living room filled with more animated people, then down a long, dimly lit hall with closed doors on each side. The number of partygoers thinned considerably.

"What's in those?" Choe asked.

"Extra rooms I don't use. The house is so big, I find that I only frequent a few rooms: the kitchen, the dining room, media room, and, of course, my bedroom."

"Why did you build such a huge house?" They stood in the hallway, surrounded by closed doors. A series of six graphite sketches lined one wall, spot-lit by accent lighting. There was no other illumination, casting them both in shadow. "I mean, if it's just you here, that doesn't make a lot of sense."

Sean chuckled. "You're certainly direct. Mainly, it's for business entertaining. I host folks from corporate for retreats and working vacations. And, of course, I have big parties."

"Vacation? Corporate retreats?" she said as she moved past him, intending to return to the party. "That all sounds awfully legit for what you do."

The air stilled. Chloe turned back to see what the problem was. The look on his face stopped her cold.

"Did I say something wrong?"

Sean narrowed his eyes. "What is it you think I do?"

Chloe smiled, trying to diffuse the situation. Her heart hammered in her chest. "I'm sorry. Did I just make a total fool of myself?" She glanced down the hallway, stifling the urge to high-tail it back to the party and the safety of other people. "Gloria told me you might be interested in hiring me."

"She was misinformed." Sean's shoulders inched down, but his jaw pulsed, telling her he'd only been partially mollified. "I'm interested in you, Chloe. I want to explore a relationship with you."

Chloe's mouth dropped open, but she clamped it shut a split-second later. "You...what?"

Sean walked toward her. She resisted the impulse to back away.

He stopped a few inches from her. "I want us to have a relationship," he said in a husky voice. He placed his hands on her hips and pulled her to him. Without thinking, Chloe put her hands against his chest and turned her head as he dipped down for a kiss.

She took a step back and shook her head. "I'm sorry. This isn't at all what I was expecting. I thought you were hiring more...employees."

Sean crossed his arms. "That's not your concern, frankly. What I don't have is companionship. You said it yourself. Life here gets...lonely."

"Surely one of your employees could keep you company."

"I'm not interested in pursuing anyone currently in my employ. I need someone who can navigate large soirees and intimate dinner parties equally well. Someone who's smart and knows how to hold a conversation."

"How do you know I can do all that?" Chloe asked.

"I've been watching you for a long time."

That's not creepy at all. "I see. But why me? Why not Gloria? She's smart."

"Gloria's a little too earthy for my taste. She's similar to many of the wives of the higher-ups in my organization. I prefer someone with more—class, for lack of a better word. Someone who is at home in a villa in Tuscany, or an exclusive resort in Cabo San Lucas."

"Why would you think I'd be comfortable in either of those places?"

"I'm a good judge of character." Sean studied her for a moment. "Of course, there'd be an incentive for you to stay. Some of my past relationships have told me I can be...difficult."

Was this guy serious? An incentive to stay because he's difficult? A cacophony of fog horns blared in the back of her brain.

"May I ask what you mean by 'difficult'?"

"Let's just say there will be ample incentive should you decide to accept the terms."

Chloe shook her head and turned back toward the party. "I'm sorry. I'm going to need some time to process—your offer."

"Of course." He caught up to her and took her elbow. "In the meantime, why not enjoy the party?"

As they walked back to the festivities, Sean said, "I expect you to keep this arrangement to yourself." He stopped and wrapped his fingers around her arm in an iron grip. "I'm not a man to play games, Chloe. If word of our conversation gets back to me in any form, I will know it was you. I'll warn you now, that's something you don't want."

Chloe swallowed hard, her throat suddenly dry. He loosened his grip, and they continued to the party. She did her best to ignore the red flags waving furiously in her mind.

15

L eine drove through the night, taking the two girls she and Derek had rescued to Sarah Two Deer, Lou Stokes's anti-trafficking contact in Minot. Derek had stayed behind in Hanson, in case Chloe ran into trouble at Sean's party.

A kindly woman named Berta gave the girls pizza and juice and sat them down in front of a big-screen television in a quiet room at the back of the facility, while Sarah scanned an online database. A nurse the organization regularly used was due to arrive within the hour.

Leine pulled up a chair from another desk and sat next to Sarah to watch her work. It didn't take long for her to find a match.

"The girls you rescued tonight are sisters named Lila and Monica. They're members of the Mandan Nation and live on the Fort Berthold Reservation. They were last seen walking home from school two days ago." She scrolled further down the screen. "Says here the parents and tribal police are exhausting every lead, and are still actively pursuing the investigation. They're going to be one happy family to get them back."

Leine leaned closer to the screen to get a better look. "Fort Berthold's about twenty-five miles from where we found them."

"How exactly did that happen?" Sarah studied Leine, a million unasked questions in her eyes.

"Let's just say we were at the right place at the right time and leave it at that."

"The tribal police may want to question you. What do you want me to tell them?"

"Tell them whatever you want, but I'd appreciate it if you kept my name out of your report."

"The people responsible need to be brought to justice."

"That won't be a problem," Leine replied.

Sarah studied her. "Lou said you had your own way of doing things."

Leine nodded. "You could say that."

"Just be careful. Powerful interests are putting down roots in the oil fields, and I'm not talking oil companies."

"Wherever there's money, there are criminals. We do what we can to stop them."

"It's going to get worse. The Super Bowl's in less than a week. My contacts tell me traffickers are ramping up from all over."

"It's in Phoenix this year, right?" Leine asked.

"It is."

"Nice weather means more visitors."

Sarah sighed. "The current levels of sex workers can't handle the influx. Get ready for an exponential growth in sex trafficking."

"The guy I'm investigating is doing the same," Leine said. "It's possible Lila and Monica were on their way to being broken in ahead of the buildup."

"Thank goodness you found them." Sarah took a drink of the soda sitting on her desk. "Ever since the #MeToo movement, we've seen an uptick in awareness about the disproportionate number of missing Native women and girls." She rubbed her eyes. "But the cases are still rising. Whenever one woman or child is found, another two go missing. It's daunting, but we keep trying."

"I get it," Leine said. "It certainly makes the victories more poignant."

"That it does. We celebrate when we can. Lately, though, the successes have been few and far between." Sarah gave Leine a tired smile. "Thank you for the two tonight."

"Hopefully they won't be the last," Leine said. "That being said, would you be able to do me a favor?"

"Sure. What do you need?"

"Can you check the database for Mimi, the girl Lou called you about? I'm curious to see if anyone's reported her missing."

"He told me what happened to Brenda," Sarah said. "She was an immense resource, and amazingly good with victims. We worked with her several times. She'll be missed."

"We spoke only briefly," Leine said, "but I got the sense she was in it for the long haul. That she really cared."

"She was and did. The best way to honor her is to keep fighting." Sarah nodded at the computer. "Give me whatever information you have on Mimi. I'll run it through the database."

Leine told her what she could about the missing girl. Sarah typed the information into the computer and waited for the screen to populate.

"I'm sorry. There's nothing. Sometimes that happens with runaways in the foster system. The foster parents want to keep getting the checks for as long as they can and don't report when the kids take off. If the parents did report the disappearance, the checks would stop."

"Great system. I ran into that before, on a case I worked in Los Angeles," Leine said.

Sarah shrugged. "It's the best we've got. Doesn't matter what system's in place. There'll always be someone willing to game it, unfortunately. Is there anything else you can give me about her?"

"No. But if I think of something, we'll give you a call."

Leine returned to her vehicle, accompanied by the sound of her footsteps crunching through the snow-covered parking lot. She climbed in and started the engine.

Her gut told her that Sean was taking Mimi to Phoenix. She doubted he'd take all of his girls. That wouldn't be good for local business. He knew Derek was looking for Mimi, so it made sense for him to get her out of town.

Leine sighed. There was no avoiding it.

She needed to call Lou.

JUSTICE NORQUIST CHECKED TO MAKE SURE THE DOOR TO THE trailer was locked tight for the evening, and retraced his steps down the stairs.

One more to go, and then he could go back and have another beer and watch Cage Fury on TV.

He checked the time on his phone as he made his way to the far trailer. Buddy hadn't checked in yet, but it was late and the lights were off, so he figured he must have been in the can when Buddy left camp with the clients.

Justice frowned at the outside light—usually Buddy turned everything off before he left. A dark spot on the ground caught his attention. He shined his phone's flashlight at it and his heart skipped a beat.

The dark spot turned into what looked like congealed blood in the snow. Several footprints surrounded the stain, leading to the side of the trailer.

One of the enforcers must have shot something.

Justice pulled his Glock free from his waistband and followed the prints to the edge of the trailer.

Might as well practice my maneuvers. A guy never knew when he might be called upon by the enforcers to bust some heads. He wanted to be ready.

With his back to the trailer, Justice raised the barrel of his gun straight up with both hands like he saw all those cops do on television. He paused, listening for movement. A slight breeze sloughed through the camp, rattling the branches of a dead bush nearby, but that was all.

In hero mode, he slipped around the corner and brought the gun down at the same time, aiming toward the imagined threat.

His breath caught in his throat. Buddy lay on the ground, propped up against the trailer skirt, his chin to his chest.

"Shit!" Justice slid his gun into his waistband and hurried to his obviously unconscious friend. "Buddy! Hey, Buddy. Wake up —" He patted the side of Buddy's face and pulled his head up, hoping to revive him. That was when he noticed a dark hole marred Buddy's forehead, accompanied by a trickle of blood that had congealed down the side of his nose. His eyes were open.

And staring at nothing.

"Gah!" Justice let go of Buddy's lifeless head and stumbled backward, falling flat on his ass in the snow. He stared at the dead body, his brain working overtime to make sense of what he was seeing.

"Damn." Justice fumbled for the radio attached to his belt. "Mayday, Mayday! This is Justice back at camp." His heart raced and his breath came fast as he stared at Buddy, waiting for a response from the radio. He was about to send out another Mayday when the handheld crackled.

"This is Cooper. What's up, Justice?"

Relief flowed through him. "I-I found Buddy."

"And?"

"Uh—he's d-dead."

There was a pause. Then, "What the fuck did you just say?"

"Buddy's dead." Gaining courage, Justice scrambled to his feet. "He was shot. In the head."

"Hold on. I'll be right there. ETA ten minutes."

"Roger that." Justice attached the radio to his belt and stared at Buddy. It was the first dead body he'd ever seen, and he was a little creeped out.

He shivered, realizing for the first time he was cold. He'd go inside, make sure the trailer was secure before Cooper showed up.

He climbed the steps and tried the door handle. It was unlocked.

What if they're still inside? Cooper would give him nothing but shit if he showed up and saw that Justice hadn't checked the structure for threats. On the other hand, the enforcer might be impressed if Justice showed initiative and cleared the trailer.

He drew his Glock for the second time that evening and eased the door open.

Upon entering, the smell of popcorn mixed with something else hit him. Sweat pooled under his arm pits as he made his way down the hall, clearing each room. By the time he reached the end of the hall, he'd recovered some of his bravado by making up a scene in his head:

The badass enforcer checked the trailer for gunmen, room by room, saving the town's grateful citizens from Dirty Dan's death and destruction...

Justice kicked open the door and entered the media room.

And promptly threw up.

16

L eine waited at baggage claim for the United Express flight from Denver to unload. Lou chose the Bismarck Municipal Airport so there was less chance that someone would recognize the former assassin or the SHEN academy recruit when they got back to Hansen. Even so, Leine wore a knit ski cap and sunglasses. She also wore a lightweight down coat in a different color she'd purchased from a department store on her way to the airport.

The previous morning's phone call with Lou didn't go well. The problems started when he recommended Jinn for the operation. Leine strenuously objected, citing the girl's inexperience.

"I understand your concerns," he replied after she'd given him an earful. "But think about it—Jinn's gotten herself out of more dangerous situations than every other recruit we have, especially one her age. She was first in her cohort at the academy, and has picked up English like she was born here. You said it yourself—she's got street smarts. And now she's had intensive self-defense and counterintelligence training. You're the one who insisted on patterning the academy after the same modules

Eric put you through at the agency. Do you really think all that training won't work?"

Leine had been silent, sifting through arguments she could make that would keep the kid from being part of the operation. None of them held water.

Lou had sensed her softening and went for the *coup de grace*: "Isn't this exactly what she's been trained to do? Let her go, Leine. She's ready. Let her prove herself. The other grads her age aren't ready for this kind of op."

Jinn had proven resilient and resourceful—both in Libya and Los Angeles. Lou was right.

"Fine. But I'm acting as overwatch," Leine responded. "Jinn will check in with me at regular intervals, and will wear a removable GPS transponder at all times. As long as I can track her, I'm good with her deployment. The moment she believes she's in trouble, I'll exfil her. And yes, Lou, before you ask—I will blow the op to save her if I have to."

"Congratulations, Leine. It's a big step—for both of you. Can you be at Bismarck Municipal by one-thirty tomorrow afternoon?"

Leine paused a moment. "You already booked her."

Lou chuckled at her droll response. "Don't forget—the minute I'm not one or two steps ahead is the minute you need to worry."

A group of passengers started trickling into the baggage claim area. Leine scanned the crowd for Jinn. Oddly enough, her slight frame and small stature hadn't kept her from being first in her class in self-defense and weapons training. Most adversaries underestimated small. And female. Leine often used the latter miscalculation to her advantage. She supposed it was one of the many reasons she'd been good at her job at the agency. Back in the day, a female assassin was a rarity. Nowadays there weren't a lot of children infiltrating the sex trafficking underworld that were trained as well as SHEN graduates.

True, the recruits would be undercover operatives, not killers. But being undercover in a criminal organization held its own dangers. Leine made sure all recruits had a thorough understanding of the risks involved. Specific modules she and others had created dealt with misdirection and staying in character for however long it took to do their job. She'd also included an intensive module on extraction, or exfil, from an operation.

Safety first.

Another group trickled into the claim area, with Jinn bringing up the rear. At the sight of Leine, the kid broke into a grin and ran to greet her with a bear hug. Leine returned the hug, then let her go.

Her cheeks coloring, Jinn took a step back. "Sorry. Am I supposed to be in character?"

Leine picked up Jinn's worn backpack and slung it over her shoulder. "You're fine. It's far enough away from where we're going. Although it's not a bad idea to practice."

Jinn studied the people from the flight waiting for their bags at the carousel. "Lou got me a window seat, so it was easy to ignore everybody." She pulled a pair of earbuds from her pocket. "These work, too."

"Are you hungry?"

Jinn nodded. "Can we get sushi?"

Leine checked her phone. "Looks like you're in luck. There are a couple of places that have good reviews here in town."

"I've been dreaming about a tuna roll covered in wasabi. Lou doesn't like hot anymore, and Nita won't eat raw fish." Nita was Lou's wife of several years. She'd enthusiastically taken Jinn into their home, even after Lou expressed his reluctance to raise another kid. She'd pooh-poohed the idea they were too old to handle another child and, predictably, Lou backed down. Leine would have adopted Jinn herself if her lifestyle and occupation had been anything close to normal.

During their lunch at the sushi place, Jinn plastered her tuna rolls with wasabi, a bright green, volcanically hot mustard, and regaled Leine with her latest obsession—a recently released video game featuring a female assassin. She didn't ask about the operation. There were several customers in the restaurant and neither wanted to risk someone overhearing their conversation.

After lunch, they drove to a gas station to fill up, then headed out of town.

"Is it always this cold?" Jinn asked, tracing a heart with her finger in the condensation on the window. Outside, the snowy landscape streamed past.

Leine shrugged. "This is my first time here. Apparently they have warm summers."

"I've never seen snow in real life."

"It's cold." Leine pulled onto the highway and headed north. "Let's run your legend. What's your name?"

"Yasmine."

"How old are you?"

"Twelve."

"What's your story?"

"I was abused at home by my stepfather, and ran away. We lived in Minot near the base. I hitched a ride to Hansen. Lucky found me going through the dumpster behind her club. She's been letting me sleep in the back room in return for sweeping up in the morning and doing odd jobs. I'm supposed to be nervous about being found out, but make friends with the dancers anyway. If I run into problems I can tell Chloe, because she's in on things."

"Good. You have the GPS?"

Jinn lifted her foot and pointed at her tennis shoe. "It's

hidden in the insole. I can take it out and put it inside something else if I have to."

"What else?"

"Depending on how the bad guy tries to recruit me, I'm supposed to act scared if he's mean, trusting if he's nice."

"What are your expectations once he makes contact?"

"Lou thinks he'll try to make me like him first. That's the best because it gives me time to find out as much as I can."

"And the worst?"

Jinn's expression hardened. "He'll be mean and try to make me do what he wants."

"What do you do then?"

"I text you and escape."

"Right away?" Leine asked.

"Right away," Jinn confirmed.

"What if they take your phone?"

"They won't. Remember, I am Jinn of the Marketplace—a ghost, a wisp of smoke. I know how to hide things, and I know how to escape."

Leine sighed. "I remember. Don't assume anything. And make sure you don't do too much on your own. I won't be far, but a lot can happen in a short time."

"Don't worry." Jinn placed her hand on Leine's. "I will be okay. I was born to do this."

"A little confidence can go a long way, Jinn. Remember that, okay?"

Jinn smiled. "I will."

IT WAS DARK BY THE TIME THEY REACHED HANSEN. LEINE PULLED off the road outside the city limits and parked. A few minutes later, a white Suburban pulled in behind them and cut the lights.

"That's Lucky's rig." Leine handed Jinn her backpack and said, "Be careful, kid. Don't take any chances, okay?"

"Don't worry, I won't." Jinn couldn't mask the excitement in her voice. She opened the door to an icy gust of air and was gone.

Using the rearview, Leine watched her approach the Suburban, her pack over one shoulder. She opened the passenger door and climbed inside. Lucky flashed her lights at Leine, then pulled onto the road and drove away.

Even though Leine had Jinn repeat everything about the op ad nauseum during their drive, a hard lump still formed in her stomach. So many things could go wrong. The world could change in a millisecond.

Lou's words rang in her head. *Let her go, Leine. She's ready.*

She hoped he was right.

17

L ucky studied the new kid, Yasmine, from her perch at the bar. She was industrious, she'd give her that. The girl swept and washed all the floors in no time and was now working on cleaning the glass shelves behind the bar. The little thing was a force of nature.

To think Lucky had almost backed out of the deal that night on the highway. *She's too young,* she told Leine in a phone call. *I can't be responsible for the kid's safety.* Leine assured her Yasmine knew what she was doing, had been trained for this kind of undercover operation. Somehow, she'd mollified Lucky enough to go through with the original plan.

But the doubts still gnawed at her.

They sure did start them early. She supposed using young girls undercover was inevitable. Who else could put the traffickers off guard and catch the bastards who exploited them for sex?

Lucky took another drag off her cigarette and exhaled a couple of smoke rings. The kid made her feel ancient. She picked a sliver of tobacco off her tongue and snorted a laugh.

Hell, she *was* old. Didn't help that Yasmine looked younger than her age, although that would surely work to her advantage since Sean liked them young. Lucky didn't have a problem with taking the guy down—and it wasn't only because he'd tried to muscle his way into her action. Lucky might have been running prostitutes out of the club, but she sure as hell never ran minors and wouldn't think of forcing anyone into the life.

No, Sean needed to be taught a lesson. And if she didn't need to involve her handlers back east, all the better.

"You missed a spot," Lucky called.

Yasmine studied her work, then turned back with a puzzled look.

"Where?"

Lucky erupted in a smoker's raucous laugh, almost hacking up a lung. "Aww, honey," she chortled, wiping the tears from her eyes. "Don't look so serious. I was just teasing. You do great work."

The relief on Yasmine's face was enough to cause the older woman to start laughing a second time. She stubbed out her cigarette and took a swig of her water bottle. The kid was priceless. Lucky suspected she wanted any feedback to the Leine woman to be good.

Gotta be her first job, Lucky mused. She mentally shrugged. The idea was to get Sean interested in Yasmine. The more Lucky exposed the kid to the characters who hung at the bar, the better and faster that would happen. Then things could get back to normal.

She figured she'd put Yasmine behind the bar as a bar back as long as no law enforcement showed. Lucky already had a cover story if that happened: she'd say the kid was her niece and needed a place to stay while her parents were off on a trip to Europe.

She doubted she'd need it, though. It was a rare night that North Dakota's finest would darken her door, unless they'd been called because of some kind of altercation. Bruce did a great job of discouraging that. Assaults had gone down measurably since she'd hired the big guy as head security. A natural manager, he'd gotten the rest of the employees in line by showing them how to treat customers, belligerent or not.

The man had respect. Hard to come by in these parts.

The door flung open and Gloria made her entrance, blasting cold sunlight into the darkened room.

"Hey, Lucky. How's it hanging?" She stopped at the bar, dry cleaner bags filled with glittery fabric draped across her forearm. "Thought I'd bring my new costumes in early." She nodded at Yasmine. "Who's the kid?"

Lucky lit another cigarette and blew smoke between them. "I'm telling people she's my niece from back east."

"But she's not?"

"Nope. Found her diggin' around the garbage bin out back. Poor thing was searching for food."

"Oh my gosh. That's terrible. Where's her family?"

Lucky shrugged. "Says she doesn't have any, but I suspect there's more to it than that." She turned to watch Yasmine wipe down a bottle before replacing it. "I'm letting her stay in the back room until I can figure out what to do with her."

Gloria wagged her finger at the older woman. "You old softie." She adjusted the bags on her arm and added, "You just let me know if there's anything I can do, okay?"

"Sure, Gloria."

Gloria walked down to where Yasmine was cleaning and leaned across the bar. "Hey there. I'm Gloria. What's your name?"

"Yasmine. But you can call me Yaz, if you want."

"Well, Yaz, it's nice to meet you. Welcome to Lucky's Club."

"Thanks."

"You come see Auntie Gloria if you need anything, okay?"

"Okay," Yasmine answered.

Lucky waited until Gloria disappeared into the back room and then motioned Yasmine over. The kid stopped what she was doing and joined the older woman at the other end of the bar.

"You watch your ass with that one," Lucky warned. "She's like a big, purring tiger—pretty and soft on the outside, but a real killer inside."

"She's one of the dancers?"

Lucky nodded. "You'll be seeing a lot of her. She's on the payroll."

"If you don't like her, why did you give her a job?"

"Because the men love her, and she earns money for the club." Lucky didn't tell the kid that those earnings had gone down over fifty percent for the other, less legal side of the business. Lucky suspected Gloria had found more lucrative venues for her talents, and that pissed her off. Damn Sean for poaching her girls. But Gloria still packed the house the nights she performed. She had a few regulars and gained new ones every week. It would be hard to find another reliable dancer who brought in the kind of business she did and wanted a permanent gig. Chloe could only do so much before she burned out.

"Pretty sure she works for Sean, so be real careful around her, okay?"

A thoughtful look crossed Yasmine's face and she nodded. "I will."

"Now get back to work. I need the coolers under the bar cleaned and restocked when you're done with the shelves."

Yasmine snapped to attention and saluted. "Yes, ma'am." Smiling, she returned to where she left off.

Lucky shook her head as she booted up her laptop to work on her beloved spreadsheets.

I could get used to that kid.

LEINE'S PHONE BUZZED, INDICATING A MESSAGE. SHE TOLD THE CAR to read the text. It was from Lucky.

"Yaz just met Gloria. I told her she works for Sean. Says she'll be careful. ~L"

She turned off the road into the parking lot of a big box store and parked.

"Shouldn't be long now," she dictated and hit send.

Things were about to get dicey. Chloe last reported that Sean wanted to be in a relationship rather than have her work for him. Chloe hadn't been enthusiastic about the prospect and delayed giving him an answer. If she wasn't working for Sean, then Derek and Leine's original plan of having Chloe introduce Jinn would be less convincing. Why would Chloe bring a kid to stay with someone with whom she obviously didn't feel comfortable? It wouldn't pass the sniff test. Sean was too savvy.

Then there was the wild card, Gloria. Leine didn't trust her. Too many uncontrollable variables. Did she have a direct line to Sean? Chloe mentioned Sean had treated Gloria as an afterthought at the party, so it appeared she didn't. True, she'd been invited, but it was a small town—everybody knew everybody. Invitations to such a large event would be relatively easy to get.

No matter how Leine sliced and diced it, for their plan to work, Chloe would have to be all in and act as though she wanted a relationship with Sean—along with everything that entailed.

She wasn't looking forward to Derek's reaction.

18

"Absolutely not." Derek paced the floor of the motel room like a caged bull. "That's a bridge too far." He stopped and glared at Leine. Chloe looked up from the magazine she was reading.

"It's the only way, other than letting Gloria make the intro," Leine answered, "and I'm not comfortable with that."

"Why?"

"Fewer controllable factors. Besides, we need Chloe there as much as possible to keep Jinn safe."

"You can't control everything, Leine." The frustration in his voice was palpable. "Jinn's trained for this. Let her go."

Echoes of Lou, she thought. "Chloe wouldn't have to—"

"You know she would. No man in his right mind would be in a relationship with her and not—"

"Enough!" Chloe set the magazine on the table. "I signed up for this. You told me I might have to take things to the point of working for Sean." She turned to Derek. "What the hell do you think that meant, Derek? That I would wash his floors?"

Still fuming, Derek resumed pacing the floor. "Yes—no. Oh, Christ. Obviously I didn't think the whole thing through."

"Look," Leine said, keeping her voice calm. "Chloe doesn't have to do anything she doesn't want to. We made that clear from the beginning. She could delay things and still put Jinn and Sean together."

"What if I bring her to him," Chloe suggested. "Tell him Lucky's been letting her sleep in the back room, and why couldn't he put her up since he's got such a big house? That plays well with his idea of me, right?"

Leine shook her head. "Not organic enough. It's a short drive to him being suspicious of your motives. We need the suggestion to come from Sean."

"Then why not let Gloria tell him about her?" Chloe suggested. "She's sleeping with one of Sean's boys—a guy named Justice. According to her, he's looking for a way to climb up the ladder in Sean's organization. I'd think scoring someone like your girl might do the trick."

"That could work," Derek said.

"I'd still be around to watch the kid," Chloe added. "Once Sean finds out about Jinn, then he'll more than likely come to me with the idea of letting her stay at his house."

"He trusts you?" Leine asked.

Chloe nodded. "He will, once I start to play his girlfriend. I can put him off if things take longer than expected. That's usually the best play with a guy like him, anyway."

"That's the extent of things, you check?" Derek looked directly at Chloe.

"Sure. Of course. It's not like I want to sleep with him, you know." She rose from her chair and joined Derek near the window. She caressed his face and murmured, "You're more than enough for any woman."

Derek's shoulders inched down as he covered her hand with his own. He gave her a tense smile. "I don't want you in danger, yeh?"

"I know," Chloe said, moving in for a full body embrace.

Leine rose from her chair and grabbed her pack off the top of the dresser.

"I'll let myself out."

19

J ustice "The Body" Norquist's face went numb as the intensity of the second orgasm hit. He closed his eyes until the sensation receded and his other brain kicked into gear, allowing him to form a coherent thought.

Jesus. How the hell does she do that? Up to that point, Justice had been a one-and-done kinda guy. Gloria helped him see the light, and he couldn't get enough.

She rolled over and handed him one of the towels she kept next to the bed, then grabbed one for herself.

"Enjoyed that, did you?" she asked with a mischievous grin.

"You can do that to me any day of the week." He lay back on the pillows, his brain swimming from all the positions they'd just tried. *I'm in love,* he thought. If she could keep doing that kind of shit in the boudoir, he'd happily let her move in, marry her, be her sex slave, whatever she wanted.

Gloria chuckled. "There's plenty more where that came from. You're fun to try stuff out on." She dropped the towel on the floor and grabbed a partially smoked joint off the night-stand. She lit up and took a hit, then offered it to Justice. He shook his head.

"Suit yourself."

Justice gazed at the side of Gloria's face as she smoked. She was the most beautiful woman he'd ever had sex with. The age difference didn't bother him—not when she had so much imagination in the bedroom. He'd rather she didn't smoke pot, but that was a minor problem, far as he was concerned.

The radiator clanked in protest in its fight against the brutal cold working its way through the cracks in the window frame. The outside temperature hit minus twenty degrees by seven o'clock that evening, bringing with it a harsh north wind. Justice made a mental note to attach another layer of plastic to keep out the worst of the weather, or pay the price in a whopper of a heating bill. He'd have to remind his landlord to upgrade the windows. Not that it would help.

Cheap bastard.

"What do you think about a trapeze?"

Justice shook himself out of his reverie. "Huh?"

Gloria gave him a sidelong glance. "You know what a trapeze is, don't you?"

"Of course I know what a trapeze is. Jeez." He struggled to a sitting position. "How would that work? The ceiling's not high enough, is it?"

She giggled. "No, silly. Not a *real* trapeze. A Yoga trapeze. It's what you call an *aid*. Something to *aid* in our adventures."

That sounded better. He couldn't imagine how much ceiling reinforcement an actual trapeze would require. His landlord wouldn't look kindly on making major modifications to the place. Still, it did sound like fun.

"Uh, yeah. Let's do it. How much does it cost?"

Gloria took another hit off the joint. "Don't worry. I've got it covered." She leaned over and blew the smoke in his face.

"Jeez, Louise." Justice waved away the acrid smelling stuff. "Would you stop that? You know I get tested."

Gloria sighed as she stubbed out the joint. "When's the last time Sean sprang one on you? Six, eight months ago?"

"Maybe. So what? I like my job. I'm not going to screw myself out of a perfect setup because of some fricking weed." He crossed his arms. "Besides, I gotta work later."

Gloria pulled the satin robe across her breasts and settled back in the pillows. Justice tried to pull the fabric away, but she slapped his hand.

"About your job." She flexed her hand and studied her fingernails. "I've got something that might help you move a little higher in the pecking order."

"Oh yeah? What's that? You got something on the Aussie?"

"Nope. Even better. Lucky found some kid scrounging food behind the club. Her name's Yasmine. Yaz for short."

"So?"

"So she's a runaway. A *young* runaway. Lucky's putting her up in the back in return for doing odd jobs around the club. I thought since your boss is gearing up for the Super Bowl, maybe he'd be interested in acquiring new talent."

Justice sat up straighter. "She's cute? Not a fatty, right?"

Gloria rolled her eyes. "She's small for her age, which makes her look younger than she probably is. And I'm pretty sure she's still a virgin. You know what that means, right?"

"No, what?" Why would his boss want a virgin? Gloria knew what kind of business Sean was in.

Gloria rolled her eyes. "Think about it. I'll bet some of those guys would pay top dollar for a girl who hadn't ever... you know."

Justice's eyes widened. "Oh. Yeah. I mean, why wouldn't they, right?" His brain raced to figure out how best to present this opportunity to Sean, while helping himself. The idea that someone would want a girl who didn't have any experience was foreign to Justice, but hey, different strokes.

"So you'll give him the information tonight?"

Justice nodded, still scheming. He reached for his phone on the nightstand. "I'll text him right now."

"Be sure to tell him where you got the information. I could use a little boost in traffic, if you know what I mean."

"Why don't you just quit? I make enough to take care of you —of us."

A slow, seductive smile formed on Gloria's face and she opened her satin robe, giving him a nice view. "Let's not talk about it. Better yet," she said, sliding the sheets off his budding erection. "Let's not talk at all."

JUSTICE SAT INSIDE HIS HUMMER H2 IN THE SUPER SAVER PARKING lot, kicking himself. Just his luck, Sean texted back that he wanted to meet ASAP. Justice would still be warm and dry and boning Gloria again if he'd just had the sense to wait on the text to his boss until morning.

Stupid, stupid, stupid.

Sean's black Mercedes turned off the main road and oozed into the parking lot. Justice didn't understand why someone with more money than God would opt for a boring old sedan when he could have his pick of four-bys. He'd been over the moon when his neighbor decided to sell his pristine Humvee. Justice had longed for one of the massive vehicles ever since they'd stopped manufacturing them in 2010, but all he could find on the market were knock-offs or beat to shit. His neighbor's was as close to a perfect Humvee as he could get. To his chagrin, Justice hadn't ever served in the armed forces, although it wasn't for lack of trying. An old knee injury disqualified him for active service, and he sure as shit didn't want to get stuck behind a damn desk.

The sedan pulled up next to the Hummer and parked. A moment later, the driver's window rolled down. Cooper was at the wheel.

"Hey, Cooper." Justice gave the enforcer a mock salute. He pretended to crack his neck so he could catch a glimpse in the backseat, but the big boss didn't appear to be in the car.

"What you got?" Cooper asked, his clipped tone broadcasting his annoyance at being called out so late.

"Thought the boss would want to know about this kid staying at Lucky's."

Cooper frowned as he lit a cigarette. "Why would he care about that?"

"It's a girl. A *young* girl. According to my source, Lucky found her scrounging for food out back of the club."

"A runaway?" Cooper asked.

Justice nodded. "Says she doesn't have any family."

"What's she look like?"

Justice shrugged. He'd have to be vague, since he hadn't seen her. "She's small for her age, so she looks younger than she is. My source says she's probably a virgin."

Cooper took a drag off his cigarette and blew the smoke out the window. "I'll pass the info along." He nodded. "And thanks again for the other night."

Justice nodded back, feeling like part of the team. "No worries."

Cooper had called in a couple of enforcers and they'd disposed of Buddy and the three bodies in the trailer by weighting them down with car parts and feeding them through an ice fishing hole on a frozen lake several miles from camp. Justice had felt a twinge of regret that they hadn't been able to notify the men's families, but Cooper had convinced him that the less people knew about the murders, the better. Sean didn't want the attention of law enforcement on his camp.

The general consensus was that the South African guy had a hand in their deaths—especially when it came to light that the two girls Buddy was supposed to bring there that night had disappeared.

"No, I mean that. You really stepped up to the plate." Cooper pointed at Justice. "Sean's keeping his eye on you. I wouldn't be surprised if you'd be hearing from him, real soon."

"Well thanks, Cooper. I appreciate that." Justice's spirits soared. He was finally making some headway with the big boss.

"Well, I'd better get going." Cooper started to roll his window up.

Justice cleared his throat. "About the kid at Lucky's."

The window stopped.

"You gonna tell Sean I gave you the heads-up?"

"Sure, Justice." The window resumed closing.

"Hey—I was thinking..."

The window stopped. The upper half of Cooper's face was still visible.

"Yeah?" Judging by his tone Cooper was becoming even more annoyed. Justice would have to make a solid case.

"If you ever find the Aussie—"

"South African, you mean?"

"Yeah, sure. Whatever." Justice waved the comment away. "I'm happy to take care of the douchebag for you."

"I thought that's what you said you were going to do anyway."

"Uh, yeah. I did."

"So? Have you found anything out?"

"Not yet, but I'm close. I can feel it. You guys have anything yet?"

Cooper shook his head. "Nothing. It's like the guy evaporated. Poof. Gone."

"At least you got Mimi back, right? Heard about the accident."

"That was pure luck. If Milo hadn't recognized the bitch with the flyers, he never would have seen the kid."

"Well, now you don't have to worry about her interfering anymore."

"That's a fact."

"Do the cops know anything?"

"Nah. The couple in the Winnebago didn't get the plate. Just to be sure, though, we retired the truck with a mechanical problem. Sean bought him a new one."

"See? Now that's the way to run a company." Justice banged his fist on the Hummer's steering wheel. "Do right by your employees, they do right by you."

"Yeah. Well, anyway. I need to go."

"No problem. I gotta bounce, too. Sayonara, dude."

The window closed and the Mercedes rolled out of the parking lot. Justice stared after the disappearing taillights, vowing to find the Aussie scumbag no matter what it took.

"It worked." Chloe draped her coat over the back of the booth and sat down across from Leine. The truck stop café was less crowded than the first time they'd met. Only two tables were occupied. "Sean asked me about Yasmine and offered to put her up until something more permanent can be found. I'm supposed to bring her over tonight."

"What did you tell him about Lucky? He knows she doesn't like him. It's doubtful she'd let a young girl she's been taking care of stay at his house."

"He thinks I told her that I'm letting Yasmine stay with me. As far as he knows, I haven't told anyone about our...arrangement."

"Have you been seen together?"

Chloe shook her head. "Not in Hansen. He had a chef make dinner the few times I went to his house. He did take me to dinner in Bismarck last week, but that's rare. He says it's because he hates the restaurants in town. I think it's because he hates being the subject of gossip."

"Or maybe he's playing it safe in case your relationship doesn't work out." Leine took a sip of her coffee and set it down in the saucer. "Let me know when you leave for his place." God, she hoped Jinn was ready.

Stop worrying, Leine. She was born for this kind of work. She's more resourceful than you were at her age.

But was that enough?

Chloe frowned and cleared her throat.

"What's wrong?" Leine asked.

"It's just...she's so young. Sean's not stupid. I'm afraid he'll put her in a compromising position and we—you—won't be able to get to her in time."

There was nothing like having someone throw your fears back at you. "She's trained to recognize if a situation is out of her control. We have to trust her. Besides, I'll be a heartbeat away." She had to be.

Chloe's shoulders inched down. "Yeah. I guess."

"Something else bothering you?"

Chloe picked up a paper napkin and started to worry its edges. "Sean has been...insistent about me staying overnight." She continued to shred the napkin until it resembled confetti. "He's planning something this evening and—"

"And you're running out of excuses." Leine finished the thought for her.

"Yes."

"What have you used so far?"

"Pulled hamstring, my period, and a nasty cold."

"So you're thinking three strikes and you're out?" Sean didn't seem like someone who would take Chloe's excuses for long. And she doubted he was a missionary-only kinda guy. He commoditized women and girls, and Chloe was just another commodity. He'd call bullshit soon enough. Leine didn't voice her thoughts, allowing Chloe to believe what she needed to continue playing the game.

Chloe leaned forward, her voice low. "I can't keep coming up with excuses. He's getting annoyed with me. I don't want him to think I'm with him because of his money."

"Why not?"

"Because that's not who I am."

"Are you who you usually are when you're with him?"

She shook her head. "I wouldn't be with a guy like him."

"Then what's the problem? If you're playing a different version of yourself, then why not make that version a woman who goes out with men for money?"

Chloe shrugged. "Because he'd probably dump me if he thought that's what I was doing."

Doubtful, but again, Leine didn't voice her opinion. "Okay. Then how about this? Turn down any gifts he tries to give you and keep acting as though you really like him, but aren't ready to commit. It'll drive him crazy."

"How do you know?"

"I know the type. Make the chase worthwhile, and he'll do anything to win."

"You said you were in security before you started to work for SHEN. Can I ask who you worked for?"

"Let's just say I came into contact with a lot of powerful people and leave it at that."

"Works for me." Chloe picked up a menu from the table and cracked it open.

"How's Derek taking everything?"

"We don't talk about it. It hangs between us every time we're together, though."

"The proverbial elephant in the room," Leine said.

"More like an aircraft carrier. Even though I reassure him that I'm not sleeping with Sean, he doesn't believe me."

"Why do you think that is?"

Chloe studied her for a moment. "If I was going to armchair-analyze it, I'd say it was because he believes most men wouldn't wait that long. And, because he thinks I'm lying to make him feel better."

"Bingo."

"You know him better than I do. What would you do?"

"I have no idea." Leine leaned back and crossed her arms. "I don't believe in playing games when my heart's involved."

"Even if it's someone you care about?"

"Especially then. If the person I'm with doesn't get that and needs to be manipulated into figuring things out, then the relationship isn't worth much, is it?"

"Yeah. You're right." Chloe scrunched the shredded napkin into a tiny, compressed ball and flicked it toward the salt and pepper.

"Listen. Derek's a good guy, but—and I can't believe I'm actually saying this—his obvious insecurities when it comes to love will only hold you both hostage."

"Unless he learns to trust me."

"That's a long, difficult road. You sure you're up for it?"

"If you're asking me if Derek's worth it, then yes, he's worth it."

Leine studied her for a moment before she nodded. "Good answer."

"So you'll tell him? I know he'll listen to you."

"Probably not. But it's good to know you're in it for the long haul." Leine finished her coffee, pulled out some cash, and put it on the table.

"This was a test?" Chloe asked, surprised.

"You passed."

"But you said you didn't play games."

Leine rose and put on her coat. "I lied."

Chloe walked into the club and waved at the bouncer. "Hey, Bruce."

He nodded at her from behind the bar. "Whassup, gorgeous?"

"Just coming to pick up Yaz."

Bruce finished pouring the beer and set it in front of one of the men sitting at the bar. "She's in back."

"Thanks." She walked through the club and down the narrow hallway. The dressing room door was open and she glanced inside as she passed.

"Hey!" Gloria greeted her. "What are you doing here on your night off?"

Chloe paused at the door. "I'm here to pick up Yaz. She's going to be staying with me."

"Oh? I hadn't heard that." She swiped some blush on her cheeks and blended it in. "You going to bring her into work every day?"

Chloe smiled. "Looks like it. Lucky's storeroom is no place for a kid."

"You've got a good heart, Chloe." She finished her routine with a dusting of powder and readjusted her breasts so they bulged from the low-cut T-shirt, almost revealing the nipples. "How are you and Sean getting along?"

"I haven't seen him in a while. Why?"

Gloria shrugged. "Let's just say a little bird told me you're seeing more of him than you're letting on." She gave her a sideways look. "C'mon. You can tell Auntie Gloria. A little rompin' stompin' happenin' over there?"

Chloe chuckled. "Hardly. Just friends."

"Uh-huh. Sure, hon." Gloria gave her a look that said she didn't believe her and continued to adjust her attire. "Next time you see him, tell your *friend* that Gloria's had some downtime. Tell him she'd prefer to keep busy. Can you do that for me?"

"Sure. Next time I see him." Chloe glanced down the hall. "I gotta go." She turned back to Gloria. "It might be a while before I see him. You should tell him yourself."

"Honey, if I thought that would work, I'd drape myself across his baby grand." She frowned at herself in the mirror. "My calls get routed to one of his enforcers, and you know how *that* goes."

"I'll do what I can. Break a leg." Chloe continued down the hallway to the office. Yasmine sat at a big wooden desk, illuminated by a banker's desk lamp. Her breath caught at the innocence on the kid's face, reminding her what was at stake—for Yasmine and all the other young girls. Her resolve hardened.

The bastard has to pay for what he's done.

21

Mimi sat against the wall of the cage and bit her last two fingernails flush with the tips of her fingers. She hated the ragged edges, but the chewing calmed her. The chill from the cinderblock wall seeped through her back, and the silver space blanket did little to warm the concrete floor. A dozen girls—the oldest looked to be Mimi's age —populated six metal cages, linked together inside a large, windowless room. Many of the girls had grown silent, having talked and cried themselves out. The older ones in the group stared stonily ahead, refusing to answer anyone's questions.

The night before, the man in the black pickup had taken Mimi from the man camp, blindfolded her, and brought her to the locked room. She slept fitfully, waking to the sound of sobbing in the next cage over.

What are we doing here? They'd never kept her in a cage before. At first she was relieved when she didn't see a mattress anywhere—she didn't think they would make her have sex with someone there. But then it dawned on her that the cages might be a holding area, that they were there temporarily. The lack of information scared her more than knowing.

A small, bookish girl wearing black rimmed glasses who was lying next to her woke up and slid to a seated position. She nudged Mimi with her elbow and said, "I'm Amy."

"Mimi," Mimi whispered back. "How long have you been here?"

Amy thought for a minute. "Three days? I'm not sure."

"What's going to happen?"

The other girl shrugged.

"Do they know?" Mimi nodded at the two older, stone-faced girls in the cage next to them.

"I wouldn't ask, if I were you. They're mean."

Mimi climbed to her feet. "They can't be any meaner than Sean's guards."

"Watch yourself," Amy warned. "Don't start anything."

Mimi walked to the edge of the cage and threaded her fingers through the metal bars. One of the older girls—the most approachable, which wasn't saying much—narrowed her eyes at Mimi. Mimi almost turned around. Instead, she took a deep breath and said, "Hi. I'm Mimi."

The older girl didn't say anything, just glared at her with a look that said, *how dare you breathe my air?*

Mimi forged ahead. The bigger girl couldn't do much worse than what had already happened to her. Besides, there was metal between them.

"You seem smart. Do you know what's going on?"

The older girl smirked and looked away. A moment passed before she turned to Mimi. "Ever hear of the Super Bowl, idiot?"

Confused, Mimi nodded. "We're going to a football game?"

The girl guffawed, drawing the attention of the others. "We're not *going* to the Super Bowl, moron. They're going to put us in rooms near the stadium." She waited for Mimi to get the implication. It didn't take long.

"No." Mimi took a step back as the full import of what the older girl said sank in.

The older girl nodded, frowning. "What the hell did you think?"

Tears of frustration and despair brimmed in her eyes, and she turned back toward the safety of her spot on the other side of the room. Blinking furiously, she joined Amy on the floor.

Amy patted Mimi's back in an attempt to soothe her and whispered, "See? Mean."

Mimi choked back the anguish threatening to derail her and clenched her fists, digging her freshly chewed fingernails into her palms. Memories flooded back—of being held inside a small room with only a bed, a toilet, and a sink, and having a seemingly endless line of dirty, stinky men hurt her; of trusting Scarf, and his betrayal, leading to more endless nights in the back of the van on a stained mattress, doing more bad things with strange men. She'd made herself numb to get through those times.

She'd have to do it again.

Why me? she thought, grateful for the feel of fingernails cutting into her skin. A girl across the room started to bang her head repeatedly against the block wall.

"She does that all the time," Amy whispered.

Mimi recognized the bleak expression on the other girl's face. She was sure it matched her own.

22

C hloe crested the top of the driveway leading to Sean's mansion and slowed to a stop. Jinn's eyes widened at her first view of the enormous house.

"Is that it?" she asked. "It looks like a castle."

"That's it. You sure you're ready?" Chloe studied Jinn, the concern in her eyes obvious.

Jinn nodded. "Ready." She was used to people thinking she needed help. She may have been smaller than average, but she knew how to fight and that always threw people off. Better yet, she was smart. And lucky. Smart got her out of trouble more times than fighting ever did, and luck did the rest.

"Leine told you what to expect, right?"

"She said the man we're going to meet will pretend to have work for me to do at his house. But he really wants to make me have sex with other men."

"And what are you supposed to do if someone tries to force himself on you?"

"Hit him in the nuts, but make it look like an accident and act really sorry. I'm not supposed to fight unless I have to."

"What's your objective?"

"To find out where he keeps the girls we're going to help."

"If you think you're in danger at all, you're going to run away and call Leine, right?"

Jinn rolled her eyes. "Leine asked me the same question a million times. Yes, I will run away."

Chloe sighed. "All right then. Let's go meet Sean."

They coasted down the hill to the portico and parked. A man in a red blazer appeared and opened their doors.

"Hey, Frank," Chloe greeted him.

"Miss Chloe," Frank answered. "Always a pleasure."

Chloe and Jinn followed Frank through the massive double doors into the huge home.

Jinn's mouth dropped open at the immense size of the front hall. She'd seen pictures in magazines of houses that had great big chandeliers and sweeping staircases, but didn't ever think she'd actually see the inside of one.

She glanced at Chloe, who smiled encouragingly. Jinn liked Chloe—she had a nice, calm feeling about her. Not like Leine, though. Leine was a lot more intense, even when she acted calm on the outside. Leine reminded Jinn of a coiled snake—quiet, patient, and waiting to strike.

Leine was her hero. She gave Jinn the feeling that Jinn could do anything. Except lately she'd been a big worrywart.

But, in Chloe's favor, the blonde dancer had an awesome tattoo of a dragon on her back and arm. She'd named him Rufus and said he protected her from harm. Jinn liked dragons. She managed to score one during an intense session of fighting magical creatures on a fantasy gaming site and had decided to save its powers for when things got sketchy.

Frank led them into a room with high ceilings and obviously expensive furniture. A bar stretched along one whole wall, with a ton of bottles on glass shelves behind it. She hoped she wouldn't have to clean them. The ones at Lucky's were a pain.

Chloe took off her coat and handed it to the man in the jacket. Jinn did the same. She wore a well-used ski coat two sizes too large, and her clothes were clean but worn. Jinn decided to stay in character from the time she met Lucky. She'd practiced for two days before coming to North Dakota, trying to get the mannerisms down so she would become the abused girl from Minot. Lou set her up with another girl who had been through what Yasmine was supposed to have experienced. She gave Jinn a crash course on the fear, helplessness, and rage someone in that position would normally feel.

Jinn could relate to a lot of what she told her. Living on the streets of Tripoli, Jinn experienced her share of fear. And rage. Especially when those men tricked her dying mother into sending Jinn with them to get an "education."

She'd gotten an education, all right. Jinn escaped before the men could make her do what they wanted, but that had been small comfort. Her mother died soon afterward. Jinn never forgave herself for leaving her, even though she didn't have a choice at the time.

Jinn shook herself out of her reverie and sat down next to Chloe on the couch. The room smelled weird, like some kind of super-sweet room freshener. She leaned over and sniffed Chloe.

"What are you doing?" Chloe whispered.

"It smells weird in here."

"And you thought it was me?" Chloe chuckled and shook her head. "I think it's Sean's cologne."

Jinn squinted at her in disbelief. "Somebody actually *wants* to smell like that?"

The door to the hall opened and a man with a shaved head and a stern face walked into the room. Chloe stood and indicated that Jinn should follow suit. The man walked over to them and extended his hand.

"Hi. I'm Sean."

Breathing shallowly, Jinn shook his hand. Chloe'd been right —the closer he got, the stronger the cologne. "Ji-Yasmine," she answered, almost forgetting to use her pretend name.

C'mon, Jinn. You can't screw up this early. What would Leine think?

"But you can call me Yaz."

"I think I like Yasmine better. You're a very pretty little girl, Yasmine."

Jinn kept her face impassive, but inside her skin crawled. There was something very wrong about him. She prided herself on being a good judge of people. This man's outsides didn't match his insides, even a little. He was hiding something bad that he didn't want anyone else to know.

This is the man Leine told you about, Jinn. He makes little girls have sex with older men. Of course he's going to hide that from people.

She suppressed a shudder and looked at the floor. *He likes it when girls are shy,* she thought. *Makes us easier to handle.*

"She's small for her age, but a hard worker," Chloe said as Sean circled Jinn. "Lucky thinks maybe it's because she didn't get regular meals growing up."

"You have family, Yasmine?" he asked.

Jinn glanced at Chloe.

"Go ahead and tell him, honey."

Jinn returned her gaze to the floor. "No. Not anymore."

"She's a runaway," Chloe explained. "She says she's from Minot. Lucky found her dumpster diving behind the club."

"Well, then. You'll need a place to stay, won't you?" Sean smiled, revealing perfect white teeth.

"Lucky says I'm good at cleaning," Jinn offered. She had to get this guy to take her in or the operation wasn't going to work. "She said she hasn't ever seen anything like me before."

Sean chuckled, sending another shiver of fear rippling down Jinn's back. His eyes looked dead when he laughed. They reminded her of Salome, the woman who tried to kill Leine. Her throat dry, Jinn swallowed hard. Leine's warning echoed in her mind: *Be careful and don't take any chances. Sean is a very dangerous man.*

"Then let's get this party started. Frank will show you to your room." He nodded at the man in the red jacket, standing by the door. "Settle in. Watch some TV. Tomorrow at breakfast we'll talk about what you'll be expected to do."

"Lucky still wants her to work at the club," Chloe said. "I can come and get her in the morning, then bring her back here before my shift."

"I don't know how to cook, but I can do everything else," Jinn offered.

"Perfect. Go with Frank, now, okay?" He gave her an insincere smile and turned his attention to Chloe.

Jinn followed Frank out the door and into the gigantic hall.

"Your room's on the second floor," Frank said, indicating the sweeping staircase. He led her up the stairs and turned left down a long hallway that stretched all the way to the far end of the house. Every door they passed was closed, except for a bathroom. Stopping at the second to the last room, he fished a key ring from his pocket and unlocked the door before pushing it wide.

Jinn sucked in a breath. The room was immense, bigger than Lou and Nita's living room back in Los Angeles. A king-sized bed, fitted with a crisp white bedspread, jutted out from the center of one wall. A huge dresser and mirror stood opposite, with an enormous television mounted in the corner. A loveseat and another comfy-looking chair had been grouped around a glass and chrome coffee table. But the furniture wasn't what captured Jinn's attention. She crossed the room to a pair of French doors leading to a balcony overlooking the snow-covered yard. The backyard lights illuminated a frozen lake stretching into the darkness.

"Wow." Jinn couldn't contain her excitement, and realized she didn't have to. Yasmine would have been impressed. She turned back to say something to Frank, but he'd disappeared, closing the door behind him.

Giddy at the idea that she would get to sleep in the luxurious room that night, she kicked off her shoes and launched herself onto the humungous bed. She jumped to her feet to test the bounce factor. *Good,* she decided, and executed several somersaults and flying leaps over the mattress. Spent, she propelled herself one last time into the air and flopped on her back, staring happily at the ceiling, trying to catch her breath.

A piece of molding near the recessed section of the ceiling over the bed looked out of place. Sobering, she got up, opened her backpack, and removed her meager belongings, which she put in the dresser, all while surreptitiously studying the molding over the bed from different angles.

Definitely a camera, she decided. One of her favorite classes at the academy was on detecting surveillance equipment. She looked around the room for something she could use to disable it, but didn't see much available.

The way the ceiling was recessed, the camera's position could only point at the bed. *That was silly,* Jinn thought. She would have positioned the camera to encompass the entire room for maximum visibility. The way it was now, the camera only recorded what happened on the bed. Why would anyone want to watch someone sleep?

Come on, stupid—what else do people do in bed? Jinn could feel her cheeks warm. Of course. According to Lucky, Sean was known to videotape people having sex so he could blackmail them.

The humongous bed she'd loved a moment ago could turn into a humongous horror if she wasn't careful.

Shaking off the images the thought conjured, Jinn walked to the bathroom and opened drawers, looking for shaving cream or toothpaste. She found an unused tube of paste, opened it, and squeezed a dollop onto her finger. Then she walked back out to the main room and dragged the chair underneath and to the back of the camera.

She climbed onto the chair and raised her hand. She wasn't tall enough. Frustrated, she jumped down, curling the finger with the toothpaste into her palm so she wouldn't lose it, and pulled the cushions off the loveseat. These she piled on top of the chair, which she then climbed.

Bracing herself against the chair back with her leg, Jinn reached up and smeared the toothpaste over the small crack in the molding. She jumped down and studied her work.

The toothpaste matched the white paint of the molding. No one would know, unless they tried to access the video of her room. Even then, it would take a while for them to figure out the camera itself had been compromised.

Jinn planned to be long gone by then.

She dragged the chair back to where she got it and replaced the couch cushions. Then she conducted her search of the furniture. Finding nothing, she continued to the walk-in closet and the *en suite* bath. She skated across the marble floors of the opulent bathroom in her socks a couple of times before searching the cupboards under the fancy clamshell sinks. Jinn ran her hand along and under every surface, including the fluffy white towels, and searched the linen closet and the separate room where the toilet lived.

What she was searching for, she didn't know, but she wanted to be thorough.

Not finding anything of value, Jinn decided to do a little

exploring. She cracked open the door and peered into the hall. The long stretch of deeply carpeted hallway was empty. Still in her stocking feet, Jinn walked along the corridor, running her hand along the chair rail, alert for noises that would indicate someone coming up the stairs. She tried each door handle, but the rooms were all locked. She flashed on Frank's keys. She needed to find out where he kept his stuff so she could steal them and look inside the rooms.

She passed the open door to the bathroom, identical to hers, before she arrived at the second-floor landing. A faint murmur floated up from the room where Chloe and Jinn had waited for Sean. Jinn sprinted across the stretch of landing that opened to the floor below, and ran into the other part of the house.

The second hallway was darker than the other. She didn't dare turn on the light. Again, all the doors were locked, except for another big bathroom. At the end of the hallway she found a pair of double doors. They were locked, too.

Maybe Sean would ask her to clean the house. She'd have to suggest it. Then he might give her the keys. That way, she could find out what lay behind each of the doors. The longer she avoided whatever he wanted to do with her, the better. She'd have to explore the rest of the house when everyone went to bed.

She was halfway to her room when Chloe called her name. She reversed course and made her way to the top of the stairs and looked down. Her coat on, Chloe stood in the foyer with Sean. Jinn studied his expression, trying to get a read on him, but his face betrayed nothing. The realization that she was going to be alone in this massive house with two strange men swept through her. She had to stop herself from running to Chloe and begging her to take her back to Lucky's.

This is your job, Jinn. Leine said she wouldn't be far away. Just keep the GPS with you, no matter what. The thought of Leine being close by helped fight the panic threatening to overwhelm her, and she managed a smile.

"I'm leaving," Chloe said to Jinn. "Sean says he's happy to let you stay here until other arrangements can be made."

"Did you see my room?" Jinn asked, injecting enthusiasm into her voice. She was totally in character. Yasmine would be excited.

Chloe shook her head. "Is it really nice?"

"Yeah. Come up and see." Jinn wanted a chance to talk to Chloe alone. She needed one more conversation with a friendly person.

Chloe turned to Sean. "Do you mind? It'll just take a minute."

Sean shrugged. "Don't take too long. We have to leave soon."

Chloe climbed the stairs and followed Jinn down the hall. Jinn prattled on about the room and the balcony until they were well out of earshot.

They walked into Jinn's room, and Jinn closed the door.

"What is it?" Chloe asked, keeping her voice low.

Jinn wrapped her arms around Chloe and held her tight for a long moment. Then she stepped back, her finger to her lips, and pointed at the ceiling.

"I just needed to..." she whispered, then stopped. She was being a big baby.

Chloe ruffled her hair. "You'll be fine." She lowered her voice to a whisper. "Leine's a minute away. All you have to do is text her. Remember the map I showed you?"

Jinn nodded. She'd memorized the roads in and around the property. She wouldn't have a problem walking in the right direction if she had to escape. Leine would be waiting to pick her up within a few minutes of her text.

"I know it's scary. Don't be afraid to leave if you think you're in danger." Chloe glanced behind her. "I don't think he's going to try anything right away. You have time."

"Okay." Jinn took a deep breath and let it go. "See you."

Chloe gave her another hug. "See you."

And then she was gone.

23

L ater that evening, Jinn turned off the television in her
room and wandered down the hallway to the top of the
stairs. The loud rumbling in her stomach reminded
her she hadn't eaten dinner.

The dark, quiet house told her Chloe and Sean hadn't come
back yet. She didn't know if Frank stayed at the house or left
after his shift. She assumed he left, too, since she hadn't heard
anything in hours. She did notice an armed man walking
around outside, and texted Leine to let her know. She assumed
he was Sean's security, which made for two gunmen—one at the
guard house, and one outside. Remembering how cold it had
been earlier, she wondered where the one guard warmed up.

At least she wasn't completely alone.

The darkness beyond the perimeter lights reminded her
how far from town they were. She missed the comfort of street-
lights, other homes, and businesses. And people.

She walked down to the first floor and headed along the
hall toward the back of the house, passing more closed doors
with locked handles. She came to a larger living area with a
huge flat- screen television, and a fireplace set waist high in the

wall. A kitchen with a large gas stove and a humongous refrigerator stood to her left, behind a long island with seating for eight.

Jinn opened the dual refrigerator doors and studied the contents. There was a lot of food, all lined up perfectly in rows. Would Sean know if she moved something? She decided to find out.

Ten minutes later, she'd prepared a spread the likes of which her mother would have been proud. Four different kinds of cheeses, three types of bread, roast beef, sliced turkey, a glass of milk, and a handful of grapes and strawberries accompanied a piece of the best chocolate cake she'd ever tasted. She'd save the rest of it for last.

She climbed onto one of the eight chairs and proceeded to devour the meal, mindful that she needed to clean everything up afterward.

"Hungry?"

Jinn startled at the voice and whirled around, knocking the glass of milk over on the counter. Frank stood in the doorway, watching her.

Milk dribbled onto the floor, leaving a puddle on the spotless tile. "I'm sorry," Jinn said. She hopped off the chair and ran to the sink. She soaked a paper towel, then ran back to the counter to mop up the spillage.

Frank walked over to a narrow cabinet Jinn hadn't explored and pulled out a sponge mop, which he used to clean the milk off the floor. Jinn stepped back, milk-soaked paper towel in hand, giving him room. When he was finished, he squeezed the excess into the sink, rinsed the mop, and put it back inside the cabinet.

He opened the refrigerator and studied the shelves. "You going to put this all away how you found it?"

"Yes," Jinn said, staring in dismay at the jumble of contents she'd left on the shelves. She remembered where things went, mostly.

Frank closed the doors and turned to face her. "You'd better make sure you do. Sean is particular how things are done around here."

"I will," she said with a nod. "I can make it neat."

He moved toward her, a calculating look on his face. "I can make it look exactly like it did before."

"Okay." She didn't like the look he was giving her and backed away with each forward step.

"Don't be afraid. I'm sure we can work something out before the boss gets back." He crossed the space between them in two strides, throwing Jinn off guard. He grabbed her arm, but she twisted from his grasp and backed away.

"What are you doing?"

"It'll be easier on you if you let me break you in." Frank unbuckled his belt.

Jinn's mind raced, trying to remember everything she'd been taught at the SHEN academy about fighting a larger opponent, but then remembered she had to make it look like an accident.

A cruel smile spread across Frank's face as he removed his belt and snapped it between his hands. In a flash, her next move became crystal clear. One of the modules at the academy had used this exact same scenario. A larger opponent who didn't expect Jinn to fight.

But it wouldn't look like an accident.

Frank stepped closer, putting Jinn on guard. She widened her eyes to look afraid, and pretended to cower near the stool. Frank's shoulders relaxed, a clear indication he underestimated her.

Just a little closer...

Frank stepped into range. Muscle memory from hundreds of practice fights locked in as Jinn brought her knee up and slammed her heel into his crotch with an explosive front kick. Frank doubled over with a wheeze and he sank to the floor, the belt still in his hand. Jinn jumped on his back, wrapped her arm around his neck, and put him in a sleeper hold, choking off his blood supply.

He grasped her forearm and tried to wrench it free, but Jinn maintained maximum pressure by straddling his ribs like an octopus and gripping her right hand with her left. Still recovering from the surprise attack, he didn't put up much of a fight. Moments later he collapsed to the floor.

Jinn made sure he was unconscious before she climbed off and checked his back pockets. Nothing. She grabbed the belt and wrapped it around his wrists—he wouldn't be out long. She rolled him onto his side and dug in his front pocket, finding the key ring she'd seen earlier. Wary that he'd recover soon, she sprinted to the staircase and up to the second floor. She raced down the hallway to her room, ran inside and closed the door, engaging the lock. Adrenaline pulsed through her as she ran to the desk and dragged the chair to the door, shoving it underneath the handle. Frank might have duplicate keys to all the rooms. Jinn wouldn't leave herself open to another attack.

Wasn't he supposed to keep away from her? According to both Leine and Chloe, a virgin brought more money. They didn't think Sean would put her to work right away.

Maybe Sean hadn't told Frank. Jinn shuddered at the thought of what he wanted to do to her. By removing his belt, he upped the stakes. He could have used it to hit her, or choke her, or tie her up, which was why she decided not to make it look like an accident. She couldn't kill him—Leine warned her not to use deadly force unless absolutely necessary—but she could defend herself. She was a runaway. According to her cover story, where she came from runaways knew how to fight. They had to, or they wouldn't survive. She'd have to explain it that way.

Jinn sat on the bed, reviewing her options. She might have messed up the whole operation. Maybe she should leave. Faced with the same decision, Yasmine would probably run. She went to her backpack, zipped it open, and started to stuff her meager belongings inside. She could show up at Lucky's again.

Maybe the operation could be salvaged.

She finished packing, grabbed her coat from the closet, and stood near the door to listen. No sounds came to her from the hallway. She dragged the chair away and eased the door open.

She slipped out of her room and sprinted to the second-floor landing, where she paused to listen once more. Nothing. She pulled out her phone and texted Leine.

Have 2 leave. Need pickup.

Leine would be waiting for her half a mile east of the guard shack. She headed down the stairs and out the door.

And ran straight into Sean.

24

Jinn staggered back from the impact and almost fell, but Sean caught her.

"Whoa. What's the hurry?" he said, gripping both shoulders to steady her.

"I—I have to go," Jinn mumbled.

"But you just got here." Sean walked her back inside. "Come on, now. It can't be that bad." They moved into the foyer and he closed the door. Chloe wasn't with him.

"I can't stay here," Jinn said, putting as much emotion into her voice as she could.

"Why?"

Jinn glanced behind her, then back to him. "Frank tried...he tried to—" With the letdown from the adrenaline rush, it wasn't difficult to muster up tears, and she let them fall.

Sean stiffened. "Frank did what?"

Jinn covered her face and cried harder.

"Where is he?" The rising anger in his voice echoed through the large entryway.

"In...the kitchen." Fresh sobs.

He grabbed hold of the strap on Jinn's backpack and propelled her toward the back of the house to the kitchen.

Still on the floor, Frank had dragged himself to a sitting position with his back against the island. His face an unnatural shade of red, he glared at Jinn when he saw her.

"What the fuck happened, Frank?" Sean demanded.

"The little bitch kicked me in the nads."

"She what?" Sean glanced at Jinn. "Is that true, Yasmine?"

Jinn nodded. "He tried to..." She let the words trail off and started sobbing again.

Sean squatted in front of Jinn, putting himself on her level. "Why don't you go up to your room? I'll take care of this...mess and come up to make sure you're okay. I'm sorry you had to deal with this."

Choking back a sob, Jinn nodded. She turned around and shuffled down the hallway toward the staircase. She hesitated, trying to make out what the two men were saying.

"What the fuck, Frank? Didn't I tell you not to touch the merchandise?"

Frank mumbled something.

"Yeah, well that excuse won't cut it. Clean this fucking mess up, and meet me out back. We need to talk."

Jinn sprinted the rest of the way to the staircase and up to the second floor. When she reached her bedroom, she closed and locked the door. Dropping her pack on the bed, she made her way to the double doors and stepped out onto the balcony. She drew the heavy curtains closed before she shut the door, cutting off the light from the room. Then she crouched in the shadows next to the house and hugged her knees, waiting for the two men to come outside.

Remembering her message to Leine, she pulled out her phone and texted her again.

Sean came home. Am ok. Will stay.

Leine texted back.

R U sure?

Yes.

Leine's reply appeared a second later.

KMP. DTC.

(Keep me posted. Don't take chances).

How many times had Jinn heard that warning? She'd taken a chance tonight, hoping that Sean would believe her and not Frank. She'd soon find out if it worked.

The door to the patio opened underneath her. She turned off her phone screen and slid the mobile into her pocket.

"I thought you'd want me to—" Frank's voice cut through the silent evening.

"You thought wrong. I told you to keep your hands off this one."

"Shit, man. If I would have known you were putting her up for bid, I wouldn't even entertain the thought."

"Right."

Jinn's ears pricked up at the skepticism in Sean's voice. He believed her story. Relief spread through her. The operation could be salvaged. She blew quietly on her hands to ward off the frigid cold enveloping her. At least she was in a semi-protected area where wind wasn't a factor.

The two men crunched through the snow toward the lake, the lights from the house illuminating their tracks. Jinn strained to hear their conversation, but they'd gone too far. She started to go inside, but froze as a flash illuminated the darkness near the lake, followed instantly by a loud *pop!* that echoed through the night. One of the two men crumpled to the ground. Jinn sank against the outside wall of the house, disappearing into the shadows. Moments later, Sean returned, typing something on his phone. Finished, he slid the phone into his pocket and stepped inside the house.

Hands shaking, Jinn took out her mobile and texted Leine.

He just killed Frank. Near the lake.

She bolted to her feet and raced inside her room, unsure of what to do next. Her phone pinged with Leine's reply.

Do you want to leave?

Jinn texted back:

No. We should keep going. I have keys. I'll hide them in the room.

There was a brief pause, then a reply.

Ok. Remember the GPS.

Jinn turned off her phone and stashed it inside her pack. She had her shoes on, so she was good with the GPS. She reached in her pocket and removed the keys she took from Frank.

She needed to hide them someplace safe. Now that Frank was dead, he wouldn't be able to accuse her of taking them.

She ran to the closet, but didn't like her options. Next she checked the bathroom, but didn't find the right place there, either. She considered hiding them under the mattress, but realized that would be too easily discovered.

As she scoured the main room, there was a knock at the door. Jinn sucked in a breath and called, "Just a minute." She scanned the room once more, and her gaze fell on the heat register in the floor.

It would have to do.

She dropped to her knees and eased the register grate out of its hole in the carpet. The ducting had a flat area before it sloped down to the furnace, and she placed the keys there. Then she replaced the register, climbed to her feet, and walked to the door.

"Who is it?" she asked.

"Sean. Can you open the door? I talked to Frank. He won't hurt you anymore."

Jinn unlocked the door and pulled it open.

Sean stood in the hallway—with a gun.

LEINE SET THE PHONE DOWN ON THE CENTER CONSOLE OF HER rental and leaned her head back. Sean killed one of his own guys, meaning events had escalated. What did Frank do to warrant getting smoked? The texts from Jinn told her an incomplete story, but she could guess the rest. He must have tried to force himself on her and she fought him off, triggering her flight response.

Leine didn't fault Jinn for running. Yasmine would have done the same, so it was within character. But now Sean knew she was a flight risk. How would he handle things from there? She doubted he'd risk leaving her at the house without ensuring her continued compliance.

She glanced at her phone, hoping for another text. It didn't come.

Shit. Leine drummed her fingers on the steering wheel, considering her options. She couldn't go in, guns blazing. Not with a robust security system and two guards. There might be more. Two guards were all Jinn had seen. Besides, their plan would go up in smoke. They weren't any closer to finding Mimi, or where Sean kept his "stable." Everything they'd done up until now would be wasted.

Sean killed Frank, which told her he wanted to keep Jinn "intact" and "pure" for his business purposes. It also confirmed that Sean was a cruel and decisive man, which did not bode well for someone as headstrong as Jinn. True, she'd been prepped to act passive, but even Leine knew Jinn could only work that angle so long.

Damn Lou for suggesting Jinn for the op. She wasn't ready.

Leine took several deep breaths, trying to calm her agitation. *She's fine. As long as she keeps the GPS on, I can find her.*

She just hoped when Jinn needed her, she'd be able to get to her in time.

25

Sean prodded Jinn down the stairs to the main level, jabbing her between the shoulder blades with the barrel of his gun.

"Where are you taking me?" she asked, her fear only partly an act.

"Somewhere safe."

The presence of the gun told her otherwise.

He steered her past the living room with the massive flat-screen television, the kitchen with the remnants of her meal still scattered on the island counter, and down a long hallway. They passed an immaculate laundry room and yet another bathroom before he ordered her to stop in front of a closed door.

He reached in his pocket and pulled out a set of keys, one of which he used to unlock the door. A series of carpeted steps led to a lower level encased in darkness.

He shoved the gun into her back. "Keep going."

"But it's dark." Where was he taking her? She'd never get the keys back, now. She willed her thudding heart to slow, but it didn't work.

"You're either walking down the steps or I'll carry you down. Which will it be?"

She walked.

As they descended the stairs, lights flickered on automatically revealing more stairs leading to a spotless basement. The open room stretched the length of the house. The sharp scent of pine permeated the air, as though the floor had recently been cleaned.

He pushed her toward a large metal door against the far wall.

"Over there," he said.

Jinn walked toward the door, her mind whirling, working out how to escape. Being locked in the basement wasn't in the plan. He pressed his thumb to the scanner on the door. The door clicked.

If he puts me in there, I'll never get out.

Sean swung the door wide. A light came on, revealing a series of cages on both sides of the room with a narrow walkway between them. Several girls sat on either side of the walkway, some on the floor on metallic space blankets, and others on metal benches situated along the wall. A small, portable toilet took up space in the corner of each cage, with rolls of toilet paper and a case of bottled water nearby.

As the girls looked on, Sean took out his keys, opened the nearest empty cage, and shoved Jinn inside.

"Take off your shoes," he said to Jinn. Panic flashed through her at the thought of losing the GPS tracker.

She glanced at one of the girls in the next cage over. She wore slip-ons. "But it's cold," she answered, hoping against hope he'd let her keep her shoes.

He considered her for a second, then said, "Give me the laces."

Relieved, Jinn untied the laces and handed them to him.

Sean locked her cage and pocketed the keys. Jinn found it odd that none of the girls said a word to him. *They must be afraid.*

Without a word, he walked out and closed the door. The ominous *snick* of the lock felt like a nail in her heart.

Don't think that way, Jinn. You were born under a lucky star. This luck has not abandoned you. She moved to the back of the cage, close to the next one over. None of the girls looked over thirteen or fourteen. The youngest looked younger than Jinn.

"I'm Yasmine," she offered. "What's going on? What are we doing here?" None of them replied. "Does anyone know what's going on?"

One of the girls stood up and walked to the front of her cage. Of medium height and slender, she had dark hair and wore a pair of leggings with a long T-shirt. She had no shoes, although she did wear socks. She leaned her face against the metal separating them.

"Some of us are going to Phoenix to be sold at the Super Bowl," she said in a low voice.

That's what Leine and Derek said Sean was getting ready to do. "When are we supposed to leave?"

"Tomorrow."

Jinn's mouth went dry. She had to get a message to Leine. The GPS would show she hadn't left, if it was still transmitting. Leine would think everything was fine. Could the signal be detected through a block wall or all the metal? She didn't know.

When it comes time to leave, the tracker will show where you're going. She'll be right there. Don't worry.

"What's your name?" she asked the girl, trying to take her mind off her backpack upstairs. Thankfully, she'd deleted the texts immediately, like she'd been trained.

"Mimi."

Mimi. The name of the girl Leine and Derek were looking for. "I'm Ji—" Jinn caught herself before she blew her cover. "Yasmine, but you can call me Yaz."

"I heard when you told them," Mimi said. "You can hear everything in here."

Someone giggled. The tension in the room lessened considerably as the girls collectively relaxed. Several whispered conversations broke out. Mimi moved to the corner closest to Jinn's cage.

"I wonder why he put you in there alone?" Mimi asked.

Jinn shrugged. "I was supposed to clean his house, but something happened and I tried to run away. I think he put me here to keep me from running away again."

Mimi looked at her with wide eyes. "You mean you've never...do you know what it meant when I said we're going to be sold?"

Jinn figured she'd better play stupid. She shook her head. "Not really."

Mimi gave her a sympathetic look. "It means he's going to sell us for sex."

"What?" Jinn played it up, trying to make it look convincing. She glanced at the rest of the girls. "All of us?"

Mimi turned to survey the group. "I think he's just taking a few of us. I overheard one of the guards talking about keeping some of the girls here for the regulars."

"I can't let that happen." Jinn paced her cell, working herself up. "There has to be some way to—"

Mimi put her finger to her lips and looked pointedly at a camera set up in the far corner of the room. Jinn nodded that she understood. He was monitoring them.

That was why no one said much. She studied the rest of the girls in the room, noting how many there were. She counted fifteen. That was good. They had numbers, and numbers could be used to their advantage.

First things first—she'd have to get them to trust her, and then she could implement a plan. Because somewhere, somehow, she would save them all.

She just didn't know how yet.

26

L eine walked through the doors of the gas station with two cups of fresh coffee, climbed back into her Tahoe, and headed toward Sean's place. Dawn was just now breaking over the horizon, outlining the gathering cumulus clouds in gold and pink. Overnight, the forecast had gone from more of the same freezing temperatures to an imminent blizzard. She was getting used to the bone-chilling temps. Ignoring them seemed to work best. What did the locals say? "It's a dry cold," a riff on the Southwestern, "It's a dry heat." She wasn't sure what to think about the snowstorm forecast. Hopefully it would blow over.

Derek had parked his truck near an abandoned oil rig, far enough away from Sean's place that he wouldn't attract attention, yet close enough to receive the signal from Jinn's tracker. She pulled up beside him and lowered her window.

"Want some coffee?" she asked, holding out one of the cups.

"You read my mind." Derek took the cup, along with two creamers. "Thanks. Trouble sleeping?"

"A little, yeah. Any change?"

He shook his head. "The tracker's been on all night. She hasn't moved."

"Let's hope the battery lasts. Activity?" she asked. Derek had a clear view through binoculars of Sean's driveway and guard shack.

"Pretty quiet. No one's been in or out."

Leine took a sip of the coffee. It wasn't half bad for gas station caffeine. The breakfast burrito on the passenger seat was another matter. The smell of beans, cheese, and shredded beef held too long under a heat lamp told her not to expect any culinary delights. She just hoped it was edible.

Of course, that's what hot sauce was for.

"I'm going to check in with Chloe, unless you already did." Derek reached over and turned up the heat.

Leine's heat was already on high, attempting to thwart the cold air drifting in through the window. She studied her friend. Derek appeared to have recovered from his bout with jealousy, although that was most likely because Chloe hadn't told him everything.

"Sounds good. Let me know if there's anything new."

"Will do. See you in four." Derek rolled his window closed and drove off, headed for town.

She closed her window, then situated her rig to get a visual of the driveway and guard shack. She pulled up the tracking app on her phone and set the device on the console. The little red dot blinked reassuringly.

Leine had managed a few hours of sleep before she jolted awake from one of her recurring nightmares. This one had children strapped to bombs, bringing back memories of Salome, the French terrorist who'd been responsible for several bombings in Paris and Las Vegas. Lou once suggested Leine get professional help to sort out her feelings, but Leine fiercely resisted the idea.

Her way of coping with humanity's dark underbelly was her kill wall—an encrypted file on her laptop.

Which reminded her—she hadn't added the photos from her recent extermination. She'd taken a group shot of the three men at Sean's man camp before she left the scene. It would have been easier to sync her phone's camera to an encrypted file in the cloud, but Leine was cautious when it came to incriminating evidence. She preferred not to take a chance on someone hacking into the online server. The kill wall had been set up so that if someone tried to access the file without the correct password, the images would be instantly deleted.

She retrieved her laptop from the backseat and turned it on. Then she opened the encrypted file on her phone containing the photos and flipped through to find the one she was looking for. Choosing the best angle, she downloaded the picture to her computer, then deleted the photos from her phone.

She resisted the urge to look at the wall—she didn't need to stir up the anger the photographs always evoked. Right now, her anger rested somewhere between simmering fury and outright rage. The three men in the picture she'd just downloaded would have attested to that.

If she'd let them live.

She was well aware that most people, if not all, would be horrified by her sense of justice, but she didn't care. She'd seen more evil perpetrated by human beings than anyone should have, and plenty of them walked away, ready to do it again. She'd finally reached a point where her conscience wouldn't allow her to let them go without exacting some kind of justice.

Right or wrong, death was that justice. Other people could worry about the moral ramifications. Leine had found her purpose.

Leine pushed her seat back and took another drink of her coffee. She eyed the burrito on the seat next to her but wasn't in the mood to play Russian roulette with her digestive tract. She could wait.

Movement in her periphery caught her attention, and she raised the binoculars. A white van with tinted windows drove down Sean's driveway toward the guard shack. The gate opened, the vehicle rolled through, then hooked a left onto the highway. Leine glanced at her phone. The red dot matched the van's trajectory.

Jinn was on the move.

Leine raised her seatback, threw the Tahoe into gear, and eased onto the road. She slid her phone into the holder on the dash, keeping Jinn's tracking icon in view. She remained far enough behind them to stay within range but not so close that they'd spot the tail. Then she called Sergeant Robinson. His voicemail picked up, and she left a message. Next, she called Lou.

"Hey, Lou," she said when he answered. "I need you to contact NDHP and let them know the make and model of my rental. Tell them I'm headed west, tailing a white Ford Transit van carrying an unknown number of trafficked kids, likely headed to Phoenix and the Super Bowl. I left a message for Robinson, but it's early, so I don't think he's in." She gave him her ETA to the Montana border and read off the license plate number.

"Is Jinn one of them?"

"Yes. Her tracking device is still transmitting, but I'm not sure how long the battery will last. I've got a visual."

"Will do."

The line went dead. Leine took another sip of coffee and hit speed dial for Derek.

"They're moving her."

"Where do you think they're going this early?"

"I'm betting Phoenix. I contacted the highway patrol. Sergeant Robinson wasn't in yet, so I called Lou to take point."

"Want me to catch up so we can double team them?"

"I think it's better if you stay close to Chloe." She glanced at the blinking red dot.

"Where are you now?" he asked.

"Headed west on 2."

"Hold on a second—let me pull up a map." Derek came back a moment later. "If I take the backroads I could be there before they head south."

"Thanks, but I've got it handled."

"What's your plan?"

"I assume the van has two drivers so they can drive straight through."

"Which means you need to not only disable the vehicle, but disable them," Derek added.

"If the cavalry doesn't show, I have two options: I could ram them and force the van into a tailspin, but I don't want to put the kids in danger. Eventually they'll have to stop to change drivers. I'll take care of things then."

"That could take hours. You sure you're up for it? You didn't look like you'd slept much when you showed up this morning."

"I can handle it. But thanks for your concern." Leine took another sip of her coffee. It was getting cold. "Did you connect with Chloe?"

"Not yet. She was still asleep when I showed up. Had a late night, apparently."

"Was she working at the club?"

"Oh, she was working, but not at the club." He sighed. "I'll wait around until she comes to and have a word."

"Jinn said something about hiding a set of keys in her room. They might unlock some of those locked doors Chloe told you about."

"I'll ask her to check. We'll have to find a way to get her inside that won't tip off Sean."

"Tell her to be careful. I doubt Sean's making the trip in the van. If he's going to Phoenix, he'll fly, so he's probably still around."

"Yeh."

"You doing all right?" Leine asked.

"Sure. Why?"

"Just checking. It has to be difficult with Chloe undercover."

Derek didn't say anything right away. Then he sighed. "I'm not sure it's worth it."

"You sound like you're giving up. I don't think that's a good idea."

"And why is that?"

"Chloe's doing what needs to be done. Take it from someone who's been there—her actions don't have anything to do with her feelings for you. Remember that."

"Ja, ja." He coughed, covering his emotion, and added, "Thanks. Text me when it's taken care of, you check?"

"I will. And keep me posted. We still need to find out where Sean's hiding the other girls."

"Roger that."

Leine ended the call and checked the tracking program. Jinn and the van were less than a mile ahead. She adjusted her seat and settled in for a long drive.

27

J inn, Mimi, two other girls, and two young boys sat huddled together in the cargo area of the van. When the driver had herded them into the vehicle, his coat flapped open, revealing a gun tucked in a shoulder holster. The woman, her expression frozen in a perpetual frown, kept her jacket zipped up, so she might have been armed, too. Jinn couldn't tell. A metal cage separated the driver and passenger from the children. The two adults spoke to each other in low voices—too low for Jinn to make out what they were saying.

Jinn glanced out the tinted back window every few minutes, willing Leine to materialize. She still had the tracking device in her shoe, so Leine would definitely know where she was.

Unless the battery died. Lou told her not to activate it until she was being taken somewhere, but Jinn had turned it on as soon as Chloe left. It made her feel less alone. She'd left the tracker on all night, realizing too late she should have turned it off. She scolded herself now, thinking that maybe Leine *didn't* know she and the others were being moved.

Wasn't Leine supposed to be watching the house? *Calm down, Jinn. She knows where you are.*

To take her mind off whether Leine was following them or not, she nudged Mimi with her elbow. "What happened to you?" she whispered.

Mimi stared at her hands—a small forest of ragged fingernails chewed to the quick. She'd ripped one of her pointer finger's nails in half. Rivulets of blood had dried in the creases. They all looked sore.

"My foster mom's boyfriend tried to have sex with me," she said quietly.

"Did you tell her?"

Mimi nodded, still looking at her nails. "She didn't believe me. He kept trying, so I ran away."

"Why did you come here?"

"I heard I could get a job at one of the restaurants in town. I remember someone telling me businesses were looking for anyone who could do the work, no questions asked. That wasn't true."

"Then what happened?"

"I met Gloria. You know her?"

"The dark-haired dancer from Lucky's?" Jinn asked.

Mimi nodded. "Yeah. She was really nice, in the beginning. I stayed at her house for a few days, doing the dishes and cleaning. Then she brought Sean over to meet me. Next thing I knew, I was locked up in a room and..." She glanced at Jinn, but then looked back down at her hands. "I don't want to talk about it."

Jinn wrapped her arm around her new friend's shoulders. "You don't have to. I'm going to find a way for us to escape."

Mimi glanced at her in surprise. "How?"

"I'm working on it. I'll let you know when I've got a plan."

Jinn counted herself lucky that she never got trapped into selling her body for money when she was on the streets. She studied the other kids—two were sitting up, their chins to their chests. The third, the youngest boy, had curled up in a ball and appeared to be asleep. The fourth one stared out the window, her expression blank.

Jinn had seen that expression on some of the other street kids she'd met in Tripoli.

"Why are you here?" Mimi whispered.

Tempted to tell Mimi the truth, Jinn made herself stick to the script. "I had the same problem, except it wasn't my foster mother's boyfriend—it was my stepfather."

Mimi nodded, absorbed by Jinn's cover story. Jinn felt a twinge of regret from the lie but shook it off.

"We lived in Minot, next to the base. I ran away and ended up in Hansen, going through Lucky's garbage to find food."

"I did the dumpster dive, too. Can you believe what people throw away?" She shook her head. "My foster mom taught me to never waste food. I guess it was a good thing. I would have starved."

"Yeah."

"What happened next?"

The woman in front turned in her seat and glared at Jinn and Mimi. "No talking," she said, the crease between her eyes deepening.

Jinn waited until she turned around before she continued. "Lucky found me and let me stay in the back room of the club in exchange for sweeping and doing cleanup. One of the dancers didn't think the back room was a good place to stay and offered to take me to her house."

"Gloria?" Mimi asked.

Jinn shook her head. "Her name was Chloe."

Mimi smiled. "She's really nice."

"She is, except she's the one who took me to Sean's house."

"She did?" Mimi's confused expression stabbed Jinn in the heart. She hated saying bad things about Chloe.

"I don't think she realized what he was going to do to me," Jinn offered, hoping to keep Mimi's good memories of Chloe intact.

"I'll bet she didn't," Mimi agreed.

"Can I ask you a question?"

Mimi nodded.

"What's it like?" Jinn asked. "I mean, I looked up intercourse online, but I don't think what I saw was right."

Mimi gave her a sad look. "It hurts. A lot. I have nightmares about it."

A spark of anger flared in Jinn's chest. "Nobody should have to do stuff that causes nightmares."

"I go away when it's happening."

"Go away?"

"In my head. I imagine I'm a princess being tortured by an evil prince, or something like that. It makes things easier."

Jinn studied her new friend. She'd have to ask Leine to make sure Mimi had someone to talk to, so she wouldn't have nightmares.

In a soft voice she said, "I'll have to try that."

28

Chloe eyed the dark clouds gathering to the south as she pulled under the portico at Sean's mansion. Her weather app warned of a snowstorm building in Eastern Montana that could spill over into the state. She hoped not. She'd had enough of snow and cold temperatures.

And it was only January.

A man in a red jacket appeared at her window, but it wasn't Frank.

"Where's Frank?" she asked when he opened her door.

"He quit."

"Oh. Well, nice to meet you—?"

"Dave."

Chloe accepted his hand and got out of the car. "Nice to meet you, Dave." She gave him her most disarming smile. "Did Sean let you know I was coming?"

Dave nodded. "He did. He said you left something?"

"My wallet. I think it's upstairs." She rolled her eyes and shook her head, giving him the dumb blonde routine. "I swear, if my head wasn't screwed on, I'd leave that somewhere, too."

Dave's lip curled in what she thought might have been a

smile, then disappeared. "Good luck finding it. I unlocked the master bedroom. If you need anything, I'll be in the garage."

"Thanks." She smiled again and walked into the house.

Her shoes clicked a staccato across the marble floor of the entryway, echoing through the empty mansion. The place was eerily still, like it was holding its breath, waiting for Sean to return. Everything looked different in daylight. She'd only been there at night.

She reached the stairs and climbed them to the second-floor landing. A quick glance behind her confirmed Dave wasn't watching her through the window next to the door, so she turned left, headed for Jinn's room. Thankfully, the door had been left open.

She closed the door and started her search in the closet. The bathroom and main bedroom came next, but she found nothing. Not the keys, or Jinn's backpack—not a trace of Jinn to be found.

Chloe sat on the bed and scanned the crown molding and baseboards, in case Jinn created a hiding place. When that didn't pan out, she started again, systematically searching for something that might tell her where the keys were.

It was when she searched the underside of the loveseat that she noticed the register seemed a little off, like it had recently been moved. Curious, she went over to it and got down on her hands and knees.

The register came free easily, and she looked into the vent. At first she didn't see anything, but when she shifted her position she noticed the tip of something shiny. She reached into the vent.

Chloe's heart beat double-time as she maneuvered the key ring out of its hiding place, careful not to make any noise. The solid metal key fob held several keys of different sizes. Three of them looked like door keys. The rest were smaller and odd shaped, similar to the kind that opened padlocks.

Chloe slid them into her front pocket and replaced the register cover. She walked to the door and eased it open, locking it from the bedroom side. The third key worked, unlocking the handle.

Good job, Yaz.

She retraced her steps to the landing, checking each of the doors. One of the three keys opened a locked door, leading to an empty bedroom or closet. She continued to the other half of the house, trying the keys on each door. She found much the same.

She avoided Sean's master bedroom and his study, walked back to the stairway, and descended to the main floor. She paused at the bottom, listening for sounds that would tell her someone was inside the house.

The stillness was complete. She couldn't even hear the wind blowing outside.

She made her way to the rear of the house, unlocking doors as she went, finding nothing of interest: one closet held cleaning supplies; another door opened onto an empty bedroom; yet another room appeared to have been completely overlooked in the furniture department. There had to be a basement. She'd never seen a house in the Midwest that didn't have one.

Chloe continued past the entertainment room and the kitchen, and followed a hallway she'd never been down before. One of the doors she passed opened onto the security room—a bank of monitors showed live feeds of various sections of the property. Chloe moved closer to the far monitor and gasped. The image showed the king-size bed in the master bedroom. When she looked more closely at the other pictures, she realized they were focused squarely on the beds of several of the other bedrooms. Each feed had a title typed below the picture: *Second floor, BR 1. Second floor, BR2.* The live feed of Sean's bedroom had been identified as simply *MBR.*

Had he filmed her? Her heart sank. Did he have incriminating photographs of their only night together? She glanced at the laptop controller, wondering how she could find the pictures and erase them.

She sat in the chair and hit the touchpad. The screen sprang to life, asking for a password. Again, her heart sank. There was no way she'd be able to guess. And what if an alarm went off when she tried to enter the wrong word?

This isn't what you're here for, Chloe. She scanned the video feeds, searching the rooms. Only nine appeared on the screen. Of those nine, only three were bedrooms. Did Sean have all the rooms monitored? Hopefully not.

Chloe slipped her shoes off and rose from the chair. She walked back into the hall, making sure she closed and locked the door. She'd have to find a way to access the feeds. She dreaded having video of herself in someone else's hands. Especially Sean. Still, if he tried to blackmail her, he couldn't do much to her reputation. Not in this town. She was a stripper. She just didn't like the idea of a video of her and Sean on YouTube, or somewhere else, for that matter. Especially if Derek stuck around.

That was a big if.

She'd have to ask Leine if she knew anything about hacking into security systems. That was one discovery she wouldn't tell Derek about.

Chloe moved along the hall, past a large laundry room, and stopped at a closed door before the mud room at the back. Although calling it a mud room was like calling the Taj Mahal a cabin. The square footage matched the size of her living room and featured comfortable built-ins to sit on and stow boots and gear.

Turning back to the door, she tried the first two keys, which didn't work. The third key was the charm. She opened the door, revealing a set of stairs to the basement.

Yes! She glanced at her phone. She'd been inside the house for over fifteen minutes. Would Dave get curious and come looking for her? How long could she realistically look for her wallet?

She decided a few more minutes wouldn't hurt.

Unable to find a switch near the top of the steps, Chloe made it down the first two stairs before a light flickered on. A few moments later, she reached the basement.

The expansive room appeared to run the length of the house. A mirror ran along one wall, with several weightlifting machines stationed in front. She scanned the ceiling, looking for security cameras, but didn't see anything out of the ordinary.

Apparently Sean didn't care to film himself working out.

A robust-looking metal door at the far end of the room caught her attention, and she walked over to investigate, her attention drawn to the digital keypad. She'd seen something similar on a friend's gun safe—a biometric lock, accessible only by a particular person's thumbprint.

Sean kept something important in there. Something valuable. Perhaps all the money he made from pimping children. He wouldn't be able to explain to the bank where he got all the cash and would have to put it somewhere. A burning desire to break open the door and take away the profit he made doing such evil roared to life. She'd donate it all to SHEN.

There was nothing like sweet justice.

She stepped closer and put her ear to the door. She wasn't sure, but she thought she heard something. Spooked, she moved away, pulled out her phone, and took pictures of the door and biometric lock. Then she slid the phone back into her pocket.

She hadn't seen any pets around the house—Sean didn't strike her as a pet kind of guy. Her next thought stopped her cold.

The children.

She was halfway up the stairs when she heard a door slam. Heart in her throat, she raced the rest of the way to the main floor, where she checked the hall. No one was there. She slipped her shoes back on, eased the door closed and locked it, then hurried to the kitchen.

She rounded the corner and almost slammed into Dave, coming from the other direction. He stumbled backward.

"Slow down, lady. Where's the fire?"

Chloe smiled, hoping he couldn't hear her heart galloping at full throttle. "I found my wallet," she said, and brandished the one she'd put in her coat pocket before getting out of her car. "I've got to get to work or I'll be late."

She moved to pass him, but he shifted his stance, blocking her escape.

"I thought you said you left it upstairs?"

"It was in the media room. Stuck between the couch cushions." Chloe shrugged and shook her head. "Like I said, if my noggin wasn't attached..."

He glanced behind her. "But you were coming from the other direction."

Chloe looked behind her, stalling. She turned back with an embarrassed grin and said, "I had to go to the little girl's room."

"Ahh." Dave acknowledged her explanation by lifting his chin. "Glad you found your wallet." He pointed to the entrance. "Your car's out front. I vacuumed it for you."

Relieved, Chloe's smile was genuine. "Gee, thanks, Dave. You didn't have to do that."

Dave gave her a little bow. "I aim to please."

Especially when it's the boss's girlfriend. "Well, I'd better be going. Thanks again." She moved past him and headed for the door, willing her heart to slow down before she had a stroke.

"Drive careful," Dave called. "Looks like the weather's changing."

"Will do." After what felt like an eon, Chloe finally stepped outside. She took a couple of deep breaths of the bitterly cold air as she walked to her car. Reaching for her keys, she realized the ones in her hand weren't hers. She glanced up to see Dave watching her from the top step and let them fall back into her pocket.

The thought occurred to her that maybe he hadn't been sucking up to Sean by vacuuming her car. What if he'd been told to go through her stuff?

Stop it, Chloe. You're being paranoid.

She grinned to hide her alarm. "Silly me. The keys are already in the ignition." She opened the driver's side door and climbed in behind the wheel. Then she started the car and pulled away, smiling at Dave as she left.

As soon as she cleared the guard house's view of the road, she pulled over, opened the door, and vomited into a snowbank.

29

S now drifted across the gray asphalt, obscuring Leine's view of the road. The wind howled, buffeting the Tahoe and flinging crusty ice pellets against her window.

The abrupt change in weather caught Leine by surprise, and she slowed to accommodate the icy highway. Normally, when a storm had been predicted in California, there was plenty of time to prepare. Not so in North Dakota, apparently.

Her visual of the van came and went as the wind blasted dry snow from one side of the road to the other. *Damn them for using a white vehicle.* She glanced at the blinking red dot, reassured that if she lost sight of the van, she'd still be able to track Jinn.

She'd never driven in a blizzard, had never planned to, but there it was. She thought of her training at the agency when they'd flown to Alaska for survival training and to learn how to drive in winter conditions. At the time, she didn't have a chance to try her newfound skills in a snowstorm but did learn how to handle a vehicle on ice. The four-wheel drive capabilities of the Tahoe wouldn't help, unless she ended up in the ditch.

Easy to do—the relentless snow drained all color from the terrain, obscuring the edges of the highway.

Squinting against decreasing visibility, she realized the van was no longer in sight. At the same time, the blinking red dot on her phone vanished.

"Shit," Leine swore under her breath. The tracker's battery had died. Either that, or someone found it and deactivated the device. She hoped it was the former rather than the latter.

Her worry for Jinn threatened to intensify and cloud her judgment. She took a deep breath and stuffed her fear in another, less prominent compartment in her mind, allowing her to regain her equilibrium and focus on the problem.

They're not that far ahead. Gradually, she increased her speed, hoping to catch up to them without drawing attention to the Tahoe. She assumed they slowed down in response to the weather. Sliding off the road would delay their arrival in Phoenix, and Sean wouldn't be pleased.

She pushed the Tahoe to the highest speed she could, relative to conditions, backing off only when the tires began to slip. Taillights were her beacon and she was losing them.

Several minutes ticked by, and still she couldn't see them. Visibility worsened to a near whiteout, and Leine slowed even more. What if she already passed them by? What if they pulled off to wait out the storm and she didn't see them?

She decided to continue on for a few more miles. If she didn't locate them by that time, she'd reverse course and conduct a more thorough search for the white van. Like a needle in a haystack.

More like a snowball in a snowstorm.

Where are you, Jinn?

JINN RETURNED TO HER SPOT BESIDE MIMI. SHE'D BEEN WATCHING

through the back windows as the storm intensified. "It's getting bad out there," she said, indicating the weather. The other kids were all awake and staring wide-eyed at each other, obviously scared of the howling sounds coming from outside.

"They're driving awfully slow. We'll never get to Phoenix," Mimi said.

"That's good," Jinn said, her mind running through possible scenarios. "We need to make them stop the van." She crawled across the floor to speak to the other kids. They all leaned closer so they could hear her.

"When they stop, everybody needs to say they have to go to the bathroom."

"Why?" one of the boys asked. Jinn wondered how old he was—he didn't look much more than nine or ten.

"I want to get them to open the door." She nodded at the two back doors. "Wait for my signal. When I say go, run away as far and as fast as you can."

The oldest girl's face tightened. "But we'll die. We've got nowhere to go." She shook her head and leaned back against the van wall. "I'm not going anywhere. Maybe you have a death wish, but I don't. Did you see that guy's gun?"

Jinn blew out an exasperated breath. "They can't shoot us if they can't see us."

The older girl just rolled her eyes and looked away.

"Fine," Jinn whispered. "Will you guys go with me?" she asked the two boys and the younger girl.

The older boy shrugged. "Maybe. She's right, though. If there's nowhere to run, we'll be worse off than if we stayed."

Jinn sighed, her enthusiasm ebbing. "You're probably right." She crawled back to where Mimi was sitting and crossed her arms. There had to be some way to escape. She just hadn't thought of it yet.

"Well? Are they going to do it?" Mimi asked.

Jinn shook her head. "They're afraid of freezing to death."

Just then, the wind howled especially loudly, and both girls winced.

"They're right," Mimi said. "You know as well as I do to stay inside during a blizzard." She peered at Jinn. "Don't you?"

"Of course I do," Jinn answered testily. But she didn't, really. She was born and raised in Libya, on the edge of the Libyan desert, and now lived in Southern California. Not exactly the frozen north. She obviously hadn't paid enough attention to the module on winter survival at the academy. The field trip to the mountains had been postponed due to conflicts in the instructor's schedule, and it hadn't happened yet. She'd have to work on that. If she made it out of there alive.

The van slowed, and the driver turned off the highway. Jinn got to her knees and looked out the windshield. Three low buildings sat clustered together in front of a large, empty parking area.

A rest stop.

Jinn's heart rate quickened and she motioned to the others to look, hoping they'd understand that once they escaped the confines of the van, they'd be able to hide in the heated bathrooms. There was also a massive semi parked in the truck parking lot several yards on the other side of the buildings. That would be a good place to run once they all escaped. Maybe the driver would help them. She didn't want to put anyone else in danger, though. She had to believe Leine was close by and would be there in time.

Jinn whispered her idea about the big truck in the parking lot to the other kids. All of them glanced out the window to see what she was talking about. The two boys spoke among themselves, then turned to Jinn and nodded.

Good. They were in. She searched the other two girl's

faces. The oldest one gave her a quick nod. That left the younger girl, although Jinn thought she'd follow the older one's lead.

"Get ready," she muttered to Mimi. Mimi grabbed her thigh and squeezed, her excitement contagious.

The driver parked the van at the curb, leaving the engine running.

"I need to go number two," Jinn called.

"Me, too," said the older girl.

"I have to pee," said the older boy.

A chorus of agreement went up from the little group in the back. The driver looked at the grouchy lady in the passenger seat, who groaned.

"Shut up," the driver yelled. The kids grew quiet. "That's more like it. Greta here will take two girls at a time. When they're finished, she'll come back and get the other two. The boys are gonna have to do their business outside the van. After the girls get back."

"But what if I have to do number two?" the younger boy asked.

Jinn hid a smile behind her hand.

The driver shook his head as he handed the van keys to Greta. "You're gonna fucking squat in the snow, that's what you're gonna do. All right?"

The little boy clamped his mouth shut.

Grumbling, the man opened the door and climbed out. Snow and wind gusted through the door before he slammed it closed and headed for the bathroom. Jinn watched as he hunched down and staggered against the wind, barely making it to the building.

Greta pulled on her hat and a pair of gloves and opened her door. The wind whipped it out of her hand, and she struggled to pull it back. She ducked her head as she exited the vehicle, and wrestled the door closed. Using the side of the van she felt her way along toward the rear door.

Jinn motioned for the older boy and bigger girl to sit next to her. "Face the door." Mimi and the other two did as she instructed. "When she opens the door, kick against it as hard as you can," she whispered. A smile of anticipation curved Mimi's lips as the three of them got into position. The other two got ready to jump.

"Ready?" Jinn asked.

"Ready," the older boy said.

Jinn held her hand up as Greta made her way around to the rear door. She imagined the dragon she'd won in the video game backing her and the other kids with its strength and fire.

Greta frowned through the back window as she inserted the key. The door lock clicked. The handle moved, and the door started to open.

"Now!" Jinn yelled. All four kicked, throwing the door wide.

Caught off balance, Greta's feet slid out from under her and she fell backward. She hit the ground, hard, slamming her head on the asphalt, as all six kids exploded from the back of the van.

The strength of the wind surprised Jinn, and she gripped the edge of the door, fighting to stay upright. Mimi held on to Jinn's upper arm, trying to do the same. The boys staggered toward the semi and the other parking lot, while the other two girls made it to the curb. Jinn glanced at Greta, but she wasn't moving.

"C'mon," Mimi yelled, and pulled Jinn's hand free of the van. They clung to each other as they moved in unison toward the semi. Ice pelted Jinn's face, and she narrowed her eyes, gaze riveted on the distant long-haul truck.

"Hey—come back here!"

Jinn turned to look behind her. The driver had emerged from the bathroom and was cutting across the snow drifts toward them, his face purple with rage.

"He's coming," Jinn told Mimi. "We have to move faster." Mimi tensed and the two girls started to run. The crusty ice proved more slippery than Jinn thought, and Mimi started to go down. She gripped Jinn's arm harder and managed to remain upright.

They were halfway to the semi before the driver caught up to them. He seized the back of Jinn's coat and knocked her face-down on the frozen ground, then drove his knee into her back. The fall knocked the wind out of her and she struggled to breathe. She strained her neck to look up at Mimi, who had stopped a few feet away. Her eyes betrayed the internal battle waging within her—should she stay and try to help, or should she keep running?

"Go!" Jinn screamed as loud as she could, cursing the lack of air in her lungs. Uncertain, Mimi hesitated, then ran at the driver, screaming as she barreled into him and knocked him over.

Jinn scrambled to her feet, but the driver was surprisingly quick. He grabbed Mimi by the arm and lunged for Jinn. Once again, Jinn found herself on the ground.

"Stay the fuck down," he growled. "Or I swear to God, I'll smash your little face in."

Jinn stayed down, her hands scraped raw from the ice.

"You little shits need to be taught a lesson." He gripped the back of Jinn's coat and jerked her to her feet. "C'mon."

The driver flashed the gun in his shoulder holster and prodded them both forward. She chanced a quick look at Mimi. Her face was the color of the snow surrounding them.

The three of them staggered to the van. The driver stopped short when he saw the woman lying on the ground.

"What the fuck did you do to Greta?" he demanded. When he didn't get an answer, he opened the cargo door and shoved Mimi inside. He slid his gun free and pointed it at Jinn.

"Get the fuck inside. Now."

Jinn shuffled toward the open door. Her mind raced, trying to think of a way to buy more time. He grabbed her arm and wrenched her forward, pushing her headfirst into the van.

"Don't move, asshole."

30

The scumbag in the camo coat spun around, his gun leading the way. Leine fired. The headshot dropped him like a sack of grain, killing him before he had the chance to pull the trigger. His body landed half in, half out of the van. Blood and bits of brain peppered the door and the ice-white snow beneath him. Leine pivoted and aimed her semiauto at the woman lying on the ground. She wasn't moving. She knelt beside her and felt for a pulse.

None.

"You can come out now," Leine called. She had to raise her voice to be heard above the howling wind. Jinn peeked through the door, the look of relief on her face palpable.

Leine retrieved the woman's weapon from her hip holster, checked the safety, and slid it into her coat pocket. Then she rifled through her pockets, looking for identification. Her driver's license showed her name as Greta Minke, with a rural address just outside of Hansen.

"I *knew* you'd come." Avoiding the driver's lifeless body, Jinn slid to the ground and ran to Leine.

Relief flooded through Leine as she wrapped her in a fierce hug. *She's safe.*

Mimi was the next to appear. She blanched at the sight of the blood and gore, and looked like she was going to be sick.

"Come over here, Mimi. He can't hurt you." Leine held out her hand, wishing like hell the girls didn't have to witness such a grisly sight. Although both had been exposed to violence in their young lives, the sight of two dead bodies would leave a mark.

Mimi edged out of the van, careful to avoid the driver's corpse, and ran to where Leine and Jinn stood.

Leine took a deep breath and let it go, the tension leaving her shoulders.

"It's okay. You're okay." Leine held the girls in a tight embrace, wanting to stop their trembling, knowing they had to deal with what happened in their own way. She glanced inside the van.

"Is it just the two of you?"

"No," Jinn answered. "I told the others to run to the truck." She nodded toward a light-blue semi idling in the parking lot across from them.

Through the blowing and drifting snow, two faces peered around the back of the concrete structure that housed the women's restroom.

"There they are," Jinn said, pointing at the building.

Leine gently extricated Jinn and Mimi, careful to keep them away from the bodies. A gust of wind blew snow in her face, temporarily blinding her. Eyes watering from the cold, Leine blinked several times to clear them.

Her sight restored, she turned to Jinn and Mimi. "Get inside the Tahoe. I'll get the other kids. If they ask, tell them I took care of these two, but no details. All right?"

Both girls nodded. Studiously avoiding the bodies and gripping each other for support, the two girls bent their heads against the wind and headed toward the Tahoe.

She watched them to make sure they could make it and then eyed the two bodies. They were both sturdy, but she thought she could maneuver them into the van. She scanned the parking lot and her limited view of the interstate to see if anyone else was heading in to park in the rest area. Thankfully, most of the cars she'd passed earlier had pulled over on the side of the freeway to wait out the storm. She doubted a lot of folks would brave the blizzard to search for a rest area. Most would end up in the ditch, making things worse.

She muscled the man into the back first, since he was already partially inside. The low step to the cargo area of the van and two functioning doors proved to be a stroke of luck. She was able to roll him to one side and bend his legs so he fit fairly easily. Messy, but doable. She picked up his gun, wiped the prints, and tossed it inside the van.

Then she turned to the woman. Ice had crusted on her eyelids and lips which, combined with her now gray skin, gave her face a frightening look. Leine lifted her upper body and grasped her by the armpits, then dragged her to the lower step of the van. A set of car keys lay on the ground where her body had been.

Once she'd stowed the other woman's body in the van, she wiped the door clean with the woman's hat, tossed it inside, and closed the door. Then she picked up the keys and slipped them into her pocket. She'd move the van to the far side of the lot next to the dog walking area, once the kids were safely inside the Tahoe. She studied the ground—drifting snow had already obscured half of the blood. It wouldn't be long before it disappeared altogether.

Until the weather warmed.

By the looks of things, that would be quite a while.

She checked to make sure she didn't have any blood on her clothes, then made her way to the women's restroom to retrieve the kids.

Chloe took a deep breath and let it go before climbing the air stairs to the Gulfstream. Derek had begged her not to go to Phoenix with Sean, but if she didn't the trafficker would be suspicious. He was paranoid enough as it was—he grilled her about her visit to the house to find her wallet, accusing her of snooping where she shouldn't. She argued that it would be impossible even if she wanted to, since he kept every door in the house locked. Thankfully, he'd relented and dropped the subject.

Besides, the few days they'd be gone would be the best time for Derek to get inside the mansion and see what was behind the locked door in the basement. That morning, she overheard Sean hiring a company to work on the garage while he was gone. After making the excuse that she had to go into work to pick up her check, she met with Derek to give him the keys from Jinn's room and the name of the contractor.

He almost talked her into staying.

The flight attendant smiled and welcomed her aboard.

"Thanks." Chloe walked past the sleek galley into the main cabin and took a seat in one of the butter-soft, white leather club chairs. The gleaming wood accents weren't familiar to her, and she asked the attendant what kind it was.

"It's an African wood called Makure. Gorgeous, isn't it?"

"Yes, it is."

"Would you like some champagne?"

Chloe shook her head. "Not right now, thanks." She needed

to stay as sharp as possible. She was in too deep now, and a slip of the tongue might get her in trouble.

She was several pages into the latest issue of *Time* when Sean appeared. He instructed the pilot and the attendant to take off, before he walked back to where Chloe was sitting.

The attendant brought him a glass of champagne. He took a sip and eyed the empty table in front of her. "It's not too early, is it?"

Chloe smiled. "No, I just don't feel like it today." She flipped the page of her magazine. "How long until we're in Phoenix?"

"Just under three hours."

"Then what?"

Sean smiled and took another sip of champagne. "Then we party like it's nineteen ninety-nine."

Chloe laughed in spite of the ever-present tension she felt when she was with Sean. She hadn't seen him this relaxed before. And she certainly hadn't heard him crack a joke.

Remember, he runs little girls as prostitutes. The thought sobered her instantly. Sean may have been paranoid, but he was also charming when he wanted to be, and she sometimes forgot herself. Leine had assured her it was normal to relax into a role when undercover. In fact, it was encouraged.

As long as she remembered she was acting when she went home.

The jet taxied to the runway and took off. Chloe watched the frozen North Dakota landscape grow smaller and smaller, and wondered when this would all be over.

31

L eine and the kids waited for the storm's intensity to abate before leaving the rest area. It was now just a "snowstorm" rather than a full-on blizzard, and driving had become much less hazardous. The semi driver hadn't appeared during the entire ordeal, leading Leine to believe he or she had most likely been riding out the storm inside the sleeper cab, and hadn't heard anything over the howling wind.

Glad to put the events at the rest area behind her, she studied Jinn as she sat in the passenger seat of the Tahoe and played a game on Leine's burner phone.

"You know that was a dangerous thing you did back there, right?"

Jinn nodded. "But it almost worked."

"Almost is the operative word." Leine sighed. "I realize it was the best you could do at the time. But what if I hadn't found you? Your tracking signal disappeared. I almost missed the rest stop."

Jinn shrugged. "But you didn't."

"I'm serious, Jinn. What should you have done?" She'd been so worried about the kid. In true Leine fashion, she expressed her concern in practical terms rather than emotional ones.

Jinn leaned her head against the seat and stared at the snow rhythmically hitting the windshield. "I should have had a plan B."

"And a C, D, and E." Leine shook her head, thankful for the teachable moment. She had to be hard on the kid, or she wouldn't realize how dangerous things had been. Or how dangerous things could have become if Leine hadn't found her.

She glanced in the rearview mirror at the rest of the children. Mimi and the older boy, whose name was Jake, were fast asleep. The younger girl, Allyssa, had the thousand-yard stare of someone who'd had too much to handle, and the other two—the older girl, Tanya, and younger boy, Ardin—were deep into a whispered conversation with each other. She'd gotten their names and called Lou to liaise between his contact in Minot and various other agencies that could reunite them with their families. According to Jinn, there were nine or ten other children being kept in the room in Sean's basement.

At least, that's where they were that morning.

"You'll be debriefed once you land in LA," Leine continued. "You should develop some other scenarios you could have used during the op. Lou will want to see that you've thought it through." Lou and Leine had both agreed Jinn should go back to LA that afternoon, effectively ending her involvement in the operation. Leine would see her off at the airport after they delivered the others to Sarah in Minot.

"You did well, though," she added, to soften her critique. "For your first op—I don't think anyone in your position could have done better."

Jinn gave her the ghost of a smile. "Thanks. I'll do better next time. I promise."

"You thought on your feet—that's invaluable during an operation. Things can go sideways—in fact, they usually do. You've got a lot of potential, Jinn."

The kid smiled a little wider, this time. Leine resisted the urge to wrap the kid in her arms and not let her go.

Leine called Derek and told him about the room. He told her about Chloe's recon of the house, confirming the basement location.

"Jinn's not sure if they're still there," Leine continued. "From what she could find out, he keeps them locked up until they're needed. Two girls arrived early this morning before the others left in the van. They were obviously traumatized, and he just left them there."

"Fucking monster," Derek replied.

"That he is. Time to shut him down."

Jinn stared out the window, the game on the phone temporarily forgotten. Leine's heart went out to her, but especially to the children Sean had used so viciously. She was going to take the dirtbag down and enjoy doing it.

A good addition to the kill wall.

"Going to do a little interrogation when you find him?" Derek asked.

"Depends on the situation. I'd like to find out who's pulling his strings, but not if it means risking his escape. I'll do my best." Either way, he was going to end up very dead.

"I'm on my way to the house," Derek said. "Chloe left with Sean for Phoenix, so it should be clear, other than security. He's having work done while they're gone. He just doesn't know it's going to be me."

"You're sure they can't ID you, right?"

"How can they? We took out everyone at the farm who saw my face."

"Just the same, better get in and get out. Once the van's discovered they'll contact the owner, which I assume is Sean. He probably won't stay in Phoenix when he realizes they never made it to their destination."

"Ja, ja. I'm almost there."

"Be careful. Keep me posted. I'll be back to Hansen late tonight."

———

DEREK PULLED UP TO THE GUARD SHACK AND ROLLED HIS WINDOW down. The guard came out to look at his credentials, asked him a couple of questions about the work he was going to be doing, and waved him through. Chloe had printed out the contractor's logo from their website, added an employee name, and then put that into a plastic badge holder with a lanyard. All he had to do was remember to speak with a Midwestern accent.

Derek closed his window and headed toward the house. He hoped the rest would be that easy.

The detached six-car garage stood several feet to the left of the house. Derek parked his rig between the two buildings. A tall guy in a bright red jacket walked over and glanced in the pickup bed. Derek had stored a large toolbox and a ladder that he borrowed from Chloe's landlord, along with an air compressor Lucky had in her back room.

Derek climbed out of the Suburban and introduced himself, glad for the bulky coat hiding his gun and body armor.

"I'm Dave," the man said, extending his hand. "Let me show you what the owner wants done."

Derek grabbed the toolbox and leather tool belt and followed him into the garage, past five bays, each with an expensive, or rare, or expensive and rare, vehicle. He whistled at the red 1962 Ferrari parked three bays in. "Now that's a car."

Dave nodded. "Yeah. And you know what? The guy *never* drives it."

"Never?" Derek asked in disbelief.

The other man shook his head. "Waste of good iron, you ask me."

"No shit."

They continued along the back of the garage to a set of stairs leading to the second floor. Upstairs was an office and a bathroom. Dave led him into the bathroom and pointed at a dark, moldy stain on the wall.

"The toilet's leaking. Ruined the drywall. And the floor's really soft." Dave stepped on a section nearby, proving his point.

"I'll have to tear out the flooring and a bunch of the wall to see how much damage there is," Derek said. "This could take a while."

Dave shrugged. "Take all the time you need. My boss is good for it." He started for the stairs. "I'll be around if you need anything. Doing some work on the icehouse down by the lake."

"Thanks," Derek called after him. He walked to the window overlooking the drive and looked out. Dave came out of the garage and climbed inside an older-model Jeep. He warmed up the engine, then rolled out a few minutes later, headed toward the lake.

Derek settled in to see if Sean had posted any other guards on the property while he was away. When no one appeared, he returned to the bathroom and tied on the tool belt.

He opened the toolbox and selected a reciprocating saw, which he used to cut into the stained drywall. Once he opened up an area wider than the damaged section, he slid the saw into the leather tool belt and headed back down the stairs to his vehicle.

Derek pretended to search for something in the back of his Suburban, covertly locating the security cameras. One had been mounted on the garage above the driveway, likely encompassing the front of the building and a swath of asphalt. The house had two that he could see, confirming Chloe's observation. When she'd been in the control room, she noticed a narrow slice of walkway skirting the house that wasn't covered by the cameras above the door. Not that it would matter much, since he planned to sabotage the security system inside the house, but he didn't want to alert anyone monitoring the feeds. Especially if Sean had remote access via his phone.

Chloe assured him she'd never encountered more security than the caretaker—first Frank, then Dave—and the rotating guards at the gate, except during the party she went to with Gloria. That night he used several of his "enforcers" to secure the perimeter and keep guests from going where they shouldn't.

Derek grabbed an extra saw battery for effect and walked inside the garage. He set the battery on a nearby shelf, then moved to the side door of the building. He cracked the door open and scanned the area above him. No camera. The cameras above the front door of the house didn't appear to encompass the garage, so he figured his short trek from garage to home would go unnoticed.

He screwed the suppressor on his gun and concealed it underneath his down vest before he slipped out the door and walked calmly to the edge of the house. He waited a beat to make sure no one surprised him. A light gust of frigid wind ruffled his hair. Other than that, nothing moved.

Hugging the wall, Derek made his way to the front door and stopped to listen. Still nothing. He tried the handle. It was locked.

He fished out the key ring Chloe gave him and tried each key in the lock. He scored on the fourth try, and the deadbolt slid free.

With one last look around, he stepped inside and closed the door behind him.

He paused to allow his eyes to adjust to the dark interior before heading to the back of the house. Chloe had drawn him a map from memory, showing where to find the stairway leading to the basement, as well as the control room with the security monitors. The rest held no interest, so he would confine his movements to the two areas.

He moved down the hall toward the basement stairwell, pausing at the control room to listen. Using the key Chloe had marked with a piece of tape, Derek eased the door open. No one was inside. An open laptop sat on the desk in front of the monitors. He scanned each monitor, mentally storing a map of each camera view. He'd been right about the side door on the garage. Only the front of the building was visible. And Chloe's recollection of a "dead space" between the front walkway and the house was also correct. Good.

He backed out of the room and closed and locked the door. He reached the door to the basement, found the correct key, and slipped into the stairwell. Overhead lights flickered on and he descended to the basement. He peeled off his coat, noting the workout equipment and wall-length mirror as he walked to the door at the back of the room.

He studied the biometric lock. Was it connected to an alarm? It didn't take long for him to find the hidden key entry. The one weakness of biometric locks, and smart locks in general, was the need for a backup way to open them in case the electronics failed.

The way this one looked, he wouldn't need the saw.

Derek took out his set of lock picks and went to work. A lip near the keyhole made it awkward to rake the lock, and it took him a bit longer than normal. Thirty seconds in, he'd unlocked the lock.

He paused to listen. If no one had come running yet, then he was good to go. There was no movement, either above him or nearby, so he opened the door.

32

C hloe set her glass of champagne on the side table next to the sofa and scanned the crowd for Sean. He'd introduced her to their host, a physically fit man in his early sixties with salt and pepper hair, who apparently owned a gigantic swath of New York. She didn't like the vibe she got from him and made her excuses, finding a quiet corner of the Presidential Suite, far from his and his friend's lecherous looks. Aside from a couple of lonely men looking for company, most everyone left her alone.

Her gaze settled on what she could see of Sean, who was animatedly schmoozing with an elderly gentleman and his trophy wife. Dripping in diamonds, the woman's earrings matched the brilliance of the two chandeliers hanging above them in the posh room.

She's got to be forty years his junior, she thought, then mentally shrugged. *To each their own.* It was probably a win-win for them both: he got a younger woman to show off and try to bang; she got security, a trip to the Super Bowl, and a house in the Hamptons.

Chloe marveled at how much people settled. Did the woman

ever dream of falling in love with her soul mate, or did the man wish he hadn't let his one true love get away, so many years before?

Stop it, Chloe. Her romantic side was obviously itching to get out. Sean's cynicism and eagerness to rub shoulders with the high and mighty for purely monetary reasons was getting old. She couldn't wait until she could go back to her real life. She'd fallen behind in her coursework playing Sean's girl-friend. He demanded a lot of her time, and she felt like she needed to give it to him to keep the lie alive. Until they rescued the kids.

The thought of those kids being used for such a horrible purpose brought things back into focus. But what if this didn't work? What if they spent all this time, working to find out where Sean kept the children, and in the end they failed?

Would it be worth it? She'd know when they got back to North Dakota. She slid her phone from her purse and checked the time. Four o'clock. Derek was probably at Sean's house by now. She drummed her fingers on the table, her impatience getting the better of her. She checked to make sure Sean was still talking to the elderly couple across the room before she texted Derek.

Find anything?

She stared at the screen, willing him to answer, but there was no reply. She tried once more.

Are you in?

"Who are you texting?"

Chloe jumped. Sean had sneaked up behind her. *Shit.* Heart hammering, she lowered the screen, plastered a smile on her face, and turned to Sean. His eyes were colder than a cornfield in an ice storm.

"Hey," she said, acting as though it was nothing. "Ready to go?"

Sean studied her for a moment before he responded. "Not yet. There are a few more people I'd like to talk to."

"Oh. Okay." Chloe sighed. "I was kinda hoping we could be alone."

"You didn't answer my question. Who were you texting?"

Don't panic, Chloe. Had he been able to see her screen? She decided to act as though he hadn't. "Lucky. I wanted to see if she found the case of Jack Daniels I shoved under the bar."

"Ah." His gaze shifted elsewhere across the room. "All right then."

He and their host exchanged glances. The other man said something to the couple he'd been talking to and walked out onto the balcony. Sean followed him.

Chloe stood and walked to the open door to see where they'd gone. They stood near the railing a good distance from anyone else, deep in conversation. How could she find out what they were saying? The host guy was bad news, that much she knew. Red flags waved every time she got near him. She trusted herself enough to know when she was in the presence of scum. She took out her phone to see if Derek had texted back, but he hadn't. Disappointed, she deleted the texts.

Then an idea struck her.

She waited a few minutes longer, pretending to be absorbed in her phone. She brought up her voice recording app, then nonchalantly walked out onto the balcony to enjoy the view. Camelback Mountain spread out before her, the ubiquitous brown smog of a big city in a basin surrounded by mountains obscuring its undulating shape. People used to come to Phoenix for the clean desert air. Hell, doctors even used to prescribe the move for their asthmatic patients.

Not anymore. Phoenix had become a victim of its own climate.

She made her way over to where Sean and their host were

talking. She wiped first one, then the other sweaty palm on the back of her dress and glanced at her screen to make sure the app was still running. It was.

Sean looked up from his conversation and narrowed his eyes. "Chloe." Their host went silent and gave her a look that made her skin crawl. Chloe pasted on a smile and continued toward them. When she was within a couple of feet, she pretended to stumble over one of the potted palms and went down on one knee. Sean stepped toward her, but she waved him away.

"I'm all right," she said. Turning her body away from the two men, she put her hand on the potted plant to help her stand and quickly propped her phone against the base of the palm. She tapped the start icon as she climbed to her feet and gave them an embarrassed smile.

"Gosh. I'm so clumsy." She brushed at her knees and then straightened.

"What do you want?" Sean's tone told her he wanted her to leave.

She walked up to him and ran her hand along his back in what she hoped was a seductive manner. "I was wondering how long you were going to be."

Sean turned her toward the door leading into the party and patted her on the ass. "Go back inside. We're talking business."

She gave him a pouty look. "All right, but it's your fault if I drink too much." Making sure she swung her hips for effect, she walked back toward the suite, casting a furtive glance at the base of the palm to make sure her phone was out of sight. It was. She continued inside, through the throng of people chatting, and steadied herself on the sofa back. Her knees were like liquid.

She dried her palms and made a beeline to the bar. The bartender had a glass of champagne waiting for her. Gratefully, she drained the drink and set the glass back on the bar.

"Was I that obvious?" she asked.

The bartender grinned and poured her another glass. "You looked like you could use some liquid courage."

"Thanks." She turned to people watch and sipped the champagne. "Whose party is this again?" she asked the bartender.

"Philip Davis." He nodded toward the door leading outside. "He's talking with your man on the balcony."

"Philip Davis the tech billionaire?"

"One and the same."

Holy crap. She thought he'd looked familiar. *Good thing I didn't know who he was when I went out there.* She would have been way too nervous to "plant" her phone. Depending on if the app picked up anything, Philip Davis could have some big explaining to do. The idea of helping to bring down someone so powerful filled her with both dread and excitement.

As long as Leine and Derek kept her name out of it.

Her heart rate had returned to normal by the time Sean reappeared. Philip Davis followed a minute later and resumed working the room. When Sean reached the bar, he ordered a gin and tonic. Chloe had become accustomed to his moods. This one wasn't good.

"Is everything all right?" she asked.

"Fine."

A second later, Sean's phone chirped. Frowning, he pulled the device from his pocket and glanced at the screen. The color drained from his face.

"What is it?" Chloe asked.

"Nothing." His expression dark, he punched at the screen, put the phone to his ear, and walked away. Philip Davis's gaze followed him, but he remained in his current conversation.

Sean's reaction didn't feel like nothing. What if Sean found out Derek was in the house? Could he know? He might have cameras she wasn't aware of—like the ones in the bedrooms.

What if he was monitoring the feeds from his phone? The thought gave her chills. Of course he was. Sean's paranoia ran deep.

I need to warn Derek. Chloe made sure Sean was still engaged in his phone call and slipped out onto the balcony. Slowing her pace so she wouldn't attract attention, she moved next to the potted palm where she'd left her phone and leaned over the railing, pretending to take in the view.

When she was satisfied no one was watching her, she walked by the pot and plucked her cell from the base of the plant. She checked to make sure nobody was looking at her before she wiped off a bit of dirt clinging to the case, then brought up her texting app.

I think he knows, she texted to Derek. *Get out now!*

Her heart raced. What if Derek got caught because she didn't warn him in time?

She willed him to look at his phone, to move, to do something. *How could I have been so stupid? Of course Sean would have some kind of alert set up on his phone. Stupid, stupid, stupid.*

Her phone dinged. She scanned the screen. Derek replied.

Leaving now.

Relief flooded her, and she leaned back against the railing. Her heart rate slowed as she slid her phone back into her purse. Hand shaking, she started for the door. Before she'd made it more than a few feet, Sean appeared.

"We're leaving." He grabbed her by the elbow and pulled her toward the door.

"What's wrong?" she asked, trying to keep up as he strode through the suite. They garnered curious stares from some of the patrons, but no one tried to stop them.

He dragged her into the hallway and repeatedly jabbed the elevator call button.

"It won't come any faster if you do that," she offered, but clapped her mouth shut at the look on his face.

"Fuck," he muttered. He paced back and forth, swearing with every step.

Chloe took deep breaths, fighting to stay calm. Finally, the elevator door whooshed open and they stepped inside. She moved to the back and leaned against the wall to give him space. And to keep her knees from shaking.

Keeping her voice calm, she asked, "Tell me what's going on."

Sean turned on her. "Things just went to shit, that's what's going on." He began to pace again.

Chloe resisted the impulse to shrink from his anger. "How have they gone to shit? You're a smart man. I'm sure you'll be able to fix whatever went wrong."

Abruptly, he stopped and glared at Chloe. "I'll tell you what happened. My client—a very powerful client—was expecting a shipment. I've just been informed that shipment never made it to its destination."

"Can you send a replacement?" she asked. What kind of shipment was he talking about? Was he trafficking drugs, too? Or maybe weapons? A chill spiraled along her spine at the thought. If that was true, then she was in even deeper than she imagined.

"No, I can't send a fucking replacement." He resumed pacing, his anger bouncing off the walls of the tiny space.

"Is there any way to find this shipment? Maybe the shipping company can put a trace on it?"

Sean turned to her and screamed, "I don't use a fucking shipping company. Are you dense? What the hell do you think I do for a living?"

Chloe fell silent and clamped her knees together to keep them from knocking. There was nothing she could say, or do, to calm him. She didn't want to stoke the fire of his anger any more than it already had been—she didn't know if he'd become more violent, and she didn't want to find out.

"They're going to have my balls for this." He was talking to himself, oblivious to her presence. She wanted to ask who but stayed mute.

As soon as the elevator opened on their floor, Sean charged down the hallway toward their room. Chloe followed at a more measured pace, unsure she wanted to be alone with him. Using her phone, she sent the audio from the balcony to Derek without listening to it and then deleted the file, followed by all her texts to and from both Derek and Leine. She shuddered to think what would happen if Sean checked her phone and found them.

By the time she reached the door, she knew she had to go inside. If nothing else than to hear his side of the conversations he was about to have.

She took a deep breath and slid her key card in the lock.

33

Derek put his phone back into his pocket and swore. If Chloe was right, then this rescue mission had just become a hell of a lot more difficult.

He turned to the half-dozen young girls he'd found in the basement room, who were standing behind him on the stairs.

"Everything's all right. Just follow me." He led them up to the main floor. At the top near the door, he turned back and put a finger to his lips. Six faces gazed at him, the fear and hope in their eyes fueling Derek's resolve. He turned and eased the door open, checking the hall to see if Dave or anyone else was nearby.

So far, so good.

He opened the door wide and motioned for the kids to file out of the stairwell. Once they were all together in the hall, he whispered, "We're going out through the front door to the green Suburban parked in the driveway. The doors are unlocked. You need to move as quickly as you can without making any noise, before anyone sees us. Okay?"

The six girls all nodded.

Derek made his way along the hall, stopping briefly at the

control room. He unlocked the door, unplugged the laptop and tucked it under his arm before returning to the girls.

They made it to the front door without incident, and Derek stopped. Maybe Chloe had been wrong? Or maybe Dave was waiting outside to ambush them. He glanced out the side window at his vehicle, a few yards away. There was no one in the driveway.

He moved aside so the girls could see the Suburban through the window. "That's the vehicle I told you about. We all need to be really quiet and walk really fast. I'll open the back door and you can all get inside. Then we'll leave, all right?"

More nods.

"Okay." Derek took a deep breath, said a little prayer to the gods of North Dakota, and exhaled. He opened the door and walked outside. The cold air hit every exposed area, making his eyes water. One of the girls gasped. Two others glared at her. She clamped her mouth shut. None of them wore coats, and he didn't have time to find any. Thank goodness they at least wore something on their feet.

Head on a swivel, he reached the Suburban and wrenched the back door open. The kids did great, following his instructions to the letter. They quietly massed near the open door. "Get in."

The girls clambered into the spacious vehicle, the older ones helping the younger ones climb onto the running board and into the backseats. Derek waited until the last kid was in before he handed the laptop to one of the older girls, pushed the door closed, and sprinted to the driver's side. His phone vibrated, signifying an incoming text.

A popping sound erupted from the second floor of the garage. Rounds pinged off the car frame. A couple of the girls screamed. Another girl shushed them.

"Stay down," Derek yelled at the girls. He slid his gun free and ducked behind the engine block, unsure which window the shot had come from.

He scanned the driveway and what he could see of the area around the garage, but there wasn't any movement, telling him the shooter was working alone.

Be the hunter, not the hunted.

Derek removed his down vest, bunched it up in a ball, and tossed it over the hood. Gunfire exploded from the second floor, third window on the left, ripping his coat to shreds. Small white feathers floated lazily through the air like fluffy snow. He returned fire, catching a glimpse of red before the shooter disappeared. Another kid screamed. Someone sobbed quietly.

Dave must have gone upstairs to see how the job was going and noticed them coming out of the house.

The lack of backup meant Dave was most likely the only shooter there at the moment. Remembering the guard shack, Derek realized it wouldn't last. Dave had probably already alerted the other enforcers.

He had to leave with the girls, now.

Staying low, he climbed inside the Suburban and started the engine.

Gunfire exploded. The windshield shattered.

More screams.

Derek shoved the rearview mirror down so he could see behind them and rammed the shifter into reverse.

"Hang on!"

He stomped on the accelerator and wrenched the steering wheel hard to the left. The Suburban careened backward in a wide arc and slammed into a concrete planter.

More screams erupted from the back. Derek slammed the shifter into drive and forced the gas pedal to the floor.

The Suburban lurched forward.

Derek slid partway up in the seat so he could see past the

dash, rounds pinging off the wheel wells and back quarter panel. He increased his speed and crested the hill.

The Suburban went airborne for a split-second before crashing back down and bouncing twice.

Derek was all the way up in his seat now, laser-focused and gripping the wheel with one hand, his gun in the other. Using the barrel, he cleared what remained of the windshield from its frame.

They blew past the caretaker's house and barreled toward the guard shack at the bottom of the hill. Derek glanced in the mirror. Six pale, frightened faces stared back at him.

"We're going through," he yelled. "Hold on tight."

Derek gripped the steering wheel, grateful for the heavy front grill on the Suburban.

The guard stood near the gate, AR-15 aimed at the hurtling SUV.

Derek floored the accelerator. "Come on, come on," he muttered under his breath. The engine screamed, straining to move two and a half tons of steel.

"Get on the floor," he yelled. A quick look in the mirror showed the girls scramble, then disappear.

Eyes front, Derek aimed his .45 through the windshield and emptied his magazine. Caught by surprise, the guard dove for cover.

The SUV-turned-missile crashed through and tore the gate off its frame, barely missing the guard.

Derek spun the wheel right, fighting to keep the rubber on the road. They skidded across the highway on two wheels, barely missing the ditch, then slammed down, hard, on all four tires and kept moving. He rammed the accelerator to the floor and sped away.

He took every back road he could think of toward town, figuring Sean's posse would be heading to the house via the easiest, most straightforward route. Adrenaline pulsed through him, keeping him ultra-sharp and aware of his surroundings. He ignored the frigid wind gusting through the open windshield, his arms and hands numb from the cold.

A few minutes in, he felt a tug on his shoulder and he turned. It was one of the younger girls. Eyes the size of half dollars graced a tiny, heart-shaped face.

"I think Sherry's hurt," she said, her voice grave. She turned to look behind her. "There's a lot of blood."

Derek's stomach sank. He scanned the flat, deserted terrain. They were miles from anywhere.

He pulled to the side of the road and parked, opened the glove box, and pulled out the first aid kit. Exiting the driver's side, he moved to the rear passenger door. Bullet holes peppered the metal. He opened the door and climbed inside, then closed it behind him.

She lay on her back on the floor between the two middle seats, surrounded by the other girls. Tears streamed down her face. Blood saturated her pant leg. Derek leaned closer to look at the wound. He used his knife to gently cut away the blood-soaked material.

The bullet had entered and exited the calf. He'd probably find it lodged in the upholstery.

In a gentle voice he asked, "What's your name, sweetheart?" He opened the first aid kit, pulled out a package of Celox and a roll of gauze.

"Sh-Sherry," she stammered.

"I'll bet it hurts a lot, doesn't it, Sherry?"

She nodded, fresh tears cascading down her cheeks.

"Well, we're going to take care of that, yeh? You're going to be okay—I promise." He opened the packet of Celox and showed her the label. "I'm going to pour this packet of powder on the wound. It's going to help stop the bleeding. Is that all right with you, Sherry?"

She nodded. "I guess so. W-will it hurt?"

"Don't worry. It won't hurt any more than it already does." Derek poured the contents of the packet over the injury, then wrapped several layers of gauze around the wound.

"I need to put some pressure on your leg, okay?"

She nodded.

Using his hands, Derek compressed the wound. Sherry winced but didn't cry out. He waited several seconds for the Celox to activate, then released her leg. "How does it feel?"

"It still hurts."

"It probably will for a while." He smiled as he rolled the remaining gauze and put it back in the first aid kit. "I'm going to get you to the emergency room where the doctors can make sure everything is all right."

"What about my mom?"

"I'll make sure to call her and tell her where you are." He looked at the others. "That goes for all of you, too. If you have someone you want me to contact, I'll do it when we get back to town. If you don't have anyone, don't worry. I've got you covered." He smiled as warmly as he could, hoping it would put everyone at ease.

God, they'd been through so much.

Derek made sure she was comfortable and checked the other kids for injuries before he climbed behind the wheel and headed toward town.

He should have contacted the sheriff's office and had them go to the house to investigate, but when he'd seen those kids inside that cage in the basement, he'd lost it.

He had to get them out.

Sean was a monster, pure and simple. Derek was going to have a talk with Chloe. The pictures on his phone of the cages and the girls inside them were proof. He'd call Sergeant Robinson and text him the evidence. Then he'd turn himself in, tell them exactly what happened. He'd show them the bullet holes in the Suburban, the kid's wound. They'd take over, call in the FBI.

Derek pulled out his phone and called Leine.

34

Chloe leaned back in her seat and tried to relax. They'd been in the air for over an hour, and so far she'd had no word about Derek or the kids.

Sean had been livid at the hotel, working his contacts to get more information on his "lost shipment," but he didn't have any luck. All she could glean from the one-sided conversations was that the shipment hadn't reached its destination in Phoenix, and no one knew where the delivery was. Sean cut their stay short at the Phoenician—they were on the plane and headed back to North Dakota in under two hours. When she asked him what was going on, he froze her out.

She checked her phone for the umpteenth time. Nothing from Derek.

What if he was dead?

She took comfort in the fact that right now, the only thing Sean seemed worried about was the shipment. If he'd heard from someone at the house, the conversations would be far different.

The flight attendant stopped next to her seat and asked Chloe if she needed anything.

"I'd love a shot of tequila and a lime," she said. She needed something to soothe her frayed nerves.

"Of course." The attendant turned to Sean. "Anything for you, sir?"

Phone to his ear, he waved her away and resumed his conversation. Chloe strained to hear, but he spoke in a low voice, making it difficult over the sounds from the jet's engines. She caught snippets of words, like "—won't be a problem," and, "I'll make it right." Obviously, he was talking to the big boss, trying to calm him or her down. It was weird to think of Sean having a boss, but of course he did. He'd alluded to "corporate retreats" and other such nonsense the night of the party at his house.

She'd just never seen or talked to them. Thinking of him as an underling gave Chloe a much-needed change in perspective. She could deal with a man who had to answer to someone.

Chloe was itching to message Derek now to find out what was going on. Sean was absorbed in his conversation, which made it an ideal time to try.

What's happening? We're on our way back, she typed.

As an afterthought, she added their estimated time of arrival so Derek and Leine wouldn't be caught unaware in case they were somewhere they shouldn't be. She deleted the text and set her phone down.

Sean finished his call and stared out the window at the darkening sky. His phone went off again, and he answered on the second ring. Chloe watched as he nodded, his movements fluid.

A minute into the conversation, his head snapped up and his shoulders went rigid. "And how did that happen?" he demanded, his voice echoing through the cabin. His tone would have put ice to shame.

That was definitely bad news. Curious, Chloe studied his profile. The tic in his jaw returned, the one she noticed every time something made him angry, but he had to maintain control of his emotions.

Did he find out about Derek? Whatever it was, she didn't want to be around to see him explode. She decided to make an excuse once they landed, tell him she needed to go home and water her plants or something.

Sean ended the call and sat completely still, his knuckles white from the stranglehold he had on his phone.

Chloe leaned forward in her seat. "Is everything all right?"

A moment passed before Sean turned to address her. His face had the pinched look of a man trying to hold on to his anger. "Not really, no."

"Can I help?"

The pinched look vanished, replaced by a deceptively calm façade, the one he wore whenever he had to deal with something unpleasant.

"I'm afraid not, no. Nothing to worry about." He released his grip on the phone and placed it carefully on the table next to him.

"Are you sure?"

"I'm very sure."

"Okay. Then you won't mind if I take the night off? I need to go home and water the plants, clean out the fridge, maybe do some laundry."

"Actually, I do mind. I'd like you to be with me right now."

"But—"

"We can stop at your place so you can do whatever you have to, but then I want you with me. Are we clear?"

"Of course. I just thought—"

"It's better if you don't."

Chloe went silent. She hated when he got this way. He was so cold—like he didn't feel anything. She wondered what happened to him that made him shut people out so completely.

She'd likely never know. He was too private. And, truth be told, she didn't really want to know.

She settled back in her chair and picked up the latest *Forbes*. She'd already read everything remotely interesting that Sean had on the plane, and the financial magazine was all that was left. She paged through, wondering how she could get out of being with him that night.

The flight attendant came by with her shot of tequila. The lime hung precariously on the lip of the glass. She threw back the shot and sucked the lime. Maybe she should get one more, to take off the edge.

Something told her the evening wouldn't be a pleasant one, and she'd had enough of unpleasant.

LEINE FOUND DEREK PACING THE LENGTH OF THE HOSPITAL waiting room. He looked haggard.

"Is she doing all right?" Leine asked, setting her coat on a chair nearby.

Derek stopped pacing and ran his hand through his hair. "She's going to be fine. It was a through and through."

"Did Robinson show?" She scanned the waiting room for the highway patrolman. Apparently it was a slow night—one guy across the room wore a makeshift splint in a sling; a middle-aged woman wearing a mask sat several rows from him; and a few rows over from her a young mother wrangled with a red-cheeked toddler.

Derek nodded. "Yeh."

"Where are the other kids?"

"They're in there." He nodded toward a closed door across from the intake desk. "He called in a woman cop to assist with contacting the families."

"Tell him what happened?"

"Just the bare minimum." He gestured toward the room. "I told him to take care of the kids first—said I'd stick around for questioning. How about you? Did Jinn get off all right?"

"She's headed back to LA. Sarah's taking care of Mimi and the other kids. Thank God. I don't know what I'd do without her."

"Looks like I stirred up a bit of a termite's nest."

"Yes, you did. And that's a good thing—those kids wouldn't be where they are right now if you'd decided to take a pass on Mimi that night." She gave him a tired smile. "That's the difference between getting involved and not."

Derek stared into space, his eyes unfocused. "But there are more out there."

"You can't let it get to you. You have to keep going or it will eat you alive." Visions of the kill wall sprang to her mind.

Everyone had their way of coping. The wall was hers.

"How do you do it? You can't save everybody."

"No, but I can sure as hell try." Leine sighed. "Have you heard anything from Chloe?"

Derek's face paled. "Shit. No, I haven't. I've been a little preoccupied." He fished his phone from his coat pocket and tapped the screen. "She says their ETA is two hours. That was"—he checked the time—"almost three hours ago."

"How much does he know?"

"According to Chloe's last text, he'd only just heard about the van. But I'm sure somebody called him from the house. I left both Dave and the guard alive."

Leine arched an eyebrow.

Derek gave her an exasperated look. "It was all I could do to get myself and the kids out of there. I wasn't about to make my last stand—not with a half dozen children at risk."

"I didn't say anything." She'd been operating on the assumption that Sean wouldn't learn of the rescue until he arrived home.

"You don't have to. You think I should have stalked Dave and put a bullet in his head before I even thought about bringing the kids outside."

Leine waited, letting him come to his own conclusions.

Derek waved away the look she gave him. "Okay. Fine. Yes, I should have neutralized him. Fuck." He propelled himself out of his chair and resumed pacing.

"Are you going to text her back?" Leine asked, changing the subject. What was done was done. Derek didn't do this for a living. Although, taking out poachers wasn't a walk in the park.

Derek pulled out his phone and tapped the screen. "I told her we're at the hospital, and that all the kids are safe." He tapped the screen once more, his eyebrows drawing into a V.

"What?" Leine asked.

He held the phone to his ear and listened. A few seconds later, he shook his head and put his phone away. "Chloe texted me a recording. It's hard to make out, but it sounds like two men talking. I'll listen to it later."

"Great." Leine rose from her chair and started for the door. She turned and asked, "Coming?"

Derek glanced at the closed door where Sergeant Robinson and his female counterpart were debriefing the kids. "I can't—I told Robinson I'd be here."

"So text him your phone number on the way. We need to go, now."

Derek hesitated for a moment, then followed her out the door.

35

J ustice "The Body" Norquist pulled his Hummer off the highway onto Sean's drive and stopped. The gate had been completely ripped off its frame and lay in the snow next to the guard house. The guard was nowhere to be found. Gloria gawked at the open driveway and shook her head.

"Holy shit. Somebody wanted to get out pretty bad."

"Yeah. Dave wasn't kidding when he said we had a big problem." Justice gave the Hummer some gas and continued up the drive to the house.

"Did he tell you what happened?"

"Some contractor found the room in the basement."

Gloria's eyes saucered. "The one where he keeps the kids? Oh my God." She glanced behind them. "Then why aren't the cops crawling all over the place?"

Justice shrugged. "Don't know, unless Sean ran interference with the sheriff and bought us some time."

"What happened to the kids?"

"The guy took them with him."

"Dave just let them go?"

Justice gave her a look. "Don't be stupid. Of course he wouldn't just let them go. The guy had a gun."

"So does Dave, right? He's trained."

"The contractor was, too, I guess."

"But—"

"Would you just shut the hell up? I don't know anything else. We'll find out when we get there."

Gloria narrowed her eyes. "Did you just tell me to shut up? Because if you did, you just lost all your privileges, asshole."

Justice took a deep breath and let it go. He shouldn't have brought her, but she wouldn't take no for an answer. He didn't know how Dave would feel about having her around. Maybe he'd ask her to stay in the vehicle.

Like that would happen.

They reached the house and Justice parked under the portico. Dave's Jeep and three other trucks belonging to enforcers were already there. Dave emerged from the house, his expression grave. Justice got out to meet him.

"What's up, man?" Justice asked. "Sounds like a load of shit just went down."

"Yeah. You could say that." He glanced at the Hummer. "What's she doing here?"

Justice rolled his eyes. "She kept yammerin' at me to take her along. I couldn't shut her up."

Dave shook his head. "Tell her to stay outside. You can come in—the boys are in the living room." He walked back inside the house.

Gloria opened the door and got out. "What's going on?"

"Look. Dave doesn't want you in there with all the guys. We're having a meeting to figure out what to do. You need to stay in the truck."

"Fuck you." She started for the front door, but he caught her elbow and stopped her short. She stared at his hand for a moment before her gaze traveled to his eyes. Danger lurked in their depths.

He took an involuntary step backward and let go of her arm.

"That's what I thought," she said. She turned and marched up the steps into the house.

Justice followed her inside. The guys would never let him live this down.

"So far, Sean's got the sheriff handled. He gave them—" Dave stopped talking as soon as Gloria walked in. He'd been addressing a group of four enforcers seated before him.

She took a seat on the sectional next to Cooper, who gave Justice a quizzical look. "What's she doing here?" he asked.

Dave stepped forward. "I thought I told you—"

"He tried, Dave," Gloria said. "But hear me out. I think I can help." She scooted over, making room for Justice to sit next to her.

"How is that, Gloria?" Dave asked. "We've got a fucking crisis going on here."

Gloria leaned forward. "Some contractor broke into the house. Have I got that right?"

Dave glared at Justice. "That's right. But I called the company and they said someone canceled the job, so they didn't send anybody out. We don't know who the guy was. Or who canceled the job."

"Where are the girls?"

"How do you know about that?"

"I work for Sean, remember?" Gloria gave him a look.

"Yeah, okay. The guy took them."

"And you didn't stop him?"

"Fuck you, Gloria. I tried."

"You mean you shot at them, right?"

"Well, yeah. What else was I going to do?"

"Did you shoot at the vehicle he was driving? By the way, what kind was it?"

"A Suburban—dark green. And yes, I shot at the vehicle."

"Did you hit it?"

"Of course I fucking hit it."

"Did you hurt anyone inside?"

"Where're you going with this, Gloria?"

"Humor me."

Dave scowled. "I don't know. Maybe. I didn't hit the guy, from what I could tell."

"But one of the rounds could have entered the vehicle?"

"More than one, yeah. The guy's rig looked like Swiss cheese." There were chuckles from a couple of other guys in the room.

"Could you have hit one of the girls?"

"Possibly." Dave thought about it for a moment. "Yeah, it's real possible. Why?"

"Because that contractor, or whoever he was, will take that little girl to the emergency room if she's hurt bad, don't you think?"

"So?"

"So, if you want to find out who the guy was, I'd start with the hospital."

Dave's eyes lit up. "You're right."

"What'd he look like?" Gloria asked.

"Tall, big shoulders, blond hair. Seemed like a nice enough guy."

"Did he have an accent?"

"Did he—" Dave thought about it for a moment, then shook his head. "Not really. I mean, he didn't sound like he was from around here, but that's not unusual with all the people coming to work the oil fields."

"Could it have been the guy who grabbed Mimi? The one in the farmhouse?"

Dave narrowed his eyes. "I don't know what he looks like."

"But it could have been, right?" Gloria arched her eyebrows, waiting for him to respond.

Justice added, "It makes sense. Nobody's seen the guy in town lately, but that doesn't mean anything. I figured he disappeared after he grabbed her."

"If it *was* him, then what happened to the van?" Dave asked.

Justice frowned. "The van?"

"The *van*, stupid," Cooper said. "The one going to Phoenix. It never showed up at the motel."

Startled, Justice cocked his head. The missing van was news to him. "What about Drew or Greta?"

Dave shook his head. "No one's heard a peep, including Sean."

"Damn. The guy must have called in reinforcements." Justice leaned back and crossed his arms. "How else would he be able to hit both places at once?"

"We don't know that." Dave crossed his arms, mimicking Justice. "It could be a coincidence."

Gloria guffawed. "Right. And I'm Britney Spears. Did you check the security footage?"

Dave shook his head. "The asshole stole the laptop. I don't have—"

"You don't need the laptop," Gloria said, the surprise in her voice obvious. "Sean monitors everything from his phone. The feed has to be stored somewhere on the cloud, right?"

Dave's cheeks colored. "Fuck. You're right."

"That's okay, Dave. You're new," Gloria assured him. "Frank was here a long time before he had a handle on everything. Did Sean give you the password to check the laptop feeds?"

"Yeah, of course."

"I'll bet the cloud account uses the same one."

Dave took out his phone. "How would I get to the account?"

"Try the name of the security company. There's probably a login."

A moment later, he shook his head. "Doesn't work. I'll call Sean to find out what it is."

"I'd wait on that until you've exhausted all options," Gloria urged. "He's not a guy who likes to be bothered."

Dave put the phone back in his pocket. "You've got a point."

"If I were you, I'd check with the hospitals and the sheriff first, see if anyone's spotted the guy or if there's been anybody admitted with a gunshot wound, and get a description of whoever brought them in. It's not like this is New York City. Somebody with that kind of injury would be noticed."

"What do you want to do to him if—when we find him?" Justice asked Dave.

"We bring him to base camp and wait for Sean." Dave glanced at Cooper, who nodded. "He'll let us know how he wants to proceed."

Cooper added, "I got a pretty good idea."

The rest of the group started to talk about who would do what. Gloria turned to Justice and said in a quiet voice, "It's the guy from South Africa—I guarantee it."

Justice nodded, watching the others divvy up the leg work of going to the cop shops and the regional hospital.

"You know who might know where he is?" she asked, still keeping her voice low so none of the others would hear her.

"Who?" Justice whispered back.

"Chloe."

Justice gave her a sharp look. "She's with Sean."

Gloria shrugged. "But it's a possibility, don't you think?"

Justice studied her, trying to figure her angle.

"You want to move up, don't you?" she asked.

"You know I do."

"Then you need to tell Sean your suspicions. Before anyone else supplies the info."

"What suspicions? That it's the foreign dude? We don't know that for sure."

She rolled her eyes again. He was beginning to really hate that about her.

"Tell him you think it's the same guy who took Mimi, and that Chloe used to date him. Have him check the online feed. I can identify him for you—I've seen them together. That way, you'll be the hero when they find him, and you won't even have to do the legwork." She batted her eyelashes and smiled. "Higher up means a bigger payday, which means"—she walked her fingers up his arm and gave him a lascivious smile—"I can move in. Just sayin'."

Justice glanced at the other enforcers, then back to her.

"That could work."

36

Chloe opened the door of the Mercedes and started to get out. "I'll just be a few minutes. I need to grab a change of clothes and water my plants."

"I'll come with you." Sean opened his door.

Chloe smiled at him. "I don't need help, really. It'll just take a minute."

Sean climbed out and waited for her to make her way around the front of the car with her roller case. "I've never seen your place. You should invite me in."

"Uh, sure. Okay." Her heart skipped a beat as she headed for the side door.

He knows something.

He'd just hung up from another call, this time from one of his guys, Justice Norquist. Sean had grown strangely quiet afterward.

"It's nothing, really," she continued, hoping he didn't notice the slight hitch in her voice. She laughed to cover her nervousness. "Pretty small, in fact."

"Sounds like you don't want me to come in."

She stopped at the door and fished her keys from her purse.

"It's not that. I'm a little embarrassed." She gave him what she hoped was an embarrassed smile.

"There's no need, Chloe. I know all about you. There are no secrets." He returned her smile. The look in his eyes made her knees tremble.

"Well, all right. But don't say I didn't warn you." She opened the door, stepped inside the kitchen, and turned on the light. Did she leave anything of Derek's lying around? She searched her memory, feverishly trying to remember if there were any photographs of her and Derek together, or if he'd left any of his clothes there.

She'd left two plates and two wine glasses drying in the dish rack, along with a frying pan that had cooked their last dinner together, but that could easily be explained. She was allowed to have friends, wasn't she?

A quick glance at the refrigerator relieved her worries, at least for that area of the house. There were a couple of funny magnets holding up her almost-due bills, but there weren't any pictures of her or anyone else.

Sean walked around the kitchen, inspecting each drawer and cupboard. *What the hell was he looking for?*

She cleared her throat. "Looking for something in particular?"

Sean shook his head and continued his perusal. "Just curious. You can learn a lot about someone by what's in their home."

"I gotta tell ya, it's kinda creepy."

Sean gave her a sharp look and then studied the dishes in the dish rack. "Do you have company often?"

"I have friends, if that's what you're asking."

"And are these friends men?"

Chloe unzipped her coat and hung it over the back of one of the kitchen chairs. Her fingers trembled. She grabbed her suitcase handle with both hands. "That's not really any of your business. Make yourself at home. I'll just be a minute."

Rolling her suitcase she walked through the living room into her bedroom, scanning for anything that might tip him off about Derek. Thankfully, there was nothing. She turned on the overhead light and went to her closet, where she pulled a few outfits down and draped them on the bed. She went to the nightstand and quietly pulled the drawer free. Inside was her Glock 26 with a full magazine. The gun went into her suitcase, hidden inside a pair of Spanx. She hoped she wouldn't have to use it, but it gave her some comfort to know it was within reach.

A pair of tennis shoes and athletic socks followed, along with her yoga pants and a workout top. She might as well make it look like she was staying a while.

What else was she supposed to do if she thought she was in trouble? She wracked her brain, trying to remember what Leine had suggested. Sean made her so nervous, she couldn't think straight.

Get it together, Chloe. Leine had given her several options. She only had to remember one of them.

She sat on the bed and searched the room, hoping something would trigger the memory. Her gaze settled on the Christmas cactus on her dresser.

That was it. Derek had told her to put the cactus in the living room window. It would act as a kind of Bat-Signal for help. She rose from the bed and picked up the overgrown plant. The pot was dry as a bone. She'd have to water it first.

She took the plant to the bathroom and ran water into the pot, allowing the overflow to run off into the drain. When she was finished, she dried the bottom and brought the plant into the darkened living room.

"Is this going to take much longer?"

Startled by Sean's voice, she almost dropped the cactus. He stood in the dark room next to the sofa, his hands in his pockets.

"Shit, Sean. You freaked me out." She took a deep breath to still her hammering heart and continued to the window. "Give me a minute—I haven't been home in a while." She moved the drapes aside and set the plant on the sill, then replaced the curtain. "Poor baby needs more light than my bedroom," she said, by way of explanation.

"Looks pretty healthy to me."

"You have a lot of experience with Christmas cactus, do you?" That was good. *Challenge him like you usually do.* She could feel her confidence returning. She had to act normally. If she let on she was nervous, he'd wonder what was wrong.

Unless he already knew.

Sean picked up the small silver Buddha sitting on her coffee table and set it back down. "Not particularly."

"Let me switch out my clothes and then I'll be ready." She returned to the bedroom and started to remove the clothes she packed for Phoenix from her suitcase. Then she remembered the special phone Leine had given her. She hadn't kept it in her purse, worried that Sean would find it and ask what it was for. He knew her other cell was an iPhone. The one Leine gave her was an Android.

She crossed to her dresser and opened the top drawer. There it was, nestled inside a pair of her panties. She turned it on, and rummaged through the drawer while it booted up, pulling out underwear and tossing them in the case. Thankfully, Leine had disabled the sound the phone made when it turned on. When she returned to the drawer, the screen displayed the few icons that came with the phone.

With the phone still in the drawer, she glanced toward the living room, then brought up the messaging app.

She'd typed the letters D-A-K-O- when Sean appeared in the doorway.

"What are you doing?" Arms crossed, his gaze lasered into her like she was a bug pinned to a bug board.

"Nothing." Heart racing, Chloe pulled her hands free, making sure she covered the bright screen with lingerie, and closed the drawer. "I was looking for my favorite pair of underwear, but they must be in the wash." She shrugged and turned to her suitcase. She zipped it closed, not sure if she'd included everything she needed. Would it matter? Hopefully, Leine or Derek would see the cactus in the window and know something was up. She would have to play the game for a little while longer.

It would be such a relief to go back to her old life.

"Ready?" he asked.

"Ready."

37

L eine and Derek cruised through the quiet neighborhood, down the dark residential street, past Chloe's small house.

The windows were dark.

"Wait a second," Derek said, craning his neck to look behind them.

"What?"

"Take another pass."

Leine hacked a U-turn and drove slowly past the house again.

"There. The plant in the window." Derek pointed to the picture window at the front of the house.

Leine pulled into the empty driveway to get a closer look. Moonlight glinted off the leaves of the lone plant.

"It's the signal we agreed on," Leine said. "She hasn't used the drop site yet, and she hasn't texted the code word."

"Yeh, but even one of those means she's in trouble. Shit." Derek pulled out his phone and checked the screen. "Nothing. We need to go to Sean's house."

Leine glanced at Chloe's modest, one-story home. "We don't

know she's there. His place should be crawling with police by now. And, if she isn't we'll have wasted precious time going to the wrong place. We need to check inside in case she left another clue." Leine didn't want to go off half-cocked looking for Chloe. It could mean the difference in her survival.

"Yeh, you're right." Derek nodded. He took his keys from his pocket and got out. Leine followed him into the house.

"I'll check the bedroom, if you want to look here in the kitchen." Derek nodded toward the other room. "Meet me in the living room when you're done."

Leine started with the upper cupboards and systematically searched both the cabinets and appliances but found nothing out of the ordinary. She made sure Chloe hadn't taped anything underneath the kitchen table or chairs, then ran her hand along the windowsills and above the door.

Nothing.

She walked into the living room. Derek walked out of the bedroom, carrying a cell phone. His face looked pale.

"It's the one you gave her. She had it stuffed in her underwear drawer."

"She was supposed to keep it with her," Leine said.

He turned the screen toward her. An unsent text message glowed blue on the screen: *DAKO.*

"It's the first part of the code word." Derek's tone hardened. "He must have been here, or she would've sent it. We have to go to the house."

His body tightly coiled, he looked as though he was spoiling for a fight—not a good mindset for a reasoned response.

"We need backup," Leine said. "Let me call Robinson, see if anyone's there yet."

She took out her phone and tapped in a number. "Sergeant Robinson," she said when he answered, "Leine Basso. Derek van der Haar is here with me."

"I was about to call him," Robinson said. "We've just finished processing the five children he brought into the hospital. The sixth is still in surgery. What can I do for you?"

"We're at Chloe Olson's house on Tipton Drive. We have reason to believe she's in grave danger. We believe she's at Sean's house on the lake. Has someone been out there yet?"

"I passed the information along to the sheriff's department, so I assume they have, yes."

"Would you find out? We're extremely worried about Chloe."

"I'll check as soon as we hang up. If they haven't, I'll go there myself. I have some questions I'd like to ask Mr. Cumani."

"Be careful. He has armed security."

"Thanks for the heads-up. Would you do me a favor and ask Derek to meet me at my office first thing in the morning? I have some things I need to clarify with him."

"Sure thing. Thanks." Leine ended the call. "Robinson's going to contact the sheriff's department. He thinks they've been up there already. If not, he'll go there himself."

"What if she's in trouble right now? I'll meet him there." He patted the gun in his holster and started for the kitchen. Leine stepped in front of him.

"Out of my way, Leine." The anger in his eyes snapped like fire.

She crossed her arms. "I'm as worried as you are, but you need to calm down—think about this strategically."

"Out. Of. My. Way."

"You'll end up getting yourself killed."

"Give me some credit."

"Your perspective is all kinds of wrong right now. What if she's not there?"

Derek took a deep breath and let it go. "I don't want to fight you. But I want to be there if she needs me. I have to be there. It's the only lead we have."

Leine studied him for a moment. "Fine. But you're not going alone."

THE MERCEDES CRESTED THE DRIVE AND ROLLED UP TO THE portico. The outside light was on, but the house looked abandoned. No one came out to greet them.

"Where's Dave?" Chloe asked.

"I gave him the night off."

That could be good news. Maybe he didn't suspect anything.

"So we have the house to ourselves?" Chloe tried to inject some excitement into her voice. She wasn't sure he bought it, but she kept up the charade. She had to buy time so that either Leine or Derek would do a drive-by, see the cactus, and investigate.

If they even figured out where she was. Too late, she realized she should have directed them to the house somehow. Sean could have taken her anywhere.

"Take your things up to the room and wait for me there." His phone to his ear, Sean walked into the library and shut the door.

Chloe didn't have any intention of waiting for him in his bedroom. This was her chance. She rolled her suitcase to the bottom of the stairs and unzipped the main compartment. The Glock fit inside her purse nicely. She pulled out the tennis shoes and socks, then zipped the case closed. She stashed it inside the powder room next to the stairs before hurrying past the kitchen to the back door. Less than a minute later, she had her shoes and socks on. She grabbed a knit hat and scarf off the coat rack before she eased the door open and slipped outside.

Taking a deep breath, she welcomed the fresh, cold air, and set off along the walkway toward the lake. She'd skirt the lakeshore until she couldn't be seen from the house, then strike off toward the highway. Chloe had made the walk once in daylight, explaining to Dave she needed fresh air and exercise. He hadn't seemed concerned at the time, and Sean never mentioned her little foray on the property.

Once she was past the range of the outside security lights, darkness swallowed her. She glanced at the sky—the stars were unimaginably brilliant, like infinitely small, bright, sparkling diamonds. Her spirits soared at the thought of never having to see Sean or the huge, empty mansion again. She'd helped Leine and Derek with the kids, and now she could go back to her old life, knowing she helped rescue several innocent children. Happiness flowed through her as she thought of the short text from Derek, letting her know he was still alive and the kids were safe.

"Chloe!"

Sean's voice cracked like a rifle shot through the North Dakota night. The obvious rage in his voice sent a chill down her spine.

Chloe stepped up her pace, putting as much distance between them as she could. She started to slip and slide on the uneven, icy lakeshore, and she swore to herself for taking tennis shoes rather than a pair of good snow boots.

Abandoning her idea of skirting the lakeshore, she veered off and struck out across the frozen lake, leaving the cover of the reeds and leafless bushes. She would cut through and hit the far side of the lake, then head south over the rise, ending up on the road. Once there, she figured she could outrun Sean, who still wore his wingtips. He'd have to go back for the car, and she'd be well hidden by then.

She looked behind her and her heart leapt. He'd seen her exodus from the shore and was transecting the distance between them. The snow wasn't as deep where he was, and it looked like he was closing the gap, fast.

Chloe reached inside her purse for the gun. She'd wait until he was within range and then fire. Whether she hit him or not wouldn't matter. He'd hesitate if he knew she was armed.

Sweat pooled between her shoulders and dripped down her spine, inviting the cold. The snow grew deeper, and she struggled to make progress. Ice caked her shoes and melted into her socks, soaking them.

The lake made a buckling sound, reverberating from deep within its watery depths. The winter had been harsh that year and the ice was thick—she wasn't in any danger of falling through. Still, the sound of it spurred her toward the opposite shore.

A gunshot shattered the air. Chloe winced, not realizing he'd had a gun, waiting for the hot sting of a round in her back. When it didn't come, she pivoted and raised the Glock. If he thought he was close enough to try and shoot her, then she'd return the favor. He was still out of range, but she needed to make him see she wasn't without options.

She took aim and fired.

And missed.

Sean froze. His posture told her he hadn't expected that.

"If you come any closer, I'll kill you," she yelled.

"I know about you and Derek." He paused, apparently expecting her to answer. When she didn't he added, "I know you tipped him off about the room in the basement."

"You don't know what you're talking about."

"Security cameras don't lie, Chloe."

"Bullshit." She squeezed off another shot. He jumped. *Reel it in, Chloe. You don't want to waste rounds.* Even though his fear gave her immense satisfaction, she wanted to see him suffer for what he did.

All those innocent kids. Anger flared inside her.

"It's over, Sean. Derek knows what you've done, and so do I."

She took a deep breath of the stinging, cold air and let it go. "How could you ruin the lives of those innocent kids? My God. What were you thinking?" Tears welled in her eyes at the thought of the fallout those kids would have to deal with.

"What the fuck do you know, Chloe? Those kids are *grateful* for the opportunities I give them. You hear that? Grateful. If it wasn't for me, they'd be living in squalor, with no way out of their pathetic little lives."

Is he serious? "You're a monster. A fucking monster. I hope you rot in hell."

An engine revved in the distance, splitting the air like an air raid. Seconds later, headlights popped over the rise and headed toward her.

Her stomach dropped. A snowmobile. Someone *had* been at the house. She spun around and glanced at the lakeshore. Too far. She couldn't outrun a snowmobile.

She turned to face both threats. Sean steadily narrowed the distance between them—but the snowmobile was the most immediate danger. Both hands on the Glock, she aimed at the approaching machine and waited.

At the last second, the snowmobile veered left and ran circles around her, forcing her to pivot to keep her aim. The driver wore a face mask, only his eyes and mouth visible. She squeezed off a shot, missed, tried again, missed. Her third shot pinged off metal.

Emboldened, she raised the gun as she tracked him. He miscalculated and came within range. She fired. The snowmobile swerved left as the driver slumped forward over the controls. A round zinged past her and she spun in place.

Sean ducked the same time she fired, and the shot went wide. *How many was that?* The Glock 26 held eleven rounds, including the one in the chamber. She had to have at least two or three left.

Sean recovered his stance and she fired again, keeping him off balance so he couldn't shoot. With a prayer to the heavens, she aimed and fired again.

Sean grimaced and the gun fell from his hand. *Yes!* She hit him. She couldn't see any blood on the dark wool coat, but she must have hit him in the arm or the shoulder. Adrenaline surged through her, and she started for him. He went for his gun with his left hand, but Chloe squeezed off another round and he staggered back.

He raised his good arm. "Stop, Chloe. Just stop."

"No." She moved through the deep snow toward him, gun aimed at center mass, unsure if there were any rounds left. *You've got this, Chloe. He doesn't know how many rounds you have.*

"Have you ever killed anyone before, Chloe?"

Without answering him, she continued toward his gun, lying in the snow several feet away. His right arm hung lifeless by his side.

"You can't kill me," he tried again. "You're not the type."

Ignoring the aching cold in her feet, she took another step forward. Something slammed her from behind and she landed face-first in the snow. The attacker's heavy weight kept her pinned against the ice. An arm appeared, and she instinctively tucked her chin as her assailant tried to put her in a chokehold. Her martial arts training kicked in, and she twisted her hips and pulled her head through the gap in his arms, ripping one of her earrings out of her earlobe in the process.

Her upper torso free, she reached for his crotch and seized his balls in a vise grip.

A strangled cry.

Dave's voice.

She hadn't killed him.

Gathering her strength, she threw him off and sprang to her feet.

Sean was too close, the semiauto in his left hand.

The gun barked.

Hot pain.

So much pain.

Chloe tilted her head to look at the dark, blossoming stain on her stomach. She pivoted and staggered from him. Tears stung her eyes as her legs went numb.

This wasn't a survivable wound. *A lot of good that EMT training did me.*

Unable to stand, she dropped to her knees. Darkness crowded her periphery and she abruptly sat down, her body too heavy to hold upright.

She was dying, and it was all her fault.

Black, ice-covered wingtips appeared at her side. A pair of raven's wings against pristine white snow.

Sean dropped to a crouch beside her, his expression strangely impassive, the weapon of her death casually held in his hand.

"I'll watch you die, and then I'm going to have your body cut into tiny pieces so no one will be able to recognize your pretty little face." He pocketed the gun and cradled his arm.

A glimmer of pride surged through her. She fucked him up. Left a mark he'd always remember.

His death would have been infinitely better.

Exhaustion overtook her, and she sank to her back. She no longer felt the cold. Would she miss people when she was dead? Could she? The lake groaned and shifted, as though protesting her death.

At least, that's what she wanted to believe.

She stared at the brilliant, twinkling stars in the infinite night sky...

...and thought of Derek.

38

J osiah "Joe" Wilson braced his hand on the open door and his one good eye on the yellow lane dividers flashing by below him, endeavoring to keep the old Ford F-100 on the highway and not end up in the ditch. Again.

His wife would tan his hide for driving when the Department of Motor Vehicles told him he couldn't.

But Joe wasn't about to let any damn autocratic, pencil-pushing, namby-pamby civil servant tell him what he could and could not do with his goddamn truck. Especially at his age.

He knew his limits.

What the hell happened to honoring your elders? That's what he wanted to know. The younger generation was all about the money—evidenced by the proliferation of strangers to his beloved town. Not that he minded new faces. He just minded new faces who didn't give a rat's ass about the history of the area, or about the people who had lived there for generations farming, ranching, and hell, digging ditches.

The rumble of the oil truck brought him back to the present and he pulled the door closed in the nick of time to avoid having it ripped off its hinges by the blasted tanker. If he'd had the time or the inclination, he would've shaken his fist at the driver just to make himself feel better.

Not that it would do any good.

Joe had conflicting opinions about big oil. On the one hand, they supplied much appreciated income for his family—the kind that would carry them through a bad harvest, or an unanticipated virus ravaging his herds. The kind a guy could use to take a nice vacation somewhere warm.

On the other hand, their presence had changed the county in ways no one expected. Now, instead of having a friendly chat with his long-time neighbors down at the Wagon Wheel Café, he'd be lucky if he recognized anybody crowding the restaurant for breakfast.

And the roads. Those big-ass oil trucks wore grooves in county roads not built for the weight. The ground beneath the asphalt would freeze, and there'd be no problem. But then the thaw would come and the roads would damn near buckle. He'd heard tell that kind of thing happened in Alaska. But never here in North Dakota.

Goddamned trucks. Those damn grooves were the reason he'd ended up in the ditch, for chrissakes.

And then there was the crime. Fights broke out almost daily between oil workers. Didn't matter what time it was, since they all worked different shifts. There'd even been a few murders in the last year—something unheard of in Hansen. And that explosion out at the old Sawyer place had been attributed to some kind of turf war between criminal elements that had supposedly taken up residence in the area. Joe didn't believe it, though. Figured it was fake news and a gas leak was the culprit. The oil companies wouldn't cop to causing damage.

Too expensive—financially and public relations-wise.

Joe heaved a long sigh, longing for the old days when things were slower and a hell of a lot more peaceful.

He flipped on his blinker and turned onto the dirt road running between two of his fields. He continued to the two silver grain silos he'd had built so he could store the soybeans and wheat close by. It beat making the run into town to the grain elevator every time he filled the big truck during harvest, and it allowed him to hold product until the prices went up.

Joe parked next to the first bin and climbed the metal rungs to the top so he could inspect the grain. The silo boasted a set of electronic sensors made to monitor the condition of the grain inside, but Joe had never trusted the latest and greatest ways of doing things. Besides, the damn silo came direct from China.

And he didn't trust the Chinese.

Sliding the access door open, he sifted the grain through his fingers, reveling in the feel of the gift from his land. Everything looked, smelled, and felt good. He backed down carefully and moved to the second one.

He hesitated at the bottom of the ladder, wondering who could have left a smear of dark red paint on one of the rungs. He made a mental note to get some turpentine out there to clean it off on his next trip.

Joe was breathing hard by the time he'd climbed three-quarters of the way, and he paused for a moment to wipe his face with a rag from his pocket. The view from the silo was one of the highlights of his day, winter, spring, summer, or fall. When he was a younger man, he could see for miles across the flat prairie, its deep, rich soil so obviously made for farming. The Creator's hand was everywhere he looked.

Nowadays, he used his imagination.

His wife would have a fit if she saw him now. Joe allowed himself a chuckle as he climbed the rest of the way to the top.

There was more reddish-brown paint smeared across the metal slats of the roof.

What the hell?

He scraped at the paint with his fingernail. It came off easily. *Cheap ass product.* Probably made by the Chinese.

Grumbling at whoever had done such a stupid thing like making more work for him, Joe slid open the access door and reached inside to assess the grain. His fingers brushed something solid, and he drew his hand back in surprise.

That wasn't right.

The grain didn't smell right, either. He pulled off his glasses and used the rag to polish the thick lenses, then put them back on and peered inside the dark bin.

He could tell there was something in there that shouldn't be, but he couldn't make out exactly what. It was most likely some animal, but damned if he could figure out how it got there.

"Goddamned eyes," he groused. Due to macular degeneration, he'd been losing his eyesight over the years, but had been able to cope up until now. He pulled out the mini Maglite he always carried and shined it inside.

The light fell across what appeared to be an arm with some kind of tattoo. With a gasp, Joe shied backward and dropped the light, saved from falling to his death by the metal cage that surrounded the ladder. The Maglite pinged off the silo as it dropped, falling with a quiet *thunk* when it hit dirt and skittered across the frozen ground.

39

L eine ended the call with Sergeant Robinson and set the phone down on the table next to her hotel window. She took a deep breath and closed her eyes.

According to Robinson, a farmer had found Chloe. Correction. He'd found part of her. The bastard hacked her arm off and left it in the man's silo.

There would be more grisly discoveries in the days ahead.

How was she going to tell Derek? They drove past Sean's place the night before, but the gate had been repaired and the guard house was dark. She'd followed Derek through the fresh snow to the lower part of the wall surrounding the property, and he climbed to the top to get a good view through the IR binoculars. He'd found nothing unusual. Sean's icehouse had been moved to another section of the lake, but that in itself wasn't cause for concern. It was common practice to change location if the fish weren't biting.

There hadn't been any law enforcement visible, but if no one was home, that wasn't odd. Either way they'd need a search warrant, and that took time. Robinson told Leine he expected to have one in hand later that morning.

Dreading what she was about to do, Leine made herself get up, walk out the door and down the hall to Derek's room.

He opened the door after the first knock. "Hey, Leine. Come on in. Any news?"

"Looks like you've been awake a while."

The dark bags under his eyes attested to the night he'd just had. He closed the door behind her.

"I couldn't sleep. Any word on Chloe?"

"Actually, there is."

"And?"

Get it over with, Leine. She took a deep breath and let it go. "Chloe's dead."

He stared at her, uncomprehending.

"Derek? Did you hear what I said?"

His face drained of color, and he started to shake. Leine moved quickly, guiding him to the edge of the bed. He sat down and stared in front of him, his silence worse than if he'd raged at her, or Sean, or the wall.

He blinked, once, and asked, "How?"

Leine shook her head. "You don't—"

His eyes flooded with pain, he turned to her and growled, "*How* do they know it's her?"

"A farmer found her arm in one of his silos. The tattoo was recognizable, and the prints match. Robinson said they're looking for...the rest."

Derek slowly rose to his feet and walked with calm precision to his nightstand. He opened the drawer, pulled out his .45, and racked the slide.

"Don't do anything stupid, Derek."

Ignoring her, he slid the .45 into his shoulder holster and walked to the closet to get his coat.

"Derek. I'm deadly serious here. You need time to absorb the news. If you act now, you'll put yourself in danger."

He started for the door. Leine stepped in his path. He drew his gun.

"Get the fuck out of my way, Leine."

"Put the gun away, Derek. You need to *think*."

"I've already done all the thinking I need. I need to act. So get the *fuck* out of my way. Now." His deadly calm delivery held menace.

She recognized the need for revenge—had seen it in herself, and others. Those able to rein in their rage had been the most effective at achieving their aim. Those who didn't ended up worse off, by far. She had to try again. She pushed the gun barrel away and took a step closer.

"Stay here. Work with me to bring Sean down. I guarantee if we do this together, we'll end his career, his life, whatever you want. I'm all in, but we have to be smart."

Derek shook his head. "I don't want to fight you, Leine."

The mixture of misery and rage in his eyes tore at her heart.

"I loved her." His voice caught. "What would you do?"

She thought of being in the same position with her old love, Santa, or April, or Jinn, or Lou. What would she do? Truth be told, she'd want to do exactly what Derek wanted to do right now.

Make Sean pay.

"I get it, Derek. I'd feel the same. But I hope that someone would help me recognize I needed to rein in my emotions before acting, or I'd put myself, and most likely others, in danger."

"You'll have to shoot me dead, Leine."

She held his gaze, searching for reason but finding none.

"Chloe wouldn't want this. You want to get yourself killed? She *loved* you. Act like you're worth that."

Derek lowered his gun and closed his eyes. "Ah, God," he said. His shoulders started to shake. Tears spilled over and streamed down his cheeks. "No, God, no, no, no, no..."

Leine led him to a chair next to the table and gently extricated the .45 from his grip as she helped him sit down. She slid it into her waistband and pulled the other chair close.

He buried his face in his hands and sobbed uncontrollably. Deep, wracking cries of despair, of loss, of hopelessness.

Leine sat with him, witnessing his anguish, and let his grief flow over her as she held vigil.

40

Lucky counted the till and closed the register. She handed the bank bag to Bruce. "Make sure this gets deposited before noon. I want enough in there so the check to the liquor guy's covered."

"Will do." He saluted as he walked out the door.

She had more than enough in the other accounts, but she preferred folks believe she was one check away from bankruptcy. North Dakotans were an odd bunch—at least compared to her friends on the East Coast. In the frugal north, signs of success were frowned upon. God forbid a gal wanted to flaunt some of that hard-earned cash. She'd be better off doing the devil's taxes in hell.

Lucky learned early on to save the big spend for her annual vacation—where nobody knew her and nobody cared.

The door swung open and Gloria walked in, bringing the cold with her. Her expression was so odd that Lucky had to stifle a laugh. She could only wonder what kind of trouble she'd gotten herself into now. Probably, she was going to ask for the night off. If that was the case, Lucky had better call Chloe.

Not like she'd been around lately.

Gloria stopped at the bar and stared at the bottles on the shelves, as though deciding which to have.

"A little early to be drinking, don't you think?" Lucky asked. She'd never known any of her dancers to be heavy into booze. Tranquilizers and painkillers, yeah, but generally not alcohol. Apparently the stuff wasn't good for the skin. Who knew?

Gloria continued staring at the shelves. Lucky waved her hand in her face.

"Yoohoo. Anybody in there?"

Gloria snapped back and her gaze cleared. "They found Chloe."

Confused, Lucky shook her head. "What do you mean, found?"

"Joe Wilson was checking his grain bins over next to the Sawyer property and found her arm."

"Her what?" Lucky's cheeks flushed warm as her blood pressure spiked. "Who the hell could want that sweet girl dead?" A mixture of confusion, anger, and suspicion crowded her mind.

Gloria shook her head. "I don't know." She wouldn't look her in the eye, giving Lucky the impression she did know, but wasn't about to say anything.

"Wasn't she seeing Sean?" Lucky asked.

"Sean? I think so, why? You don't believe he's capable of killing her, do you?"

Lucky studied Gloria. An avid student of human nature, she decided Gloria's posture and facial expression screamed deception. And a high stress level. She definitely knew more than she was letting on.

And Gloria was scared.

"Who told you?" Lucky asked.

"It's all over town. Joe was at the Wagon Wheel, telling anybody within earshot that he found her."

Lucky closed her eyes, pulled in a deep breath, and let it go.

Chloe was dead. Not only her best dancer, but a genuinely good person. She'd seen a lot in her life, and some of it included the reason why she ran a strip club in the Great White North.

No one bothered her.

But here she was, in the middle of a shitstorm once again. An innocent getting caught in some criminal's crosshairs. She opened her eyes and shook a cigarette out of an open pack she'd left on the back bar. The lighter flared, and she sucked in the welcome shot of nicotine, giving her time to figure out what to say to the woman standing in front of her. Lucky had her suspicions about Gloria—did she have a hand in getting Chloe killed?

Leine's face from the other day flashed in her mind. Lucky'd asked the boys back east to do a little investigating on the mystery woman, but they'd found nothing prior to 2006. The only people she knew of who didn't have histories were either in witness protection, criminals using a false ID, or were working as spies. The first two categories didn't fit, so that left spy.

What would Leine do when she heard about Chloe? As soon as Lucky heard that Sean and Chloe had hooked up, she suspected the blonde dancer was working with the woman with no past. A woman as smart as Chloe wouldn't put herself in the position of girlfriend to a criminal. Gloria, however, was another matter.

Not that she wasn't smart—more that her ambition took precedence over pretty much anything else.

Maybe a little booze would loosen Gloria's tongue. Couldn't hurt. She grabbed the good tequila off the higher shelf and poured them each a shot.

Gloria threw back the drink and set the shot glass on the bar. Lucky poured her another but left her own drink alone. Gloria didn't notice and drank the second one.

"What are we going to do?" Gloria said. "I can't work all of Chloe's shifts. I have a life."

And now Chloe doesn't, you self-absorbed, callous bitch. Lucky kept her thoughts to herself and poured another. It never failed. A person's true colors tended to display themselves the more a person drank. Gloria sucked that one down, too.

"Then why don't you just quit?" Lucky poured another for her, curious to see how many she'd consume. "Sounds like you aren't interested in pulling your weight around here." She shrugged.

Gloria downed the fourth shot and frowned at Lucky. "Are you firing me? I'm one of your best earners."

"Not when you spend all your time with that wannabe douchebag, Justice Norquist."

"I don't spend *all* my time with Justice. He has a job, you know."

"Sure he does."

"He takes care of things for Sean." Gloria slid her glass toward the bottle of tequila and tapped the rim. Lucky looked at the clock and poured her one more before she capped the bottle. She'd better ease up, or Gloria wouldn't be worth shit later that night. She put the bottle back on the shelf.

The door slammed open with a crash. Lucky and Gloria both startled and turned to see who'd walked in.

It was the South African guy with the hots for Chloe. The bulge under his arm told Lucky he was packing.

Gloria's face paled, and she stepped back from the bar. "I have to go." She continued backward and ran into a four-top. She steadied one of the chairs stacked on top to keep it from crashing to the floor and turned to leave.

"Stop right there."

Gloria froze at his steely tone. Lucky nonchalantly moved behind the bar to where she kept the shotgun and quietly pulled it from its mount. If anybody was about to shoot up her bar, it was going to be Lucky.

Plastering a fake smile on her face, Gloria turned to him and said, "What are you doing here, Derek?"

Derek strode over and got up in her grill. Gripping the shotgun below the bar, Lucky waited to see if he drew his weapon.

"You damn well know what I'm doing here. Chloe's dead. Did you know that?"

"Of course I knew," Gloria sputtered. "The whole town knows."

"I *know* you had something to do with it. I can feel it in my bones." Derek's face was red and he was breathing fast, a sure sign he was in stress mode. "Chloe mentioned you were the cold, calculating type. Did you tell Sean we'd been together? Hmm? Or did you just play along until her being dead worked out better for you?"

That was the first time Lucky had ever seen Gloria at a loss for words. She relaxed her grip on the gun but kept it handy. The poor guy probably needed to let off some steam.

Gloria cleared her throat. "Listen. Derek. I'm as torn up about it as you are—"

Lucky snorted. Derek gave her a sharp look.

"Lucky doesn't seem to think so."

Gloria tried again. "Look. Chloe and me had a friendly rivalry, that's true—emphasis on friendly. The customers loved it. Why would I do anything to put my income in jeopardy? That little rivalry brought in a hell of a lot of cash. Right, Lucky?"

Lucky shrugged, nodded. She was right. But holy Jesus, could the bitch lie.

"You're a lying piece of shit, Gloria." Fists clenched, Derek took another step toward her. "Chloe's death is on your head."

Lucky raised the shotgun and aimed it at Derek's back. "You'd best leave, Derek. I don't want to kill you, but if you lay a hand on my dancer, you'll be picking your balls up off the floor."

Derek caught a glimpse of the shotgun and slowly raised his hands in the air. "I've got no quarrel with you, Lucky. I'm going to take a step back, now. All right?"

"All right." She stared through the sights as he took two steps back, then three.

Gloria eased away from Derek, putting as much distance between them as she could.

"Good," said Lucky. "Now, if you don't mind, I'd like to get back to running my damn bar."

Gloria skirted the rest of the tables and hurried into the back, casting a quick look at Derek to make sure he didn't follow her.

Derek's shoulders slumped. He lowered his arms and turned to face her. Lucky stood down. She couldn't remember ever seeing a bleaker expression on a man's face.

"It was my fault. I wasn't there. I didn't order her to stop seeing him." He closed his eyes.

Lucky returned the gun to its rack and shook out another cigarette. "I like to think I knew Chloe—at least some. She was a headstrong, romantic fool. Ordering her to do something would never have worked. You know that."

He walked up to the bar and leaned against the glossy wood. "Don't you want to see Sean pay for what he did?"

Lucky nodded. "I do."

"Then tell me how to get to him. Where do his guys hang out? How much security does he run?"

"You're too close to it, Derek. Too emotional. That right there is a recipe for disaster."

"You sound like Leine."

"She's a smart lady."

"I'm going after Sean whether you help me or not. It will work out better if you give me something to go on. I don't have a lot of time."

Lucky studied him, trying to decide if she should tell him anything. Either way, the fool would probably get himself killed.

Derek tried again. "If you won't do it for me, then do it for Chloe."

She had a feeling she was going to regret this. She sighed. "If I knew how to get to him, I'd have my own people take him out."

Derek gave her a look. "Your people?"

"From back east. Only thing is, they aren't interested in a small-time hustler like Sean."

"What if he was the front for an international ring of pedophiles?"

Lucky narrowed her eyes. "You got proof?"

"Sort of."

"I already told my people about Sean muscling in on my business. If he's as big into the underage trade as you say, I guarantee they'll show. Enzo hates pedophiles. He's got a couple kids about Mimi's age."

"Call them."

41

Early in the afternoon, Leine carried the takeout to Derek's hotel room and knocked on the door. She figured he hadn't eaten since the night before so she'd picked up a couple of sandwiches from the local deli.

When he didn't answer, she knocked again.

"Hey, Derek. It's Leine. I've got lunch."

There was still no answer. Leine balanced the bag of food on one arm, pulled out her phone, and called his mobile. There was no corresponding ring from inside the room. She ended the call when his voicemail picked up.

Shit. Leine checked the time. He could have been gone for hours. Cussing Derek under her breath, she went back to her vehicle, tossed the food on the passenger seat, and peeled out of the hotel parking lot.

THE DOOR TO LUCKY'S BAR SWUNG OPEN AND LEINE WALKED IN, blinking against the dark interior. The woman was on a mission, Lucky thought.

"Figured you'd be by, eventually." Lucky's gravelly voice carried across the empty room. Leine made her way to the bar where the older woman sat, laptop open in front of her.

"I'm looking for Derek."

Lucky retrieved the smoldering cigarette from the ashtray next to her computer and took a deep drag. She exhaled the blue-gray smoke in a rush, matching the sigh that escaped her lungs.

"He was here a few hours ago. Pissed off and looking for revenge. He about killed Gloria." She covered her mouth and hacked, the phlegmy cough subsiding a few moments later. She stubbed out her cigarette. "Damned things."

"Where did he go?"

Lucky shook her head. "I gave him some ideas where Sean might be, but I doubt he'll find him. If Sean doesn't want to be found, he won't be."

"What if he does?"

"Why would Sean make it easy for Derek?"

"It'll make it easier for Sean. To kill Derek."

Lucky narrowed her eyes. "You really think he'd risk it all just to kill him?"

"My contact in the highway patrol told me there's no sign of Sean. They got a warrant and searched his place on the lake. There's nothing there that can connect him to Chloe—no finger-prints, no obvious signs of struggle, nothing."

"What about all that fancy forensics shit? Wouldn't she have left something behind with her DNA? Hair? Blood?"

Leine shook her head. "No blood, and the hair and anything else they find can be explained by her having been at his last party, and the fact that they were in a relationship. There are several witnesses."

"So he'll go free? You *know* he's responsible."

"He's a person of interest, obviously. But if they can't find him, they can't prosecute. Someone with his means most likely has access to a fake passport and enough money to disappear. His business here is finished, except for getting rid of witnesses. And Derek's heading straight into his trap."

Lucky put her head in her hands. "Christ. I suggested he try Sean's man camp outside of town."

"I know it. Who gave you the information?"

"Gloria's banging one of the wannabee enforcers. She let it slip that they like to hole up there in their off hours."

"Thanks." Leine turned to leave.

"Hold on a minute." Lucky cleared her throat.

The other woman looked at her expectantly.

"I have some people who might be able to help." She hesitated to call Enzo and his crew *friends*, exactly—more like her ace in the hole when—and if—the shit hit the fan. "Acquaintances from the old days."

"The old days back east?" Leine asked.

"Yeah." She stubbed her cigarette out in the ashtray. A thin gray contrail of smoke wafted toward the ceiling. "They'll be here this evening. I can set up a meeting, if you want."

"Let's see how things go. I'd appreciate you giving them a heads-up. I'd hate to take out your friends by mistake."

"You're worried about hurting Enzo and his crew?" Lucky snorted. "You've got some balls, I'll give you that. I'll be sure to tell them you're out there, though. Wouldn't want you to get hurt."

Leine's lips quirked up for an instant, giving Lucky the impression she was trying to suppress a smile. Without another word, she walked out the door. Lucky stared after the mystery woman, wondering who in hell she really was, and whether she should warn Enzo.

JUSTICE NORQUIST CHECKED HIMSELF IN THE MIRROR ONE MORE time, making sure he looked the part of an enforcer. Aside from the razor burn on his chin, he thought he looked menacing enough.

He adjusted his shoulder holster for the fifth time, uncomfortable with the new addition. He usually just slid his piece into his back waistband, but Cooper made him stop doing that. Something about it being unprofessional and easy to lose. But Justice had never lost a gun.

Of course, it wasn't like he'd been super active. The most action he'd had was driving customers to and from the camp for their rendezvous with the hookers and fixing a burned-out lightbulb or a stopped-up toilet. Hell, he hadn't even been tasked with monitoring the camp perimeter, even though Buddy's death revealed a glaring hole in security.

Justice slid his down coat over his tactical vest and walked outside, locking the door behind him before making his way to the Hummer. The winter sun cast long shadows across the fresh snow covering the yard, reminding him to check for his flashlight. Daylight didn't last long this time of the year, and he'd definitely need light for what he and the enforcers were going to do.

Thirty-five minutes later, Justice pulled up to the camp gate and entered the passcode on the digital pad. The gate swung open, and he pulled into the parking lot next to the main trailer. His anger flared at the sight of Dave's dark-blue Dodge parked in his designated space. Five other vehicles, all belonging to enforcers, took up the rest of the spaces.

Grumbling, Justice parked behind Cooper's pickup and went inside.

A group of enforcers sat in the living room and kitchen area. Cooper stood in front of a whiteboard showing a crudely drawn aerial view of the camp. He paused as Justice removed his coat and had a seat on the arm of the sofa.

"As I was saying, we need to cover each quadrant—we don't know for sure that he'll try to breach the same section as before. Stay out of sight. Key the mic once for the gate, twice for the north section, three times for the south, four times for the west. As soon as you hear the mic, get your ass to that quadrant—let's overwhelm the motherfucker. And try not to kill him. Once we've got him subdued, zip-tie his ass and bring him back here. We'll have a welcoming party ready."

"What if he brings backup?" one of the enforcers asked.

"Then we deal with that, too. Sean wants the African dude alive. He doesn't care what we do with anyone else. Shoot to kill. We'll get rid of the body, pronto, so no need to worry about the law." He turned to Dave and grinned. "Thanks to Dave here, we've got a couple new ways to do that."

The others hooted, and the enforcers sitting next to Dave grinned and elbowed him. Dave smiled and looked at the floor as the others congratulated him on disposing of Chloe's body in such a creative way.

Justice's cheeks burned with jealousy at Dave's show of false modesty. Everybody knew the cartels used acid to dissolve bodies. It wasn't brain surgery. On the other hand, the severed arm in the grain bin was a wicked good tactic. Because of an anonymous tip from Dave, the sheriff's department was convinced they had a maniac on the loose, targeting strippers.

Anything to take the heat off Sean and the enforcers.

"How do you know he's coming here?" one of the enforcers asked. "We could be proactive, go out hunting for him."

"That'd be like looking for a needle in a haystack. Look, the dude's already been here—remember, he killed Buddy and the other guys in cold blood. Sean's convinced he'll be back to look for him. If nothing else, he might think he can get some information out of one of us."

"Gloria told Lucky that we all tend to hang here," Justice offered.

"Why would that matter?" Cooper asked. "Lucky's not after him."

"Gloria said she saw him at the bar earlier today." Justice shook his head, remembering how freaked out Gloria had been. "He was out of his mind angry. She thought he was going to kill her."

A thoughtful look crossed Cooper's face. "That's good. Means he's more prone to mistakes. I'll make sure to tell Sean."

"Where *is* Sean?" Justice asked.

The group fell silent and Dave glanced at Cooper.

"He'll be here later on," Cooper answered. "He's taking care of some things."

Surprised, Justice wondered what those things could be. Gloria figured Sean was long gone, at least until things died down. That worried Justice, but he kept it to himself. If Sean bounced, they'd all be out of a job. The others must have known something he didn't, or they'd probably be gone, too.

Which worried him even more. Justice hated being kept out of the loop. He doubted Gloria would stick around if he lost his job working for Sean. He'd have to go back to the oil and gas people. It was good money but a lot harder, and the hours were shit.

Cooper finished briefing them, and they all got up to leave. Justice asked Cooper if he could stay behind to talk.

"Sure. What's up?"

Justice pulled his coat on slowly, waiting until the last enforcer had left. "I didn't want to say this in front of everybody else, but have you heard whether Sean's gonna keep the operation here? I mean, since the cops are looking for him and all?"

Cooper looked away when he answered. "I haven't heard yet."

"Yeah, well. What about a bonus for this extracurricular activity?"

"I'll talk to Sean, see what I can do."

Justice nodded. "Thanks. Appreciate it. I just don't want to get caught with my pants down if he decides to pull up stakes, you know?"

Cooper patted him on the shoulder as they walked to the door. "I hear you. Don't worry. I'm sure Sean will take care of everybody. Doesn't he always?"

"Yeah. He does that."

"Now let's go out and find this asswipe and give him an enforcer send-off, all right?'

Justice tipped his head and smiled. "Let's do it."

42

Derek's breath ghosted through the cold air as he screwed the suppressor onto the AR-15. It'd still be loud enough to alert someone nearby, but if he played it right, he wouldn't have to fire.

He dug in at the rear of the property and studied the camp through the night vision scope. Things looked quiet. When he and Leine had been there before, two gunmen guarded the perimeter. Tonight, he'd seen one. There was one truck parked in front of the main trailer.

Which meant the rest of Sean's guys were out in force—and probably looking for him.

That didn't bode well for Sean being somewhere inside the compound. Derek half expected he wouldn't be there. That would make things too easy. At least this way he'd be able to question whoever he found without the distraction of having to fight off the other enforcers.

Derek timed the guard's rounds, estimating he had at minimum fifteen minutes before the gunman returned. Plenty of time to cut through the fence. He'd wait in the shadows next to the far trailer and quietly neutralize the guard when he walked by. If things went as planned, the guy wouldn't be able to alert his buddies, and Derek could work on extracting information about Sean.

Derek waited until the guard had moved out of sight before he slid down the rise to the base of the chain link. The heavy-duty wire cutters made fast work of the fence, and Derek slipped through, disappearing into the shadows.

The minutes ticked past. Derek strained to listen for the guard. The sound of footsteps came at him from the opposite direction.

He lifted the AR and scanned the fence line through the scope. Did the guard cut through the compound and double back?

The footsteps stilled. Derek checked the area again.

Nothing.

He took a deep, quiet breath in and exhaled. *Calm down, Derek.* This wasn't much different than waiting for prey to break cover. He'd given up killing wildlife—his preference was to poach the poachers. As far as he was concerned, killing Chloe and tricking young girls and boys into a life of sexual slavery put Sean and his men in the same category as the hunters who killed elephants for ivory or rhinos for their horns.

They had no respect for life. And he had no respect for them.

His grief for Chloe had morphed into cold calculation—killing Sean was the only way he knew to appease the guilt he felt for not being able to save her. He'd either succeed or die trying. If it was the latter, he'd do his best to take Sean with him.

A good death is hard to find.

The quote from some poem he'd read years before flickered unbidden through his mind. Hopefully, he'd get lucky and find a good one.

A shuffling sound came from the left and he pivoted.

Again, there was nothing.

He swiveled back to his original position. Something moved in his periphery, and he shifted into combat stance. He locked in on a shadow near the edge of the next trailer. The shadow moved and he fired. There was a grunt, followed by the sound of something heavy hitting the ground.

Derek stepped forward to see where he'd hit him, but something hard jammed against his left temple. He froze.

"Drop the gun," a man's voice commanded.

Derek's stomach clenched as his plan evaporated. *Shit.* Time for Plan B. He could take out these assholes, but that didn't get him any closer to Sean. They hadn't killed him on the spot, so he assumed Sean wanted to do the honors.

That could work. His captors would get him close. Derek would do the rest before...

He didn't finish the thought.

Feigning a resigned sigh, Derek chucked the AR to the ground and lifted his hands. A man holding an AK emerged from the shadows nearby and picked up his rifle. Derek didn't recognize him, but he was obviously one of Sean's enforcers.

The man behind him holding the gun to his head barked an order to pat him down. A man Derek recognized walked out from behind the trailer.

"Dave," he said, nodding at Sean's caretaker.

Dave slammed his fist into Derek's face. Derek saw stars as his head snapped back. Warm blood dribbled from his mouth. He worked his jaw back and forth—it wasn't broken. Yet.

Hurt like a bitch, though.

Apparently Dave wasn't in the mood to chit chat. Derek tried to smile, but it hurt too much and he abandoned the idea. The enforcer gave him a rough pat down and discovered his backup gun and tactical knife.

"Take me to your leader," Derek quipped, but no one found

it funny. Hopefully he'd survive long enough to put Sean in a world of hurt.

If the shit stain was still in North Dakota.

Three more ugly looking dudes emerged from behind the trailer. One of them seemed familiar, although Derek couldn't quite place him. A cruel smile curved the man's lips, giving Derek a preview of things to come.

He'd walked into a trap. Leine had been right—her words of warning flitted through his head. He'd done it this time.

He'd gotten his ass killed.

THE BOYS ZIP-TIED DEREK'S HANDS AND DRAGGED HIM TO A trailer on the far side of the compound. They shoved him up the stairs at gunpoint and pushed him through the door. The layout was like the one where Leine found the pedophiles—a kitchen area immediately to the right, a laundry room, bathroom, and bedrooms beyond that. This time, instead of three disgusting assholes in the media room, there was just one —Sean.

"Good. You didn't fuck him up too bad." Sean studied Derek's face. "I want him to be able to hear what I have to say. Then you can take him."

"I'm surprised you're still here, dickwad," Derek said. "Everybody's looking for you." Derek wondered why his right arm was in a sling.

"There's no evidence linking me to a crime, so even if they did catch me, they wouldn't have enough for an arrest. Asshole," he added.

Despite the pain, Derek smiled. "Once the FBI cracks that laptop I took from your place, they'll have quite a lot more to go on. Combine those files with the footage I took on my phone of the kids in that room downstairs, and you've got a lot of explaining to do."

Sean tilted his head and gave him a look. Pity? Anger? Derek couldn't decide.

"Let's do the math, shall we?" Sean said. "Say I'm brought up on sex trafficking charges. Maybe there are victims who will testify, maybe not. These are kids, remember? With fanciful imaginations." He wiggled his fingers in mock fear. "Ooh. Scary. Who's going to believe them?" He leaned forward and smiled. "I've also got footage of powerful politicians doing some awfully embarrassing things. One of them is good friends with the state's attorney general. I doubt the AG would allow a trial this scandalous for his friend to move forward.

"So, a nice little plea deal for me, if they don't drop the charges altogether." He shrugged. "Besides, when I post bail— and it could be any amount, believe me, my employer will pay— I'll be so far gone it'll take a dedicated task force with a big budget to find me. Nobody's going to waste tax dollars on an international manhunt for some small-time sex trafficker."

"But are you really, Sean?" Derek asked, tilting his head to mimic the other man's posture.

"Am I really what?"

"Small time?"

He shrugged again. "Ask anyone."

"That's not what Chloe said."

Sean smiled. "Good luck getting her to testify."

Laughter erupted from a few of the enforcers surrounding Derek.

At that moment, Derek had never wanted to kill another human being more than he wanted to kill Sean. *Easy, Derek*. He couldn't take Sean down here, not with his goons behind him.

But he could make him squirm.

"I guess that's the beauty of video, isn't it?" Derek said.

"Of what?" Sean narrowed his eyes. His body tensed.

"Chloe shot footage of you and Philip Davis discussing business on the balcony of the Presidential Suite at the Phoenician."

"That's a reach. We're acquaintances. We might have been talking about a business venture—but it didn't involve sex trafficking."

"There's audio, too."

Sean studied him for a moment, then shook his head. "You're bluffing. We were outside. The ambient noise would be enough to fuck up any audio recording."

"Do you really want to take that chance? If I'm not mistaken, the FBI has some phenomenal audio-enhancement equipment, not to mention talented lip readers."

"Were you full of shit in South Africa, too?" Sean waved him away. "Glad we had this little talk. I'm going to let my boys take over from here." He leaned forward, his eyes gleaming with anticipation. "You're going to wish you were back on the savannah, being ripped to shreds by a pack of hungry lions."

"I've met my share of lions. Your guys aren't lions."

Sean sat back in his chair. "Get him out of here."

"You want us to get rid of the body?" one of the enforcers asked.

"Nah. Leave him on the side of the road. I want him used as a warning to anybody else trying to take me down."

"How cartel-ish of you," Derek said. Someone slammed him in the kidney and his knees buckled.

This would not be a good death.

43

L eine followed the boot prints through the scrub behind the man camp to the bottom of the chain link fence. The prints were roughly Derek's size and the tread looked similar. She pressed on the wire and the metal separated. He'd repeated what they'd done the other night and broken into the camp.

She paused to listen. A slight breeze skated through the bushes, rattling the dried leaves, but that was all. After a few minutes she spread the fence and slipped through, following the footprints. Several more prints joined Derek's near the back of the rear trailer. Two distinct pairs of footprints flanked two parallel troughs carved through the snow, indicating he'd been dragged away.

With grim determination, she followed the tracks along the far side of the camp until they turned into the bottom step of a different trailer. A set of similar tracks radiated outward from the bottom step and skirted the fence, punctuated by dark spatter against the blue-white snow.

Derek had been hurt. But was he still alive?

The perimeter lights were off, and all the windows were

dark. No sound, light, or movement came from the other structures, and there weren't any cars parked at the complex,
confirming her suspicions that the place had been abandoned.

She followed the intermittent, bloody trail to the main
parking area where it abruptly ended. A set of tire tracks led
through the gate and toward the highway before disappearing
into the night.

She was too late.

"I THINK YOU CAN STOP NOW, JUSTICE. HE'S DEAD."

Cooper's voice cut through the fog of bloodlust coursing
through Justice Norquist's brain. He gave the inert form another
taste of his steel-toed boot before standing back, panting from
the effort.

"Fuck yeah!" he shouted. He puffed out his chest, the adrenaline shooting through his veins like heroin. The other enforcers
cheered and clapped him on the back.

He'd just killed a man. Kicked the ever-lovin' shit out of him
and killed the motherfucker dead.

They'd all had some fun, at first, but when Justice started
going to town on the piece of shit Aussie, the others stepped
back to watch. He'd kidney-punched him, snapped his forearm,
then body slammed him like he'd seen on MMA. The pussy had
stopped fighting a few minutes in, but that didn't stop Justice.
He'd never felt so powerful, so important. The praise from the
other enforcers only made him work harder.

Justice recovered his breath and grinned. Cooper punched
his shoulder and shook his head in amazement. "Damn, brother.
I didn't think you had it in you."

"Me neither," he said. It was the truth. They'd accept him
now. He was part of the group. He hoped Sean stuck around—or

maybe set up shop somewhere else and hire them all again. Either way, Justice Norquist had found his true calling.

Cooper's phone buzzed, and he pulled it from his pocket. "Cooper here." He paused. "Yeah. Got it. Be right there." He ended the call and whistled to get everyone's attention.

The enforcers grew silent.

"That was Sean. He wants to meet us at the old granary. He's got something for us."

Whistles and hoots followed his announcement. Cooper turned to Justice. "Looks like you get in on the bonus, Justice."

Pride filled Justice's chest. He couldn't stop smiling. The enforcers all walked back to their cars, but Justice stopped. "Shouldn't someone put a bullet in him, just to be sure?" he asked.

Cooper turned to look at the motionless, bloodied form lying on the ground and shook his head. "Why waste the ammo? If he's not dead now, he will be." He nodded at the windswept prairie covered in snow. "We're a long way from anywhere. He won't survive the night."

Justice shrugged. "I guess." With one last look at his handiwork, Justice Norquist walked away, eager to take his rightful place among the enforcers.

44

Leine turned left onto the old county road and continued the search for Derek. She'd already logged over one hundred miles, methodically searching the desolate roads in a grid pattern. Every so often, her headlights flashed on one of the relentlessly active oil rigs in the continuous search for black gold, but nothing else.

She checked oil rig sites and abandoned farms, and anywhere that could hide a body, but there were too many possibilities in the vast farm country.

Her heart sank with each mile. If he was still alive somewhere—and that was a huge if—with temperatures sinking to the low teens he'd die of exposure in a matter of hours. Her mood bleak, she kept going, refusing to give up until she found him, dead or alive.

Was what she did really worth all the death and desperate measures? She had enough money—she could retire perfectly well in some small, warm country—forget her past, reinvent herself, start over.

Enjoy her life.

Then she remembered the two sisters from Fort Berthold

she and Derek had rescued. And Mimi. And the girls from the van destined for Phoenix. And Jinn. And the children that Derek liberated from Sean's basement.

Damn right it was worth it.

Her determination restored, Leine cruised the frozen backroads, searching for cutoffs and other tracks that may or may not lead her to Derek. She'd given as much information as she could to Sergeant Robinson, and he'd assured her he would pass it along to the FBI. She'd also contacted Lou and let him know about Chloe, Derek, and Sean's disappearance.

Lost in thought, she almost missed the silhouette in the shallow ditch alongside the road. She slowed down, hacked a U-turn, and doubled back to where she thought she'd seen something.

Parking on the opposite side of the road, she got out of her vehicle and crossed to the other side. A frigid north wind whipped her face. She zipped her coat to her chin and pulled her knit cap lower onto her forehead. As she drew closer, the outline became a formless heap, which became a pile of clothes, which became...

"Derek?" she breathed. She sprinted the rest of the way to him, afraid he was dead. The nearer she got, the more afraid she was that he'd survived.

A soft moan came from the mass of blood and hair and shredded clothing.

"Oh, God. Derek. I'm here. Hang on." She took off her coat and tucked it around him as well as she could, then raced back to the Tahoe. She laid rubber wheeling the SUV closer, grabbed a blanket from the back, and vaulted out of the cab.

She draped the blanket over him and checked her phone for service. No bars. Cursing under her breath, she bent down and brushed a strand of blood-caked hair away from his face.

"I've got to move you, Derek. Your ribs are likely broken so it's going to hurt like hell, but I've got no choice. If I don't get you to the emergency room you're going to die. I can't let that happen. Not now that I finally found you."

Leine carefully rolled him onto his side, grimacing at the guttural moan emanating from his throat. Blood bubbled through his lips. She straightened the blanket underneath him and rolled him onto his back. Then she grabbed two corners and heaved him toward the Tahoe.

The adrenaline spike from finding him in such a horrifying condition added a burst of strength, and she managed to hoist his upper torso into the cargo area on the first try. His legs were next. The overhead light shone on his bruised and battered face. They'd done a number on him. He'd need reconstructive surgery, and his arm hung at an odd angle. The blood on his lips told her he suffered from internal bleeding.

He didn't have much time.

She was about to close the door when his arm moved and his mouth quivered as though he was trying to speak. She leaned in so she could hear his words.

"Lucky."

"What about her?"

He tried to say more, but instead lowered his arm and closed the eye that hadn't already swollen shut. Leine shut the door and climbed into the driver's seat. If she floored it and didn't hit a patch of ice and end up in the ditch, she could make the emergency room before he died.

———

LEINE STRODE THROUGH LUCKY'S, GARNERING SURPRISED LOOKS from the patrons sitting at the bar, waiting for the next dancer to appear. The first dancer had left the stage, which was now littered with empty cans and bottles. The soft lighting cast the tired, worn furnishings in a warm glow, allowing for the carefully crafted illusion of fun, excitement, and glitz.

The bouncer made his way down the bar, rousting the obviously impaired customers.

"Where's Lucky?" Leine asked him.

He gestured toward the rear of the building. "In her office."

"Mind if I go back there?"

The bouncer, whose nametag read Bruce, shook his head. "She's got company and doesn't want to be disturbed."

"Text her that Leine's here and wants to see her."

He cocked his head as he slid his phone from his back pocket. "You sure she'll want to see you?" He thumbed a message and turned to the next drunk occupying a stool. "C'mon, Bart. Time to go home."

Bart held up his long neck beer. "But I still got a partial."

Bruce plucked the bottle from his hand and shook his head. "Now, Bart. You know the rules."

Grumbling, Bart slid off his barstool, wavered a second until he got his bearings, then staggered toward the door.

Bruce's phone pinged and he glanced at the screen. "Looks like you're in." He pointed to the hallway next to the stage. "Go straight back and hang a right. Can't miss her."

Leine thanked him and walked down the hall, passing an open door to what appeared to be the changing room. One of the dancers was busy wiping off her makeup. Leine turned right and stopped at the door marked *Office*.

She knocked and the door swung open, revealing a small office with several cases of booze stacked against one wall, a calendar with a beer logo on it, and a couple of filing cabinets squished in a corner. Lucky and two big guys dressed in dark suits sat around a scarred wooden desk, the telltale bulge of a shoulder holster evident on each man.

Leine walked the rest of the way in and closed the door behind her. The men simultaneously stood as she entered.

Old school. How charming.

"Leine Basso, meet Enzo Delmonico and Ramón Hart. Enzo and Ramón, Leine."

Leine shook their hands while Lucky grabbed a folding chair.

"We heard a lot about you," Enzo said, his Brooklynese coming to the fore. "Lucky here says you got some major balls. Either that, or you're full of shit, pardon my French." Enzo shrugged. "We'll know soon enough."

Leine sat down on the folding chair. "I'm not full of shit." She sized up the two men. They were both muscular with thick necks and hard stares. Enzo was taller by about six inches, but what Ramón lacked in height, he more than made up for in presence. Leine would put money on Ramón being the more brutal of the two.

She looked at Lucky. "I found Derek."

Lucky blew a cloud of smoke toward the ceiling. "Alive?"

"Barely." She tamped down the molten anger roiling through her at the thought of what Sean and the enforcers did to him. "He's in surgery. The doctors are giving him a thirty percent chance of survival."

"Jesus." Lucky shook her head and stubbed out her cigarette. "Enforcers?"

Leine nodded. "Pretty sure, yeah. But I'm more concerned about getting to Sean before he disappears."

"The enforcers are Sean's muscle I was telling you about," Lucky explained to her two other guests. "They're brutal, but mainly a bunch of wannabe Special Forces types."

Enzo leaned back in his chair and crossed his arms. "So what's your proposal?"

"I've got a good idea where to find Sean. Two sources

mentioned the same place and I believe it's my best chance." As she drove Derek to the hospital, she'd remembered what both Mimi and Scarf had said about Sean using the abandoned granary on the outskirts of town. It felt like more than a decade had passed since that day at the farmhouse. "I can't be in two places at once, and I want to close the loops so Sean can't escape."

"Which would be?"

"I need someone to cover the airfield outside of town, make sure Sean doesn't slip away on his private jet while I look elsewhere."

"How do you know he isn't already gone?"

"I don't. But my gut tells me he's still in play."

"What kind of bird does he have?" Ramón asked.

Leine gave him the information Chloe had texted her when she and Sean flew to Phoenix.

Enzo and Ramón exchanged a look. Enzo studied Leine for a moment. "Tell you what. Lucky and me will go to the airfield to keep an eye on his jet. If it ain't there, Lucky'll let you know. Ramón will go with you to check out your hunch."

"There's really no need," Leine said. She didn't relish working with someone she didn't know and trust. Too many variables. Still, the idea of someone covering her six had merit. She'd gotten used to working with Derek.

Enzo leveled his gaze at her and smiled. His expression reminded her of a predator before the kill. "Look. I want this shit bird as bad as you do. Lulu here tells me he's been trying to muscle in on her business ever since he blew into town." He wagged his finger at Lucky. "Shoulda come to us sooner, Lulu. We coulda run his sorry ass outta town before any of this shit went down." He shook his head. "Especially when you found out he was runnin' kids." He put his hands together like he was praying and looked at the ceiling. "Jesus, Mary, and Joseph. I got two girls—both under ten years of age. That mother—excuse my French—fucker deserves a very slow, very excruciating death."

Lucky lit another cigarette and nodded. "Sorry, guys. I thought I could handle it myself." She turned to Leine. "Ramón's good people. You can trust him."

Leine studied the little group for a moment. Then she leaned forward and extended her hand to first Enzo and then Ramón. "Let's bring the motherfucker down."

45

L eine parked on the side of the road and cut the lights. Ramón snapped a fresh magazine into his pistol. He hadn't said much on the ride over, which Leine appreciated. She'd never liked small talk and didn't appreciate it in others. Yappers, both animal and human, annoyed the hell out of her.

She brought up the binoculars and focused in on the abandoned grain elevator.

It didn't look abandoned. In the old days, people referred to grain elevators as the Cathedral of the Plains for the church-like shape of the tower that normally housed the grain. The sorry-looking receiving office attached to the side had a sloped roof and appeared to be occupied—a faint glow could be seen from the windows. The bed of a white pickup poked out from behind the structure. She handed the binoculars to Ramón.

"What's your plan?" He leaned forward as he dialed in the focus to get a better view.

"First, find out how many we'll have to go through to get to Sean—if he's even there."

"And then we light the fuckers up." Ramón bared his teeth in what passed for a smile.

All righty then. Leine shook her head. Revenge made for some interesting associates. "Let's not go all *Rambo* on them, all right? We need to think about this before we go in guns blazing."

"Sure." Ramón handed the glasses back to her.

Leine exited the Tahoe and walked around to the back. Ramón joined her.

She opened the door to reveal a pair of fully automatic MP5-SDs, several grenades—both concussion and fragmentation— two armored vests, night vision goggles, and extra ammunition. Ramón grinned as he picked up the submachine gun with the built-in suppressor.

"Where'd you get these?" he asked, testing the sights.

"A friend."

That friend was Lou. The man never threw out a phone number or email and had contacts in every state and most countries from his days with the agency.

"Here." She handed Ramón an armored vest, which he tossed to the side. "You know they shoot back, right?" she asked.

"Too bulky. I got to be able to move." He flexed his thick shoulders to make the point. "Besides, I'm all muscle. That's all the protection I need."

She frowned and slid on hers. "I'd feel better if you wore the vest. You know, so you'll stay upright long enough back me up."

"Don't worry about me, lady. I got it dialed in just fine. Besides, I figure if it's my time, it's my time. I'm not going down alone."

The evening temperature had plummeted to single digits. Leine came dressed in thin layers, an insulated hoodie, and her down vest. Ramón wore a new-looking faux-fur-trimmed parka lined with bright safety-orange over a dress shirt and sweater, and shiny new lace-up rubber snow boots. For someone who needed to move and not attract attention, the guy hadn't chosen the best options.

They pocketed grenades and secured the night vision goggles. Then she reached into her backpack and fished out two ear mics and radios. She handed a set to Ramon.

"Key the radio once for yes or to tell me you're in position, twice for no. Anything above two means the number of gunmen. Keep chatter to a minimum."

She closed the back of the Tahoe and slid the NVGs in place. "We'll split up once we get to the elevator. I'll get a visual on the occupants through a side window while you cover the back. Once we know what we're up against, we move in and take them down."

"Sounds good."

They set off through the snowy field lying between them and the building. Halfway there, Leine stopped, alarmed at Ramón's labored breathing. She slid the NVGs onto her forehead.

"You okay?" she asked.

Ramón nodded as he bent over, his hands on his knees. "Yeah, I'm good," he said between gasps. "I'm just not used to hiking through fields of deep fucking snow. Give me a minute."

Leine bit her lip, opting not to tell him that the "deep fucking snow" he referred to wasn't all that deep. She dropped down to her haunches and looked at his boots.

"Mind if I retie these?" she asked.

"Knock yourself out." His breathing had gone from alarming to a more manageable wheeze.

Leine checked the laces and found a sloppy job that left his feet shifting with each step. *City boy.* She untied them, then cinched them firmly from the bottom to the top. Satisfied, she stood and nodded at his parka.

"Might want to zip up that monster jacket. It'll make things a little easier to navigate."

Ramón looked down at the bright orange liner. "But I'm already sweating like a menopausal hooker."

"That sweat's going to make you a hell of a lot colder with these temps. But hey, knock yourself out."

Ramón scowled and zipped his jacket.

Leine started for the grain elevator, wondering if she should knock Ramón out and continue on her own. She abandoned the idea—he'd never survive the frigid temperature, and there was no way she was going to drag his ass back to the Tahoe.

Besides, he'd draw fire, giving her a better chance.

When they were near enough, they split up and approached the structure from opposite directions. The white pickup they'd seen from across the field morphed into five vehicles parked behind the smaller building. The back door had been left ajar— light leaked onto the crumbling step leading inside.

She ghosted up to one of the side windows and keyed the radio once, letting Ramón know she was in position. He answered with the same, telling her he was near the back door.

She eased closer to the corner of the window, glanced inside, then quickly pulled back. Several men with guns stood or sat on tables and chairs, surrounding another man dressed in khakis and a fleece sweatshirt.

Sean.

She recognized him from newspaper articles she'd found online, and from Chloe's description. Chloe had sneaked a few photographs of their target and texted them to Derek and Leine, but those had been suboptimal images, at best.

Leine keyed her mic seven times and said, "Target acquire—"

An explosion of automatic gunfire cut her words short.

"Shit!" Leine sprang into action and sprinted to the rear of the building. The back door had been thrown wide open. There was no sign of Ramón.

He'd gone in solo.

46

S houts mixed with the continuous gunfire ricocheting inside.

Pop-pop-pop-pop-pop.

Leine leaned against the wooden slats of the building and cursed the Mafioso's showboating. She took a deep breath and let it go, adjusted the MP5, and moved inside.

The thick smoke and acrid smell of propellant underscored the number of rounds discharged. Apparently, Ramón was holding his own or the shooting would have died off. She edged through the small entry and paused near the door to the receiving office.

"Ramón! Where are you?" she said into her mic as she took a flashbang grenade from the side pocket of her cargo pants.

Seconds ticked by. More automatic gunfire.

Ramón's voice crackled over her earpiece. "I'm pinned... south wall of the tower. Two of 'em."

"Incoming," Leine warned him. She pulled the pin and tossed the grenade, then turned away and covered her ears.

The grenade detonated with a bright flash. Leine shot out

the lone ceiling light and moved into the room, head and weapon on a swivel, scanning the space through the NVGs.

Something shifted to her left. She dropped low and fired. Her adversary fell to the floor with a thud.

Now from the right—muzzle flash as bullets punched the air above her. She pivoted and fired a burst through the haze.

Another body hit the floor.

Two down. She checked for more gunmen. Muzzle flash wasn't a problem with the MP5-SD, and she continued through the haze, confident she wouldn't give away her position when she fired.

Most of the gunfire was coming from the tower, and she moved through the gap between the two buildings. A torrent of bullets had shredded the sliding barn door separating the office from the granary. Splintered wood and bodies littered the floor.

Stepping carefully, she gave each dead gunman a quick glance, but none were Sean.

Ramón had been busy.

Leine eased further into the tower. More smoke and gunfire. She turned left, headed for the south wall.

"Where the fuck are you?" Ramón's voice crackled over her earpiece.

Leine keyed the mic.

"Can't hold them...longer—" A barrage of automatic gunfire erupted from the other side of the cavernous room, cutting his transmission short. She keyed the mic once more, telling him she was on her way.

She cleared her section of the tower and moved toward the south wall.

There.

Two shooters crouched behind a hulking piece of machinery bolted to the floor, their backs to her. They aimed their weapons at a sheet of rusted metal stacked against a bullet-riddled wall.

Leine eased behind a stanchion and sighted in on the target. She sent a three-round burst into the first gunman, and then the other, systematically cutting them down. Both slumped to the floor like marionettes with their strings cut.

"Clear," Leine said into her mic.

Ramon emerged from behind the sheet metal, clutching his right arm. Blood soaked the sleeve of his parka and saturated the bright orange liner. His MP5 hung limply from its sling.

"You okay to move?" she asked as she scanned their exit, making sure it was clear.

"I'm good."

"Can you shoot with your left?"

His eyes cut to the side. "Sure."

"Let me rephrase. Can you hit a target using your left hand?"

He shrugged. "Why not?"

Leine turned back to the main room and started for the door. "Well, at least you can fire, right?"

"Yeah. At least."

They moved past the bullet-pocked barn door and into the receiving office. The smoke had cleared, revealing four dead enforcers. None resembled Sean.

Outside, a car door slammed and an engine started. Leine and Ramon exchanged looks.

Someone had left the building.

JUSTICE NORQUIST'S HEART WAS BEATING SO HARD HE THOUGHT his chest would burst as he shoved Sean through the open door and into the parking lot.

"Get in the Hummer, now!" he hissed, keeping his voice low in case the assault team shooting up his homies heard him.

Fat chance of that happening over the volley of gunfire inside.

"Holy shit," Sean sputtered, sliding across the ice on his loafers as he made a beeline for the vehicle. "What the fuck was that?" Blood spattered his face and clothes, but beyond the sling on his arm, he didn't appear injured.

"I don't know, but it wasn't good," Justice said. The words were unnecessary but helped center him. He covered Sean's six as the boss climbed into the vehicle and slammed the door closed. Justice winced at the sound.

Thankful he'd backed into the space and could make a fast exit, he reached for the driver's door handle.

Rounds pinged off the side of the Hummer, narrowly missing him. He dropped to the ground and low-crawled to the front of the vehicle, putting the engine block between him and the shooter. He rolled to a seated position and checked the rounds in his Glock.

Three left. And no spares.

More rounds slammed into his precious Humvee, shattering the glass and most likely putting some major hurt on the side panels. Jesus, he had to stop them before they totally destroyed her. He climbed to his knees and brought up his Glock, and the engine turned over. It didn't catch the first time.

Too cold, Justice thought. Sean was in the driver's seat. *That's good—I can jump in the passenger side and we can blow this pop stand.*

It turned over again. This time the Humvee coughed and sputtered to life. Exhaust billowed into the air.

Using the high-strength steel bumper, Justice pulled himself to his feet and waved over the hood at Sean to make sure he knew he was there.

Their eyes met.

Sean threw the Hummer into gear.

Stomped on the gas.

Eyes wide, Justice windmilled his arms and tripped over his own feet trying to get out of the way.

But the Hummer was too fast.

Three tons of American-made steel mowed Justice Norquist down, its current driver barely registering a bump as the behemoth all-wheel-drive crawled over the heavily muscled torso and squashed his head.

47

L ucky lit another cigarette and blew the smoke outside Enzo's SUV. For a surveillance detail, the digs weren't too bad. His rental—a Lincoln Navigator with all the bells and whistles—included separate temperature zones, heated seats, and a moon roof the size of Manhattan. They were parked on the outer edge of the gravel lot at the private airstrip Sean used. They had eyes on his Gulfstream while they waited for the call or text telling them whether Leine and Ramón had found Sean.

Enzo had gone in to schmooze the woman at the front counter and ask if she could tell him if his good friend Sean Cumani had checked in yet for their departure to the Caribbean.

"I'm not supposed to give out that kind of information." She'd giggled and batted her lashes as she pulled up the right screen. "But I suppose since you're his guest and it's almost closing time it won't hurt this once." She'd smiled and checked to see if any recent flight plans had been filed, but told him there hadn't.

Enzo had thanked her and told her he'd try calling Sean again to make sure he had the correct date and time. He winked as he handed her his card, urging her to look him up whenever she might find herself in New York City. She said she'd be delighted.

Half an hour later, the woman closed up shop for the evening and drove off. So now they waited.

"The boys say hello," Enzo said, his eyes on the section of the jet visible through the partially open hangar door.

Lucky nodded, blew another cloud of smoke through the crack in the window, flicked the ash off the end.

"Just so you know, I was going to call you guys." She shrugged, looking through the windshield. "I thought I could handle things."

"It ain't like you haven't taken care of your share of things."

Lucky gave him a quick smile, nodded. "Yeah." She cleared her throat and moved a little in her seat, getting comfortable. "I'm grateful Monty left me alone this long. Tell him that when you go back, would you?"

Enzo sighed and leaned his head on the leather headrest. "Yeah. About that."

Lucky froze, cigarette halfway to her lips. She didn't want to hear the rest.

"You know, when you were short on vig that first month, Monty said, 'Not to worry. Lulu always makes good.'" He shrugged. "Then, when revenue fell in the second and third quarter, we started to worry. Maybe our Lucky wasn't so lucky anymore."

"Yeah, but I made up for it in November and December."

He nodded his agreement. "That you did, that you did. But now we got this asswipe child rapist trying to take the lion's share of the revenue by poaching your business. That pisses Monty off. The man's not happy. And neither am I."

Lucky blew out a long breath. "Look. It's just a bump in the road. I've got it handled."

"Be that as it may, Monty asked me to stick around a while. Make sure things run smoothly, you know?"

"What the hell? I mean, he did?" She flicked the cigarette butt out the window and reached for another. "You and Ramón both?" The two wise guys would stick out like a pair of snowballs in hell. Not only that, but Lucky didn't need, or want, oversight from the boys back east.

"Yeah. Go figure." He shook his head and gestured at the snow-covered plains surrounding the airfield. "I ask you, who the hell would want to stay in this Godforsaken place? No offense."

"None taken."

"Maybe a fuckin' Yeti." He stared out the windshield. "I ain't no Yeti."

There went her carefully crafted cover story. She'd never be able to explain Enzo and Ramón's presence at the bar. Not in tiny little Hansen. Shit, she might as well blow town—sell the bar and set up somewhere Monty and his friends couldn't find her.

Wherever that might be. If they'd travel all the way to Bum-Fuck, North Dakota, they'd go anywhere.

"Look, Enzo. You don't want to be here. Not that I wouldn't love having you around and everything, but I don't need anybody looking over my shoulder." She lit the next cigarette, took a deep drag, and blew it out the window. "Once we take care of Sean and his thugs, the town's pretty quiet. The only excitement we get around here are bar fights and the occasional arrest for being drunk in public."

"Really? Then how come there's been so many murders in the past couple weeks?"

Lucky waved his question away. "That was on Sean. And the South African guy who rescued a kid Sean forced into tricking. After tonight, we won't have either problem.

When Sean disappears, Leine assures me that she'll be gone, and the other guy will, too. Then, *voila*—no more problems."

Enzo narrowed his eyes and growled. "That Sean mother-fucker deserves to suffer for what he did."

"I have no doubt he'll—"

The phone in her satchel buzzed. She cut herself short and fished out her cell. It was Leine.

"Did you get him?" she asked.

"No, although the enforcers won't be a problem," Leine replied. "Sean took off in a black Hummer. We're on our way, but he got a good head start. If I were a betting woman, I'd say he's headed for the airfield."

"Got it. We'll keep an eye out. You coming?"

"Ramón's been shot. He's conscious, but he's lost a lot of blood. I'm going to drop him at Emergency. Then I'll head your way."

Lucky repeated what she'd said to Enzo. He shook his head and reached for the phone.

"Give it to me."

Lucky handed the cell over.

"Enzo here. What the hell happened?" He fell silent, listening. Then, "Tell that crybaby to suck it up and get his whiny ass over here. We got no time for the emergency room—we don't need any what you call 'extra attention,' if you catch my drift." Enzo paused, listened. "Good." He handed the phone back to Lucky.

"Hello?" she said, in case Leine was still on the line. Dead air. She pressed the end call button and slid the phone back into her purse. "What'd she say?"

Enzo shrugged. "Let's just say they both saw it from my perspective."

Twenty minutes later, Lucky leaned forward and pointed

through the windshield. A pair of headlights had popped over the rise and appeared to be headed toward them.

"That a Hummer?"

Enzo squinted at the two dots of light. "Could be. Looks like a wide body."

The twin lights morphed into a shiny black Humvee racing along the county highway toward them. The vehicle hooked a left and fishtailed into the private airfield's parking lot. A jagged line of bullet holes pocked the side.

"That's him."

The Humvee continued through the lot and disappeared around the corner of the office building.

Enzo put the Lincoln in gear and eased toward the hangar where Sean had his jet parked. Lucky double-checked the magazine of her Sig Sauer P225, then snapped it back into the well.

Lock and load.

When they reached the hangar, Enzo stopped, killed the engine, and reached in the back for his Mossberg pump action shotgun. Sean was on his cell phone, pacing back and forth in front of his jet. They exited the SUV and started toward him. Enzo kept the barrel of the shotgun pointed toward the ground and behind him, while Lucky hid the Sig in her coat pocket.

"Get your ass back here," Lucky heard Sean say.

"I don't give a shit what you think I said," he continued. "I'm telling you we're leaving *now*."

Sean glanced up as they approached. His expression morphed from anger to puzzlement. He ended the call and slid the phone into his coat pocket. "What are you doing here?" He addressed his question to Lucky but shifted his gaze to Enzo.

"We're here about you musclin' in on Lucky's business." Enzo pulled out the shotgun. Sean blanched.

"Now, wait a minute." He held up his good hand and looked from Enzo to Lucky and back again. "This isn't a problem."

"Oh, yeah? How is you taking revenue out of my pocket not a problem?" Enzo fed a shell into the shotgun and pumped the Mossberg. For effect.

Eyes riveted to the gun, Sean took a step backward.

Lucky drew her Sig. "That's far enough."

Sean froze. "What do you want? Money? I've got money. Lots of it. Name your price."

Lucky cocked her head. "What do you think, Enzo? Should we shake him down for some cash?"

Sean's lips pulled back in a tentative smile as he looked to Enzo for his reaction.

Enzo shook his head. "Nah. I guarantee he don't carry that kind of juice."

"Good point. So what should we do?"

Enzo aimed the Mossberg at Sean's chest. "I think we need to have a little talk—New York City style."

Sean's face paled, matching that of the drifting snow of the fields outside the hangar. He lowered his hand and took off running. Enzo aimed for his leg and fired the big Mossberg, the report echoing through the metal hangar. Sean screamed as he staggered. A second later, he recovered and kept going, dragging his leg behind him.

Hop. Drag. Hop. Drag.

"That's for Lucky," Enzo called, still walking after him. This time he aimed higher.

Lucky grimaced at the trail of blood Sean left behind on the concrete floor. Being shot by a blast from the Mossberg at close range had to hurt like a bitch. She reminded herself he ruined little kids' lives and made money by selling them for sex, and immediately cheered up.

Bam! Sean wheeled counterclockwise as the second blast destroyed his right shoulder.

"And that was for using little kids, *children*, to fill your own personal piggy bank." The madder Enzo got, the darker red his face became. "I got children, you asshole. How can you sleep at night? You piece of shit. You rip their beautiful, sweet innocence away from them *for money*? What kind of monster does that?"

Sean shook his head as though to clear it, and gripped his shoulder with his left hand, dragging his leg behind him, frantically hopping toward the open hangar door.

Hop. Drag. Hop. Drag. Hop. Drag.

Little pools of blood trailed behind him as he edged forward.

Hop. Drag. Hop. Drag.

Enzo followed him to the hangar door. Sean paused and leaned against the corrugated metal, his shoulders heaving as he gasped for breath from the pain and the shock and the effort. A sharp wind whistled through the opening. Enzo stopped a short distance away, not saying a word. Sean half-turned toward him, eyes pleading for mercy.

"Yeah. I don't think so." Hands gripped around its barrel, Enzo raised the Mossberg, Louisville Slugger-style, wound up, and let fly, smashing the stock of the shotgun against the other man's head.

48

Six months later...

L ucky placed her laptop in the backseat of her white Suburban and closed the door. She took one last look at the lush flower baskets lining Main Street with an expansive blue sky for a backdrop. She always did enjoy summers in Hansen.

She'd have to find another place with as much potential. And maybe a little warmer in the winter.

Hell, a LOT warmer.

Derek handed her a thick envelope, which she slipped into her jacket pocket.

"Thanks," she said, and meant it. "This will do a damn good job of helping me get lost."

"Well, don't stay lost too long. I want postcards, or at least a text every once in a while."

He still looked rough, what with the bandages and the cane. Still, Derek was one tough guy. A guy who wouldn't take shit from anyone that might try to muscle in on his new club.

She eyed the familiar old building and smiled. Instead of the neon sign that read Lucky's Bar, Derek had changed the name to Chloe's. He'd replaced the big green shamrock—an afterthought when she bought the place—with a glittery palm tree.

It fit.

He was in the middle of a big remodel, which the old girl certainly needed. From the looks of the plans, it appeared he was going to class up the joint. Lucky approved.

Times changed.

She shook a cigarette from her pack and lit up. She blew the smoke toward heaven and offered up a little prayer, in case Chloe was somewhere nearby looking down on them. Leine emerged from the club, with the highway patrol sergeant who'd helped all those kids she and Derek had rescued coming right behind her. What was his name again? Roberts? Robinson? Something like that.

"Everything looks great, Derek." Leine turned to look at the new sign and smiled. "She'd love that."

Derek nodded. "I just wish she was here to see it."

The small group grew silent, remembering the woman whose name now graced the new club.

Lucky broke the pall by turning to Leine and saying, "It means a lot that you came all the way out here to see me off."

"The least I could do. Besides, I wanted to see what Derek was doing with the place."

Lucky pressed the key fob and opened the driver's door. "Don't forget, Derek—if you run into any trouble, don't hesitate to call the boys, all right?"

"Sure, Lucky."

When she'd told Enzo she was selling out and heading to parts unknown, he'd passed it along to Monty, who gave her his blessing. She paid up the loan, and added a little for the trouble she'd caused, and then asked if they wanted to keep in touch via email. Enzo had laughed and said there was no need. If they needed her, they'd find her.

Yeah, that didn't give her the warm fuzzies.

Not that she'd ever rat out Enzo. The Feds had arrived the day after the woman from the office discovered what was left of Sean in the hangar. Enzo and Ramón had left town immediately after Sean and Enzo's "meeting." When the Feds interviewed Lucky, she'd mentioned why, yes, some East Coast thugs had been hanging around her place, trying to muscle their way in and take over the bar. Then she gave them the same name and number that was on the fake business card Enzo handed to the woman at the airfield.

Local law enforcement attributed the massacre at the grain elevator to rival gangs thought to be active in the area, ever since the explosion at the old Sawyer place. Which meant more federal scrutiny, but that would die down once everybody figured out there really weren't rival gangs.

In Hansen, at least.

"Did you hear about Philip Davis?" Lucky asked.

"The billionaire they brought up on charges?" Sergeant Robinson asked.

Lucky nodded. "Yeah. Apparently, he's disappeared. No one's seen him in weeks." At Lucky's request, Derek had sent her a copy of Chloe's audio recording of Sean and Philip Davis talking business at the Phoenician. Turns out the recording was clear enough to establish that Philip Davis was heavily involved in sex trafficking of minors, and Derek had given a copy to the Feds. But in her opinion the Feds always took too long, what with trying to make an airtight case.

So she forwarded it on to Enzo.

"Well, time to shove off."

"Safe travels, Lucky."

She climbed into her Suburban and pulled away from the

curb, waving goodbye to the motley crew that had assembled on the sidewalk to see her off. Lucky wasn't much for sentiment. Her motto had always been "If it ain't working, move along."

For some reason, this time leaving tugged at her heart.

Shit, Lucky. You're getting soft.

She sighed and shook another cigarette from the pack on the console.

She'd land somewhere interesting, she had no doubt.

AFTER LUCKY LEFT, LEINE TURNED TO SERGEANT ROBINSON. "Do you want to tell him or should I?"

"Go right ahead."

Derek eyed them with suspicion. "Is this something I should brace myself for?"

Leine laughed. "It's all good, Derek. We just received confirmation that every single kid we rescued who didn't have a family to go home to has been placed with foster families who intend to adopt."

"Including Mimi?"

"Including Mimi."

"That's great."

Sergeant Robinson added, "All because you took action and rescued Mimi when you saw her in that van." He shook his head. "I wish more people would pay attention to what's happening—not just in Hansen, but all over the United States. We need more people like you two." He nodded at Leine and Derek. "Child sex trafficking—trafficking, period—is a cancer that needs to be eliminated. Law enforcement can't do it alone. We need people who care to get involved."

"Apparently," Leine said to Derek, "the state of North Dakota is taking a closer look at human trafficking—especially child sex trafficking—all because of some foreigner who couldn't stand by and watch a young girl be exploited." She smiled and patted him on his hand—one spot where he hadn't been injured by the beating. "You did good, Derek."

Derek's cheeks colored as he looked back at the club, obviously embarrassed. "Anyone else would have done the same."

"No, I don't think anyone would." Sergeant Robinson gave him an appraising look. "It takes a lot to get involved—most folks are afraid to risk it."

"So Derek," Leine asked, changing the subject. "Think you'll be able to withstand the long, cold winters?" If she knew him, he'd be on the first plane to Nairobi come snowfall.

He gave her a look she couldn't read and answered, "I've got a bit of business to finish here first."

"Meaning the club?"

"That's one thing, sure. I didn't tell Lucky, but I've already got a partner-manager lined up once the remodel's finished. Someone from back east."

"Then what?" Leine asked. Although she had a pretty good idea. Derek had mentioned something about taking care of the reason he'd come to North Dakota in the first place. Something having to do with a guy named Bart.

She didn't want to know the rest.

"Leine here tells me you're an avid hunter," Robinson said. "You sure can't go wrong with North Dakota in that regard. Duck season is just around the corner. And then there's moose and elk, if you're so inclined."

Derek gave Leine a sidelong glance. "Yeh. I definitely plan to do a little hunting."

Leine smiled at her friend.

So did she.

THE END

ACKNOWLEDGMENTS

Writing novels never seems to get easier, but the people you meet and work with along the way certainly makes it a lot more fun and interesting. Many thanks to a stellar editing team: Ruth Ross and Laurie Boris—your attention to detail is second-to-none, and I am so grateful to have you both in my corner. Thanks to the North Dakota Highway Patrol; my amazing writer's group: Ali, Jenni, and Michelle; early readers Mark, Ruth, and Brian; the incomparable ARTeam (you guys know who you are); TSODA 134 for all things weaponry and tactical; Bruno De La Mata and Bob Metz for accuracy re: the oil and gas industry; and last, but not least, my best friend and plotting partner, Mark. Thanks for all the amazing dinners, love.

.

ABOUT THE AUTHOR

DV Berkom is the USA Today bestselling author of two action-packed thriller series featuring strong female leads: Leine Basso and Kate Jones. Her love of creating resilient, kick-ass women characters stems from a lifelong addiction to reading spy novels, mysteries, and thrillers, and longing to find the female equivalent within those pages.

After years of moving around the country and skipping off to locations that could have been movie sets, she wrote her first novel and was hooked. Over a dozen novels later, she now makes her home in the Pacific Northwest with her husband, Mark, and several imaginary characters who like to tell her what to do.

Her most recent books include *Dakota Burn, Absolution, Dark Return, The Last Deception, Vigilante Dead, A Killing Truth, Cargo, The Body Market, A One Way Ticket to Dead,* and *Yucatán Dead.* Currently, she's hard at work on her next thriller.

To find out more, go to DVBerkom.com. For free books and to be the first to hear about new releases, go to bit.ly/DVB_RL

ALSO BY D.V. BERKOM